LIN CARTER SELECTS . . .

Here are eleven stories of wonder running the gamut from pure heroic fantasy such as Charles R. Saunders' "The Pool of the Moon" or Lin Carter's own "Black Moonlight" to C. J. Cherryh's unique treatment of an ancient myth and Clark Ashton Smith's and Lin Carter's post-mortem collaboration on post-mortem horror.

This sojourn through myriad worlds of romance, singing swords and magic begins with L. Sprague de Camp's "Eudoric's Unicorn," an hilarious and masterfully written fable of mundane foibles in an enchanted setting which never slackens its standards. You know immediately you are in the hands of the best of anthologists in a vintage year for fantasy.

The Year's Best Fantasy Stories: 3

Edited by
LIN CARTER

DAW BOOKS, INC.
DONALD A. WOLLHEIM, PUBLISHER

1301 Avenue of the Americas
New York, N.Y.   10019

COPYRIGHT ©, 1977, BY DAW BOOKS, INC.

All Rights Reserved.

Cover art by Josh Kirby.

Acknowledgments for the individual stories will be found on the following page.

FIRST PRINTING, NOVEMBER 1977

1 2 3 4 5 6 7 8 9

PRINTED IN U.S.A.

ACKNOWLEDGMENTS

"Eudoric's Unicorn" by L. Sprague de Camp, "The Dark King" by C. J. Cherryh, "The Snout in the Alcove" by Gary Myers, "The Goblin Blade" by Raul Garcia Capella, appear here for the first time by arrangements with the authors.

"Ring of Black Stone" by Pat McIntosh, from *Anduril* #6, August 1976, © 1976 by John Martin. By permission of John Martin.

"Two Suns Setting" by Karl Edward Wagner, from *Fantastic*, May 1976. © 1976 by Ultimate Publishing Co., Inc. By permission of the author and his agent, Kirby McCauley.

"The Stairs in the Crypt" by Clark Ashton Smith and Lin Carter, from *Fantastic*, August 1976. © 1976 by Ultimate Publishing Co., Inc. By permission of the Estate of Clark Ashton Smith.

"Black Moonlight" by Lin Carter, from *Fantastic*, November 1976. © 1976 by Ultimate Publishing Co., Inc.

"The Pool of the Moon" by Charles R. Saunders, from Dark Fantasy #8. © 1976 by Charles R. Saunders. By permission of Howard E. Day.

"The Lonely Songs of Laren Dorr" by George R. R. Martin, from *Fantastic*, May 1976. © 1976 by Ultimate Publishing Co., Inc., by permission of the author.

"Shadow of a Demon" by Gardner F. Fox, from *The Dragon*, Aug. 1976. © 1976 by Gardner F. Fox. By permission of the author.

DEDICATION

To the memory of
Mary Gnaedinger
Thomas Burnett Swann
and
Ruth Plumly Thompson

CONTENTS

The Year in Fantasy: *An Introduction*	9
Eudoric's Unicorn: L. Sprague de Camp	12
Shadow of a Demon: Gardner F. Fox	31
Ring of Black Stone: Pat McIntosh	59
The Lonely Songs of Laren Dorr: George R. R. Martin	77
Two Suns Setting: Karl Edward Wagner	99
The Stairs in the Crypt: Clark Ashton Smith	129
The Goblin Blade: Raul Garcia Capella	141
The Dark King: C. J. Cherryh	164
Black Moonlight: Lin Carter	176
The Snout in the Alcove: Gary Myers	204
The Pool of the Moon: Charles R. Saunders	213
The Year's Best Fantasy Books: *An Appendix*	233

Introduction:

THE YEAR IN FANTASY

Well, the *Silmarillion* still didn't come out, and the Conan books remained in limbo, but in many respects 1976 was a rich year for those of us who love fantasy.

In the first place, my good friend and colleague and sometime collaborator, L. Sprague de Camp, received the Gandalf to a standing ovation at the World Science Fiction Convention in Kansas City. He was only the second living writer to be so-honored, the first being Fritz Leiber. (The Gandalf, more correctly The J. R. R. Tolkien Memorial Award for Achievement in Fantasy, is a handsome bronze statuette given out each year to a writer for his entire lifetime work in our field; the award bestows the title of Grand Master of Fantasy on a deserving scrivener. And few scriveners are more deserving of it than Sprague. In fact, none that I can think of, after Leiber.)

In the second place, after allowing the Adult Fantasy Series to dwindle and die some years back, Ballantine Books finally got back in the fantasy business and picked editor, author, and outspoken critic Lester del Rey to launch a new line of originals and selected reprints. Thus far, his reprints have been, if anything, a trifle over-cautious, and he has brought back into print such obviously deserving books as Pratt's *Well of the Unicorn,* and the (almost) complete Harold Shea series. The originals he has chosen are equally safe bets: a new Deryni by Katherine Kurtz and a very *Unknown*ish new novel by Gordon R. Dickson.

It remains to be seen what Lester will give us when he gets up enough confidence to venture a little further out on the limb. But it's a good sign to have Ballantine back in the ranks, again.

Other good news: Mike Moorcock has begun writing a new series, Chronicles of Count Brass, and—more importantly—has revamped and revised and refurbished the whole Elric Saga, adding thereto some new stories and new novels.

And, I'm afraid, some bad news. Thomas Burnett Swann, one of the most popular, prolific and talented of fantasy writers, succumbed to cancer at his family home in Florida on May 5, 1976. He was only 47—cruelly young, with many good and productive years ahead of him—and he spent his last weeks in the hospital putting the finishing touches on a new novel about Dido and Aeneas, which will be among several posthumous works.

He will be missed.

And I (at least) am going to miss Mary Gnaedinger, who died at her home in the Bronx at the age of 78 this year. For nearly thirty years she edited *Famous Fantastic Mysteries* and its siblings, *Fantastic Novels* and *A. Merritt's Fantasy Magazine,* and did yeoman service by tirelessly getting back into print many of the best of fantastic fiction. I owe her a personal debt, for it was in the pages of her magazines that I first read the great romances of H. Rider Haggard and A. Merritt, and such unusual works as Chesterton's *The Man Who Was Thursday,* Hodgson's *The Boats of the 'Glen Carrig',* Cutcliffe Hyne's *The Lost Continent*—books which I, in my turn, reissued during my years with the Ballantine Adult Fantasy Series. She did good work for the cause of fantasy, and many readers beside myself are indebted to her.

And this past year we lost another writer to whom I owe a deep personal debt—Miss Ruth Plumly Thompson, of Oz and Philadelphia. When in her twenties, she picked up the Oz books after the death of L. Frank Baum, and continued to write them, one a year, for most of her life. Her twenty-second Oz book, *The Enchanted Island of Oz*, has just been published posthumously. She died on April 6, 1976.

The Oz books are the best and the greatest children's books in American literature. And their excellence, their sparkling sense of fun and adventurous swagger and endless color and variety, are due in very large measure to Miss Thompson. It was these books (and, in particular, *her* contributions to the series) that first caught and held my interest in my boyhood. I owe it entirely to Miss Thompson that, early on, I was turned in the direction of fantasy. Bless her . . . she was a lovely lady.

I'm sorry to have to take up so much space in this introduction with these unhappy duties. But there were things that had to be said somewhere, and they might as well be said here.

The Second World Fantasy Convention was held in New York City over the Halloween weekend, and the guests of honor were two excellent writers we seldom get to see here on the East Coast: C. L. Moore, the creator of Northwest Smith and Jirel of Joiry, and Michael Moorcock, the creator of Dorian Hawkmoon and Elric of Melniboné. Also joining in the fun were H. Warner Munn, Edmond Hamilton, Leigh Brackett, L. Sprague de Camp, Karl Edward Wagner, and plenty of other interesting people.

If you're interested in attending next year's World Fantasy Convention, it will be held over the same Halloween weekend in October, 1977, in Los Angeles, California, at the L. A. Hilton. The guest of honor will be Richard Matheson.

—LIN CARTER

Hollis, Long Island, New York

L. Sprague de Camp

EUDORIC'S UNICORN

This is the second in Sprague's new series of comical Sword & Sorcery yarns laid in the pixilated, slightly wacky world of Sir John de Mandeville's mostly made-up Travels and Voyages. With a fine, careless disregard for the world as it actually is, Sir John's bogus memoirs shaped a gaudy geography that maybe ought to be, but isn't. (The first yarn in this series, "Two Yards of Dragon," appeared in Flashing Swords! #3.) The de Campian sense of the ridiculous in human affairs was never headier than in this hilarious poke-in-the-ribs to heroic fantasy, which appears here for the first time in print.

—L.C.

When Sir Eudoric Dambertson's stagecoach line was running smoothly, Eudoric thought of expansion. He would extend the line from Kromnitch to Sogambrium, the capital of the New Napolitanian Empire. He would order a second coach. He would hire a scrivener to relieve him of the bookkeeping. . . .

The initial step would be to look over the Sogambrian end of the route. So he posted notices in Zurgau and Kromnitch that, on a certain day, he would, instead of turning around at Kromnitch to come back to Zurgau, continue on to Sogambrium, carrying those who wished to pay the extra fare.

Eudoric got a letter of introduction from his silent partner, Baron Emmerhard of Zurgau, who once had almost become Eudoric's father-in-law. The letter presented Eudoric to the Emperor's brother, the Archduke Rolgang.

"For a gift," said Emmerhard, fingering his graying beard, "I'll send one of my best hounds with thee. Nought is done at court without presents."

"Very kind of you, sir," said Eudoric.

"Not so kind as all that. Be sure to debit the cost of the bitch to operating expenses."

"At what value?"

"Klea should fetch at least fifty marks—"

"Fifty! Good my lord, that's absurd. I can pick up—"

"Be not impertinent with me, puppy! Thou knowest nought of dogs. . . ."

After an argument, Eudoric got Klea's value down to thirty marks, which he still thought much too high. A few days later, he set out with a cage, containing Klea, lashed to the back of the coach. In seven days the coach, with Eudoric's helper Jillo driving, rolled into Sogambrium.

Save once when he was an infant, Eudoric had never seen the imperial capital. By comparison, Kromnitch was but a small town and Zurgau, a village. The slated gables seemed to stretch away forever, like the waves of the sea.

The hordes who seethed through the flumelike streets made Eudoric uneasy. They wore fashions never seen in rural parts. Men flaunted shoes with long, turned-up toes, attached by laces to the wearer's legs below the knee; women, yard-high conical hats. Everyone seemed in a hurry. Eudoric had trouble understanding the metropolitan dialect. The Sogambrians slurred their words, dropped whole syllables, and seldom used the old-fashioned, familiar "thou" and "thee."

Having taken quarters at an inn of middling grade, Eudoric left Jillo to care for the coach and team. Leading Klea, he made his way through a gray drizzle to the archducal palace. He tried on one hand to take in all the sights but, on the other, not conspicuously to stare, gape, and crane his neck.

The palace, sheathed in stonework carved in fantastic curlicues, in the ornate modern style, rose adjacent to the Cathedral of the Divine Pair. Eudoric had had enough to do with the court of his own sovran, King Valdhelm III of Locania, to know what to expect at the palace: endless delays, to be shortened only by generous tipping of flunkies. Thanks to this strategy, Eudoric got his audience with the Archduke on the second day.

"A bonny beast," said Rolgang, stroking Klea's head. Clad in gold-and-purple Serican silks, the Archduke was a fat man with beady, piercing little eyes. "Tell me, Sir Eudoric, about this coach-wagon enterprise."

Eudoric told of encountering regular coach service, unknown in the Empire, on his journey to Pathenia. He recounted bringing the concept back to his home in Arduen, Barony of Zurgau, County of Treveria, Kingdom of Locania, and of having a coach of Pathenian style constructed by local wainwrights.

"This bears thinking on," said the Archduke. "I can foresee some effects adverse to good government. Miscreants could use your coach to flee from justice. Bankrupts could leave the site of their indebtedness and set up in business elsewhere. Subversive agitators could travel 'bout, spreading discontent and rousing the rabble 'gainst their betters."

"On the other hand, Your Highness," said Eudoric, "if the business prosper, you may be able to tax it some day."

The beady eyes lit up. "Aha, young sir! Ye've a shrewd instinct for the jugular vein! With that consideration in mind, I'm sure His Imperial Majesty will impose no obstacle to your enterprise. I'll tell you. His Imperial Majesty holds of levée at ten tomorrow. Be there with this pass, and I'll present you to my 'perial brother."

Leaving the palace cheered by this unexpected stroke of good fortune, Eudoric thought of buying a fashionable new suit, although his thrifty nature winced at the thought of spending capital on another such garment before his present best had begun to show wear. He cheered up at the thought that he might well make a better impression as an honest rustic, clean and decent if not stylish, than as an inept imitation of a metropolitan dandy.

Next morning Eudoric, stocky, dark, square-jawed, and of serious mien, stood in plain russet and black, in line with half a hundred other gentry of the Empire. Emperor Thorar IX and his brother passed slowly down the line, while an official introduced each man:

"Your Imperial Majesty, let me present Baron Gutholf of Drin, who fought in the Imperial forces to put down the late rebellion in Aviona. Now he doth busy himself with the reconstruction of his holding, dyking and draining a new polder."

"Good, my lord of Drin!" said the Emperor. "We must needs show our deluded subjects, stirred to rebellion by base-born agitators, that we love 'em in spite of all." Thorar was tall, thin, and stooped, with a gray goatee, an obvious hair piece, and a creaky voice. He was clad all in black, against which blazed a couple of jeweled decorations.

"Your Imperial Majesty," said the usher, "this is Sir Eudoric Dambertson of Arduen. He hath instituted the coach line from Zurgau to Kromnitch."

" 'Tis he of whom I told you," said the Archduke.

"Ah, Sir Eudoric!" creaked the Emperor. "We know of your enterprise. We'll see you anon on this matter. But—are ye not that Eudoric who slew a dragon in

Pathenia and later fought the monstrous spider in the forest of Dimshaw?"

Eudoric simpered with modesty. "Indeed, 'twas I, Your Imperial Majesty, albeit I came through more by good hap than by good management." He did not add that Jillo had killed the dragon, largely by accident, and that Eudoric, when he had the giant spider Fraka under his crossbow, had let her go on a sentimental whim.

"Stuff, my boy!" said the Emperor. "Good luck comes to those prepared to make the most of it. Since ye've shown such adroitness with strange beasts, we have a task for you." The Emperor turned to the Archduke. "Have ye a half-hour to spare after this, Rolgang?"

"Aye, sire."

"Well, bring the lad to the Chamber of Privy Audience, pray. And tell Heinmar to dig Sir Eudoric's dossier out of the file." The Emperor passed on.

In the Chamber of Privy Audience, Eudoric found the Emperor, the Archduke, the Minister of Public Works, the Emperor's secretary, and two bodyguards in silver cuirasses and crested helms. The Emperor was turning the pages of a slim folder.

"Sit down, Sir Eudoric," said Thorar. "This bids fair to take time, and we'd not needlessly inflict sore knees 'pon loyal subjects. Ye are unwed, we see, albeit nearly thirty. Why is this?"

Eudoric thought, the old boy might give the appearance of doddering, but there was nothing wrong with his wits. He said: "I have been betrothed, Your Imperial Majesty, but chance hath each time snatched away my promised bride. That I am single is not from lack of inclination towards the other sex."

"Hm. We must needs 'mend this condition. Rolgang, is that youngest daughter of yours promised yet?"

"Nay, sire."

The Emperor turned back. "Sir Eudoric, the gist is

this. Next month, the Grand Cham of the Pantorozians comes on a visit of state, bringing a young dragon to add to the 'perial menagerie. As ye may've heard, our zoological collection is, after the welfare of the Empire, our greatest passion. But, for the honor of the Empire, we can't let this heathen Easterling outdo us in generosity.

"Dragons are extinct in the Empire, unless a few still lurk in the wilder wastes. We're told, howsomever, that west of Hessel, in your region, lies the wilderness of Bricken, where dwell many curious beasts. Amongst these is the unicorn."

Eudoric raised his eyebrows. "Your Imperial Majesty wants a unicorn to give to this Pantorozian?"

"Aye, sir; ye've put the bolt in the gold. How 'bout it?"

"Why—ah—sensible though I be of the great honor, Your Imperial Majesty, I know not whether I could manage it. As I told you, my previous escapes were more by luck than by skill or might. Besides, my coach line, requiring constant attention to detail, takes all my time—"

"Oh, stuff, my boy! Ye crave a just wage for your labor, as do we all, however we bluebloods affect to be above base thoughts of material gain. Eh, Rolgang?"

The Emperor winked. Eudoric found this ruler's genial cynicism refreshing after the elaborate pretence of the country gentry, among whom he lived, to care nothing for vulgar money. Thorar continued:

"Well, at the moment we have no vacant baronies or counties to bestow, but my brother hath a nubile daughter. She's not the fairest of the fair—"

"Petrilla's a *good* girl!" the Archduke broke in.

"None denies it, none denies it. Neither doth anyone propose her for the Crown of Beauty at tournaments. Well, Sir Eudoric, how about it? One unicorn for the hand of Petrilla Rolgangsdaughter?"

Eudoric took his time about answering. "The young

lady would have to give her free consent. May I have the honor of meeting her?"

"Certes. Rolgang, arrange it, if you please."

Eudoric had been in love several times, but the outcomes of these passions had given him a cynical, practical view of the battle of the sexes. He had never found fat girls attractive, and Petrilla was fat—not grossly so yet, but give her a few years. She was dark, dumpy, blunt of feature, and given to giggles.

Sighing, Eudoric totted up the advantages and disadvantages of being joined with this unglamorous if supremely well-connected young woman. For a career of courtier and magnate, the virtues of being the Archduke's son-in-law overbore all else. After all, Petrilla seemed healthy and good-natured. If she proved too intolerable a bore, he could doubtless find consolation elsewhere.

Back in Arduen, Eudoric sought out his old tutor, Doctor Baldonius, now living in semi-retirement in a cabin in the woods. A wizardly scholar who eked out his pension by occasional theurgies, Baldonius got out his huge encyclopedia and unlocked its iron clasps.

"Unicorn," he said, turning pages of crackling parchment. "Ah, here we are. 'The unicorn, *Dinohyus helicornus,* is the last surviving member of the family Entelodontidae. The spirally twisted horn, rising from the animal's forehead, is actually not one horn. This would be impossible because of the frontal suture, along the mid-line of the forehead. It is, instead, a pair of horns conjoined and twisted into a single spike. The legend that the beast can be rendered mild and tractable by a human virgin appears to have a basis in fact. According to the story. . . .' But ye know the tale, Eudoric."

"Aye," said Eudoric. "You get a virgin—if you can find one—and have her sit under a tree in a wood frequented by unicorns. The beast will come up and

Eudoric's Unicorn

lay its head in her lap, and the hunters can rush out and spear the quarry with impunity. How could that be?"

Baldonius: "My colleague Doctor Bobras hath published a monograph—let me look—ah, here 'tis." Baldonius pulled a scroll out of a cabinet of pigeonholes. "His theory, whereon he hath worked since we were students as Saalingen together, is that the unicorn is unwontedly sensitive to odors. With that great snout, it could well be. Bobras deduces that a virgin hath a smell different from that of a non-virgin human female, and that this effluvium nullifies the brute's ferocious instincts. *Fieri potest.*"

"Very well," said Eudoric. "Assuming I can find me a virgin willing to take part in this experiment, what next? It's one thing to rush upon the comatose beast and plunge a boar spear into its vitals and quite another to capture it alive and unharmed and get it to Sogambrium."

"Alas! I fear I have no experience in such things. As a vegetarian, I have avoided all matters of chase and venery. I use the latter word in its hunting sense; albeit, *scilicet,* the other meaning were also apt for an adept like myself."

"Then who could advise me in this matter?"

Baldonius pondered, then smiled through his waterfall of beard. "There's an unlikely expert dwelling nigh unto Baron Rainmar's demesne, namely and to wit: my cousin Svanhalla."

"The witch of Hesselbourn?"

"The same, but don't let her hear you call her that. A witch, she insists, is a practitioner, of either sex, of black, illegal goëtics, whereas she's a respectable she-wizard or enchantress, whose magics are all beneficient and lawful. My encyclopedia traces the derivation of these words—"

"Never mind," said Eudoric hastily, as Baldonius began to turn the pages. "I've not met her, but I've heard. She's a cranky old puzzle, they say. What would she know of the techniques of hunting?"

"She knows surprising things. 'Twas always said in the fraternity, if ye wish some utterly useless bit of odd information, which nobody on earth could rightly be expected to have—say, for example, what Count Holmer the pretender had for breakfast the day they cut off's head—go ask Svanhalla. I'll give you a letter to her. I haven't seen her for years, for fear of her raspy tongue."

"So ye be a knight now?" said Svanhalla, sitting with Eudoric in the gloom of her hut. "Not by any feats of chivalry, ta-rah! ta-rah! But by shrewdly taking advantage of what luck hath brought you, heh? I know the tale of how ye slew that Pathenian dragon—how ye missed clean with the Serican thunder-tube and ran for your life, and how Jillo by chance touched off the sack of fire-powder just as the beast waddled o'er it."

Silently cursing Jillo's loose tongue, Eudoric kept his temper. "Had I been twice as brave and thrice as adept with the thunder weapon, Madam, 'twould have availed us nought had luck been against us. We should have made but toothsome morsels for the reptile. But let's to business. Baldonius says you can advise me on the capture of unicorns in Bricken."

"I mought, if ye made it worth me while."

"How much?"

After a haggle, Eudoric and Svanhalla agreed on a fee of sixty marks, half then and the rest when the unicorn was secured. Eudoric paid.

"First," said the witch of Hesselbourn, "ye must needs find a virgin, of above fifteen years. If the tales I hear be true, that may take some doing in Arduen, what with you and your lecherous bretheren . . ."

"Madam! I have not carnally known any local lasses for nigh a year—"

"Aye, aye, I ken. When the lust becomes too great

to endure, ye fare to the whores of Kromnitch. Ye should be respectably wived by now, but the girls all think you a cold-blooded opportunist. Therein, they're not altogether wrong; for, whilst ye love women, ye love your gold even more, heh!"

"You needn't rub it in," said Eudoric. "Besides, I seek advice on hunting, not love."

"Heh! Well then, your brother Olf doth cut a veritable swath amid the maids of Arduen. Not that I blame the lad overmuch. He's good-looking, and too many peasant maids think to catch a lordling with their coyntes for bait. They hope, if not for lawful wedlock, at least for affluent concubinage. So they all but shout: 'Come, take me, fair sir!' 'Tis a rotten, degenerate age we live in."

"Since you know so much about affairs in Arduen, who, then, *is* still a virgin?"

"For that, I must needs consult my familiar." She issued further instructions on the mechanics of capture, ending: "Come back on the morrow. Meanwhile go to Frotz the rope-maker to order your net and Karlvag the wainwright for your wheeled cage. Be sure they be big and strong enough, else ye may have less luck than ye had with the dragon, heh!"

When Eudoric returned to Svanhalla's house, he found her talking to a bat the size of an eagle. This creature hung upside down from her rafters, along with smoked hams, bags of onions, and other edibles. When Eudoric jumped back, the witch cackled.

"Fear not Nigmalkin, brave and mighty hero! She's as sweetly loving a little demon as ye shall find in the kingdom, heh. Moreover, she tells me what ye be fain to know."

"And that is?"

"That in all of Arduen, there's but one wench that would fill your bill. True, there be other virgins in fact, but none suitable. Cresseta Almundsdaughter is ill and like to die; Greda Paersdaughter's father is a religious fanatic who won't let her out of his sight; and so on."

"Then who is available?"

"Bertrud, daughter of Ulfred the Unwashed."

"Oh, gods! She takes after her sire; one can detect her down-wind at half a mile. Is that the best you can do, Svanhalla?"

"So it is. Take it or leave it. After all, a proud, fierce adventurer like yourself shouldn't mind a few little stenches, now should he?"

Eudoric sighed. "Well, I shall imagine myself back in that prison cell in Pathenia. It stank even worse."

Bertrud Ulfredsdaughter would, if cleaned up, have been a handsome girl; some would say, even beautiful. Ulfred the Unwashed had once been told by a fortune-teller that he would die of a tisick caught from washing. He had therefore forsworn all external contact with water, and his daughter had fallen into similar habits.

Eudoric rode roundabout from Arduen back to the wilderness of Bricken. He avoided the demesnes of his old foe, Baron Rainmar of Hessel, and tried to keep on the windward side of Bertrud.

Besides Bertrud, with Eudoric rode Jillo's younger brother, a simple farm worker named Theovic Godmarson, to help with the heavy work. Jillo followed, driving the wheeled cage. Eudoric left Jillo with this vehicle at the edge of the forest, into which no road wide enough for it ran.

After a day of searching, while watching cautiously for the nearly-invisible webs of the giant spiders, Eudoric chose a spot. Here grew a giant beech, with enough boughs near the ground to make for easy climbing. It also stood near an affluent of the Lupa, by which they pitched their camp.

It took the rest of the day to rig the net, attaching it by slip knots to the higher branches of the beech and two nearby trees, so that one good pull on the release lanyard would bring the whole thing down. Leaden weights along the edges of the net assured that, when it fell, it would envelop the prey. They made the net heavy, and the summer day was hot. By the time they completed their task, Eudoric and Theovic were bathed in sweat. They threw themselves down and lay panting and listening to the buzz and chirp of insects.

"I'm for a bath," said Eudoric. "You, too, Theovic? Bertrud, if you go round yonder bend in the stream, you'll find a pool where you can wash in privacy. 'Twould do you no scathe."

"Me, wash?" said the girl. " 'Tis an unwholesome habit. An ye'd risk your death of cold, 'tis your affair."

During the night, Eudoric heard the snort of a unicorn. The next morning, therefore, he caused Bertrud to sit at the base of the beech, while he and Theovic climbed the tree and waited. Peering through the bronze-green leaves, Eudoric held the lanyard that would release the net. Bertrud languidly waved away the cloud of flies that seemed to follow her as a permanent escort.

When it arrived, in the afternoon, the unicorn did not look much like the dainty creatures, half horse and half gazelle, shown on tapestries in the Emperor's palace. Its body and limbs were like those of a buffalo, six feet at the shoulder hump, while its huge, warty head bore some resemblance to that of a gigantic hog. The twisted horn sprouted from its head above the eyes.

The unicorn approached the great beech, under which Bertrud sat. The beast moved cautiously, one step at a time. When it was almost under the net, it halted, sniffing with big, flaring nostrils.

It sniffed some more. Then it threw up its head and gave a colossal grunt, like a lion's roar but more guttural. It rolled its eyes and pawed the earth with cloven forehooves.

"Bertrud!" Eudoric called. "It's going to charge! Get up the tree, forthwith!"

As the unicorn bounded forward, the girl, who had watched it with increasing dismay on her soil-caked face, scrambled to her feet and swarmed up the low branches. The beast skidded to a halt, glaring about with bloodshot eyes.

Eudoric pulled the lanyard. As the net began to fall, the unicorn sprang forward again, swerved to miss the tree, and continued on. One of the leaden weights of the net struck the unicorn's rump as the net settled to the ground.

With a frightful bellow, the unicorn whirled, champing its great dog-teeth or tusks. Seeing no foe, it galloped off into the forest. The crashing and drumming of its passage died away.

When the unicorn-hunters were back on the ground, Eudoric said: "That settles it. Baldonius said these creatures are sensitive to odors. You, my dear Bertrud, have odor for six. Theovic, you shall go to Hessel Minor and buy a cake of soap and a sponge. Here's money."

"Wouldn't ye rather go and leave me to guard the lass, me lord?" said Theovic with a cunning gleam.

"Nay. If I were recognized, Rainmar would have his bully boys after us; so keep a close mouth whilst there. Go, and with luck you'll be back for dinner."

With a sigh, Theovic saddled his horse and trotted off. With a trembling lip, Bertrud asked: "What—what will ye do to me, sir? Am I to be beaten or raped?"

"Nonsense, wench! I won't hurt a hair of your head. Don't think that, because I have a 'Sir' before my name, I go about bullying the commonality. I try to treat folk as they merit, be they serf or king."

"What will ye do, then?"

"You shall see."

"Ye mean to wash me, that's what! I'll not endure it! I'll run away into the wildwood—"

Eudoric's Unicorn

"With unicorns and other uncanny beasts lurking about? Methinks not."

"I'll show thee! I go—"

She started off at random. Eudoric imitated the grunt of the unicorn. Bertrud shrieked, ran back, and threw her arms around Eudoric's neck. Eudoric firmly unpeeled her, saying:

"When you're cleaned up and the unicorn's caught, then, if you're fain to play such games, we shall see."

Theovic returned at sunset, saying: "Here's your soap and all, me lord. Jillo asked after you, and I told him all went well."

Since Bertrud was cooking their supper, Eudoric let the bath go until morning. Then, stripped to his breech clout and with gleeful help from Theovic, he pushed and hauled Bertrud, struggling and weeping, down to the branch of the Lupa. They pulled off her skirt and blouse and forced her into the water. She shrieked:

"Gods, that's cold!"

" 'Tis the best we have, my lady," said Eudoric, scrubbing vigorously. "By the Divine Pair, wench, you have layers of dirt over layers of dirt! Hold still, damn your arse! . . . Hand me the comb, Theovic. I'd get some of the tangles out of this hair. All right, I can manage the rest. It's time you fed the horses."

Theovic started back towards the camp. Eudoric continued soaping, scrubbing, and ducking his victim.

"Now," he said, "does that feel so dreadful?"

"I—I know not, sir. 'Tis a feeling I never have felt ere now. But I'm cold; let me warm myself against you. My, beant you the strong fellow, though?"

"You're no weakling yourself," said Eudoric, "after the struggle I had to get you in here."

"I work hard. There's none to do the chores, since me mother ran away with that pedlar, but me father and me. What thews!"

She felt his biceps, inching closer until her big, firm teats rubbed his chest. Eudoric felt a familiar stirring in his loin cloth.

"Now, now, my dear," he said. "I said, *after* the brute's captured, not before." When she continued her attentions and started to explore Eudoric's person, he barked: "I said nay!" and pushed her away.

He pushed harder than he intended, so that she fell backwards and got another ducking. When she scrambled up, her expression had changed.

"So!" she said. "The high and mighty knight won't look at a poor peasant lass! Too grand for aught but them perfumed, painted whores of the courts! Ye may take them all to Hell with you, for all of me!"

She strode out of the pool, picked up her garments, and vanished towards the camp.

Eudoric looked after her with a troubled smile. He devoted himself to his own bath until the smell of breakfast reminded him of the passage of time.

He and Theovic rigged the net again. This time, the unicorn came around noon. As before, it seemed about to approach the seated Bertrud but then went into a frenzy of rage. Again, Bertrud had to scramble up the tree to safety.

This time, the unicorn did not even wait for Eudoric to pull the lanyard. It blundered off into the forest at once.

Eudoric sighed. "At least, we shan't have to haul that damned net up into the trees again. But what could have gone wrong this time? . . ." He caught a faint smirk on Theovic's face. "Oho, so thither lies the wind, eh? Whilst I was bathing this morn, you were futtering our frail, so she's no more a virgin!"

Theovic and Bertrud giggled.

"I'll show you two witlings!" howled Eudoric.

He whipped out his hunting falchion and started for the pair. Although he meant only to spank them with the flat, they fled with shrieks of mortal terror. Eudoric ran after them, brandishing the short, curved sword, until he tripped over a root and fell sprawling. When he had pulled himself together again, Theovic and Bertrud were out of sight.

On the borders of the wilderness, Eudoric told Jillo: "When that idiot brother of yours comes in, tell him, if he wants his pay, to return to finish his task. Nay, I won't hurt him, for all his loonery. I should have foreseen what would happen. Now I must needs leave these nags with you whilst I ride Daisy back to Svanhalla's hut."

When Eudoric came again to the cabin of the witch of Hesselbourn, Svanhalla cackled. "Ah, well, ye did your best. But, when the devil of carnal desire reaves a youth or a maid, it takes one of monkish humor to withstand it. That's something neither of those twain possesses."

"All very true, Madam," said Eudoric, "but what next? Where shall I find another virgin, sound of wind and limb?"

"I'll send me familiar, Nigmalkin, out to scout the neighboring holdings. Baron Rainmar's daughter Maragda's a filly unridden, but she's to wed in a month. Besides, I misdoubt ye'd find her suitable."

"I should say not! Rainmar would hang me if he could lay hands on me. But. . . . Harken, Madam Svanhalla, would not *you* qualify for the part?"

The witch's bony jaw sagged. "Now that, Sir Eudoric, is something I should never have hit upon. Aye, for all these years—an hundred and more—I have forsworn such carnal delights in pursuit of the highest grades of magical wisdom. For a price, mayhap. . . . But how would ye get an ancient bag of bones like me to yonder wildwood? I'm spry enough around this little cabin, but not for long tramps or horseback rides."

"We'll get you a horse litter," said Eudoric. "Bide you here, and I shall soon be back."

Thus it came to pass that, half a month later, the aged witch of Hesselbourn sat at the foot of the same beech tree on which Eudoric had rigged his net. After a day's wait, the unicorn approached, sniffed, then knelt in front of Svanhalla and laid its porcine head in her bony lap.

Eudoric pulled the lanyard. The net fell. As Svanhalla scrambled to safety, the unicorn surged up, shaking its head and snorting. Its efforts to free itself only got it more entangled. Eudoric dropped down from the branches, unslung the hunting horn from his back, and blew a blast to summon Jillo.

Eudoric, Jillo, and the forgiven Theovic rolled the beast, exhausted but still struggling, on an ox hide. Avoiding thrashing hooves and foaming jaws, they lashed it down. Then the hide was hitched to three horses, which towed the ungainly bundle along the trail to where they had left the wheeled cage.

It took most of a day to get the animal into the cage. Once it almost got away from them, and a soaking thunderstorm made their task no easier. At last the brute was securely locked in.

Eudoric and his helpers shoved armfulls of fresh-cut grain stalks through the bars. The unicorn, which had not eaten in two days, fell to.

The Archduke Rolgang said: "Sir Eudoric, ye've done well. The Emperor is pleased—nay, delighted. In sooth, he so admires your beast that he's decided to keep the monster in his own menagerie, 'stead o' sending it off to the Cham of the Pantorozians."

"I am gratified, Your Highness," said Eudoric. "But meseems there was nother matter, touching your daughter Petrilla, was there not?"

The fat Archduke coughed behind his hand. "Well, now, as to that, ye put me in a position of embarrassment. Ye see, the damsel's no longer to be had, alas, no matter how noble and virtuous her suitor."

"Not dead?" cried Eudoric.

"Nay; quite otherwise. I'd have saved her for you, but my duty to the Empire overbore my private scruples."

"Will you have the goodness to explain, my lord?"

"Aye, certes. The Grand Cham paid his visit, as planned. No sooner, howsomever, had he set eyes 'pon Petrilla than he was smitten with a romantical passion. Nor was she 'verse.

"Ye see, laddie, she's long complained that no gallant gentleman of the Empire could ever love a squatty, swarthy, full-bodied lass like her. But here comes the mighty Cham Czik, master of hordes of fur-capped nomads. He, too, is a short, stout, swart, bowlegged wight. So 'twas love at first sight."

"I thought," said Eudoric, "she and I had exchanged mutual promises—not publicly, but—"

"I reminded her of that, also. But, if ye'll pardon my saying so, that was a hard-faced commercial deal, with no more sentiment than a turnip hath blood."

"And she's—"

"Gone off with the Grand Cham to his home on the boundless steppes, to be his seventeenth—or mayhap eighteenth, I forget which—wife. Not the husband I'd have chosen for her, being a heathen and already multiply wived; but she'd made up her mind. That's why my 'perial brother did not deem it necessary to send the Cham your unicorn, since Lord Gzik had already received from us an unthridden pearl of great price.

"But, even if Petrilla be no longer at hand, my brother and I mean not to let your service go unrewarded. Stand up, Sir Eudoric! In the name of His Imperial Majesty, I hereby present you with the Grand Cross of the Order of the Unicorn, with oak leaves and diamonds."

"Ouch!" said Eudoric. "Your Highness, is it necessary to pin the medal to my skin as well as my coat?"

"Oh, your pardon, Sir Eudoric." The Archduke fumbled with fat fingers and finally got the clasp locked. "There ye are, laddie! Take a look in the mirror."

"It looks splendid. Pray convey to His Imperial Majesty my undying thanks and gratitude."

Privately, Eudoric fumed. The medal was pretty;

but he was no metropolitan courtier, swanking at imperial balls in shining raiment. On his plain rustic garb, the bauble looked silly. While he could let Petrilla go without uncontrollable grief, he thought that, if they were going to reward him, a neat life pension would have been more to the point, or at least the repayment of his expenses in unicorn-hunting. Of course, if times got hard and the order were neither lost nor stolen, he could pawn or sell it. . . .

He said nothing of all this, however, endeavoring to look astonished, awed, proud, and grateful all at the same time. Rolgang added:

"And now, laddie, there's the little matter we spake of aforetime. Ye are authorized to extend your coach line to Sogambrium, and beyond, if ye can manage it. By a decree of His Imperial Majesty, howsomever, all fares collected for such scheduled carriage shall henceforth be subject to a tax of fifty per centum, payable monthly. . . ."

Gardner F. Fox

SHADOW OF A DEMON

When I was in my teens, I remember reading some swell swashbucklers by Fox in the old Planet Stories—a marvelously sleazy pulp magazine of the sort they just don't make any more. These were yarns full of juice and vinegar, with marvelously evocative titles like "The Man the Sun Gods Made," and "Sword of the Seven Suns," and like that. They were "almost"-fantasies; that is, while there was plenty of sword-play and sorcery going on in them, there was usually an extra moon or two in the sky, just enough to suggest the setting was really on another planet and the story could, if you wished, be taken for sf.

Much more recently, though, Gar Fox has been doing some more-or-less straight Sword & Sorcery: a brace of novels about Kothar the barbarian swordsman, and a new series about Kyrik that is much the same sort of stuff.

And even, occasionally, a short yarn in the genre, such as this one.

—*L.C.*

He came into Angalore from the eastern deserts, a big man wearing a kaunake of spotted fur over his linkmail, his legs bare above warboots trimmed with miniver, with a sense of his own doom riding him. Niall of the Far Travels had not wanted to come to Angalore, for an old seeress had prophesied that he would be taken from this world by demons, should those warboots carry him into that ancient, brooding city.

Yet he had come here because his fate had so decreed.

He was a mercenary, a sell-sword, a barbarian out of the forested mountains of Norumbria. A wanderer by nature, he earned his keep wherever he went by the might of his sword-arm, by his skill with weapons. He feared no living thing, man or animal, though the thought of demons put a coldness down his spine.

Now he paused on the crest of a hill and stared at the city. Massive it was, and old, so old that some men said it had been here since men had first learned to walk upright. It lay between the river and the desert over which the caravans came from Sensanall to the south and Urgrik to the north. Ships lay in the little harbor that was formed by the river, riding easily to the lift and fall of its tides.

Angalore was the city of Maylok the magician.

An evil man, Maylok. Niall had heard tales about him, over campfires and in the taverns where men drank wine and watched dancing girls perform. Rumor had it that he used demons as men used pawns when they played their games of chance. Gossips also said that in the dungeons and stone labyrinths below his palace, Maylok had stored the treasures of his world, gold and silver, diamonds and rubies and emeralds, and golden vessels carved and fashioned by famous sculptors.

Niall moved his heavily muscled shoulders, uneasy as a wild animal might be, walking into strange country where it knew nothing of the dangers to be faced. Yet he had to go to Angalore. There was no way out, if he wanted to eat and drink. The desert had offered no oasis, no plant from which to pull the roots to allay his hunger. He had been offered employment by a captain of mercenaries, and was on his way to join up with the black eagle banner of Lurlyr Manakor of Urgrik when he had been attacked by a huge mountain lion out of the Styrethian Hills. He had killed the lion but not before it had broken the neck of his horse.

On foot, he could never reach Urgrik. He had known that, and so he had set his feet to the westward, to reach the river that ran through these lands. On the river he might find a boat to carry him to Urgrik.

His wandering had brought him to Angalore, instead.

Niall hitched at his swordbelt and gave the city a hard grin. There would be food in Angalore, and cold wine. Niall had a need for both, maybe even a wench if he could find an agreeable one.

His feet carried him down the slope toward the landward gate. Niall was not a fearful man, nothing frightened him; still, that threat of demons made him wary. He was not one to put overmuch confidence in the babblings of soothsayers, but old Thallia was not your usual prophetess.

He had stumbled onto Thallia in Cassamunda, where he had met that mercenary captain. She was an old woman, clad in rags, but she carried a small bag that clinked as she moved, and two ruffians had tried to take it from her. Niall had been passing, had leaped to her protection, had buffeted the ruffians with his big fist and knocked them senseless.

Old Thallia had been grateful. Her bag held her wealth, such as it was, a few coins and some jewels which she kept by her to sell when she needed food. He had escorted her to the cheap little room above the tavern where she lived, and she had insisted on giving him some wine and a barleycake.

She had read his fortune, too.

'Beware of Angalore,' she had whispered, her rheumy eyes wide and fear-filled. 'There are demons there, who serve Maylok the wizard. They will snatch you away with them when they come. And—there is no return from a demon world.'

The landward gate was closed, at this time of day, with the late afternoon shadows black and ominous. No caravans were expected in before the morrow, and guards stood their watch on the walls, half drowsing in the sunset. Niall stopped before the wall and shouted upward that he was a stranger in need of food and drink, and desired also a cot on which to lay his body.

After a time, a small door inset in a larger one creaked open. Two warriors wearing the griffin insignia of Angalore scowled at him suspiciously. Niall grinned and moved forward.

"There is a fee to be paid," one of them said, "It is after the hour when we admit travelers."

Nial shrugged. He had no wish to remain outside these high stone walls, knowing that inside them he would find what his belly told him he so desperately needed. His big hand fumbled at his worn leather belt-pouch, extracted a few coins, and dribbled them into the outstretched palms. The stink of bribery was strong in his nostrils, but beggars had little choice.

He moved off along a cobbled street, his eyes hunting a sign that might tell him where a tavern waited with its warmth and merriment. These buildings past which he walked were warehouses where were stored the goods that came by caravan, with no hint of roasting meat nor smell of chilling wine.

Niall had never been in Angalore before and so he lost his way, moving down narrow little alleys and into cul-de-sacs, always aware that his hunger and his thirst were growing with the darkness. And then in a narrow passageway between buildings which seemed to lean their walls together, he saw the girl.

She was clad in leather rags that fluttered in the wind moving off the river. Her long legs were brown and shapely, and the hair that fell almost to her haunches was black as Corassin ebony. She was turning her head to stare back at him, shrinking against the wall behind her.

Niall grinned. "You seem as lost as I am."

Green eyes studied him. "I am not lost. I know my way." She added, almost ominously, "To where I want to go."

"There's no need for hurry." His gaze took her in, seeing the tatterings of her worn leather tunic, its stains and spottings, the manner in which it failed to hide the curve of her breasts and revealed almost the complete length of a bare leg. "Come eat with me, I'll pay the fare. And I'll give you as much wine as you might care to drink."

The green eyes softened, but her voice was cold. "Go your way, barbarian. Let me go mine."

Niall shrugged. It mattered little to him whether she went with him or not, but she was pretty enough, with full lips and a tilted nose. She would have made a good bed-companion for the night. He might even have taken her to Urgrik with him and—if he could afford it—buy her some decent clothes.

He walked away, putting her from his mind.

And then he heard the clank of metal.

The Far-traveler turned his head. Behind him four men were moving out of a little alley toward the girl. She had seen them and was shrinking back, away from them. The men were grinning at her.

"Come along now," one said, putting out a hand to grasp her arm.

The barbarian turned and waited.

"No," she whispered. "I know you men. You serve Maylok."

"And Maylok needs female blood for his incantations."

They leaped, all four of them, and the girl disappeared behind their big bodies. Niall snarled and went on the run, not bothering to draw his sword. His big fist should be able to handle these carrion.

He caught a man, swung him about, drove knuckles

against his face, pulping his nose. A second one he caught and rammed his head against the stone wall so that he went limp and crumpled.

The other two yanked out their blades, swung them at him. Niall laughed softly, put his own hand to sword-hilt and drew out Blood-drinker. The barbarian had little wealth, except for his sword, that had been forged long ago and far away and that Niall had found in a tomb which he had looted, early in his youth. He had been offered fortunes for that blade, he had always refused to part with it.

He fought swiftly and terribly, did Niall of the Far Travels. With parry and thrust and overhead blows he drove the two ruffians before him until their backs were to the building wall, and there he ran them through.

The girl had never moved, but stood erect and as coldly disdainful as ever. Niall felt surprise at sight of her, he was certain she would have run away when given the opportunity. He growled as he wiped his steel clean, "What are you waiting for? Why didn't you run?"

"You fool," she breathed. "You *fool!*"

She stamped her sandaled foot. Her cold anger beat out at him like a living entity, and the sell-sword stared. "Has Emelkartha the Evil stolen your wits? Or did you want to go with those men to be sucked dry of blood for Maylok's wizardries?"

Her eyes lidded over and she drew a deep breath. "You would not understand. You are only a common warrior. Besides, what do you know of Emelkartha?"

"She is the mother of demons, that one. I've heard it said that all demons regard her wishes as commands."

The girl shrugged. "I pray to her for vengeance."

"She ought to hear your prayers, then. She's malevolent, that one."

The green eyes glowed. "Is she, warrior? I hope so. Perhaps she will grant me my revenge on Maylok then."

Shadow of a Demon

He caught her bare arm, drew her with him. "Tell me about it. Mayhap I can help a little, though I've no fancy for wizards myself, and usually I stay clear of them."

She went with him readily enough, but cast a look behind her where two men were stirring and two others lay in pools of their own blood. Was it only fancy, or did that face of hers mirror a faint regret?

"What's your name? Where are you from?" he asked.

The green eyes slid sideways at him from under long black lashes. "Call me—Lylthia. And—does it matter where I come from?"

"Not to me," he chuckled. "Are you hungry? Thirsty?"

His eyes ran over the cheap leather tunic that barely hid her body. She carried no money pouch, the only thing on her besides the tunic and her tattered sandals was a rope belt about her slim middle. As the river-wind grew cooler, she began to shiver.

"We'll get you into a warm tavern and put some meat in you," he said. "Also some Kallarian wine."

"Little good it will do you," she muttered.

Niall grinned. He had a way with wenches like this. Yet as he walked with her along the torchlit streets, he failed to notice that while those torch flames cast his shadow, there was no shadow for the girl.

The tavern was warm and noisy, filled with seafarers of the Aztallic Sea, with wanderers from the western lands, with mercenary warriors and with women who plied their ancient trade between the tables, to sit where they were welcomed and join in the feasting and the drinking. A great hearth held a huge log that blazed with a sullen roar and threw a scarlet hue across those nearest it.

Niall pushed Lylthia onto a bench and waved an arm at a serving maid.

"Thort steaks and Kallarian," he ordered, then

turned his attention to the girl. She was staring around her with wide eyes, almost as though she had never been in such a hospice before.

"So you seek vengeance on Maylok," he murmured. "But why? What has Maylok done to you?"

The green eyes regarded him. "He has taken that which was mine. He has not offered to pay for it, nor will he."

"What could you own that's so valuable?"

Her leather tunic was stained and discolored, it hardly hid the swells of her breasts nor the lengths of her supple thighs. She was a poor girl, that much Niall would swear on the Wargod's sword.

She shrugged. "You would not understand."

Something about those green eyes made him murmur. "If I can help you, I shall. Though I don't fancy warlocks."

She smiled suddenly, and those eyes lost their coldness. "I need no help. Though I thank you."

Niall was not so sure that she could not use a blade like Blood-drinker to side her when she went hunting Maylok in his palace, and said so. "No man can take him by surprise, it's rumored. He has set spells and cantraips on all the doors and windows so nothing can catch him unawares. At least, so I've been told. Only by his will can a man or a woman enter his stronghold."

"That is true enough."

"Yet you think you can gain revenge on him? Unarmed and—well, practically naked? Without coins with which to bribe a way in?"

"I need neither sword nor gold. Here's your food. Eat it."

Niall glanced at her in surprise. There had been an imperiousness in the way she had spoken that indicated she expected to be obeyed. It was almost as if she were a princess in disguise. Niall felt uneasy at that, he had no experience with people of royal blood. Servingmaids and tavern wenches were more his familiars.

Shadow of a Demon

Still, he ate the savory meat, slicing it with his knife, using his fingers to wolf down the blood-dripping meat. He loaned his knife to Lylthia, watched how daintily she ate. He filled her leathern jack with wine, drank his own empty and then refilled it.

Lylthia drank sparingly, as if not quite trusting the Kallarian. There was suspicion in her, he knew; she expected him to take her into a bed and enjoy her body. Well, that was what he meant to do, all right; he didn't blame her for eyeing him so watchfully.

By the Wargod! She was a pretty thing. He liked her. And she had a body on her, he could tell that easily enough because of that scanty leather tunic. She would be fun when he got his arms around her. If she was enough fun, he would carry her to Urgrik.

An almost naked woman came into a cleared space and danced. Niall was torn between the dancer and watching the disdain that was so easy to read in Lylthia's pretty face. As applause rang out and the girl sniffed, Niall leaned close to her.

"You can do better, I suppose?"

"I would drive you mad were I to dance for you."

She said it calmly, but there was a ring of truth in her voice. Niall shifted uneasily on the bench. There was a mystery about this girl, he knew that much; she was not as other women he had met in his far travelings, willing to offer smiles and a soft body for a good meal and some glasses of wine, and a part of him regretted that. He thought of Lylthia in a warm bed with himself beside her, and stirred restlessly.

He asked, "Will you stay the night with me? It grows late, and Maylok may have other men searching the streets."

She nodded. "I will stay with you."

He paid for the meal with the last of his gold coins, accepting silver in change. Then he walked behind Lylthia's swinging hips along the narrow stairway to the upper rooms.

There was a bed and a washstand in the room he

selected, and a single window that looked out on the stars and the glittering ring of matter which wisemen said was the remains of the moon which had circled this world once, and had been shattered many eons ago, to be caught and held by gravity in the sky. Niall unbuckled his swordbelt and hung it over the back of a chair, slipped out of his linkmail shirt and kicked off his warboots.

He lay down on the bed and beckoned to the girl. "Come here, Lylthia. I want to taste the sweetness of your mouth."

To his surprise she walked toward him and sat on the edge of the bed. She leaned closer as if to kiss him, but his gaze was caught and held by her green eyes that seemed to swell and swell until they were all that existed in the room.

"Sleep, Niall of the Far Travels," those eyes commanded. "Sleep!"

And Niall slept, and Niall dreamed.

He sat on a stone throne in his dream in a great hall, dark except where tall torches glowed in sconces, forming a pool of light in which Lylthia danced. Naked she danced, and her body was a pallid white and disturbingly sensual. She was all the lusts, all the sensuous dreams of man, every need he had for that which would satisfy his animal nature.

In that dream, Niall hungered for her flesh but he could not leave the stone throne which seemed almost to hold him back. His arms stretched out, he called to her to come to him. She was a dainty promise whispered in the ear, a shapely seduction with her white legs and quivering haunches. She turned and dipped, pranced and swirled, and always the need in him for her flesh grew more sharp.

Niall woke to the first pink rays of dawn, sitting up in bed and gasping. His dream was still strong upon him, his eyes went around the room hunting for the girl. She was not there, he was alone.

He shook himself as might a shaggy mountain bear

roused from its winter sleep. Under his breath he muttered curses as he stumbled to the washbasin and poured cold water from the pitcher over his head. The water shocked him to full wakefulness and he lifted his head and stared out the window.

She was out there, in this city. He knew that. He thought he also knew where she had gone. He could not see Maylok's palace but he would find her there. He reached for his swordbelt and buckled it about his middle. A flash of light from the corners of his eyes caught his attention and he stared into a cracked mirror, seeing his face.

His skin was bronzed and his black hair hung uncut almost to his shoulders. A scar was white against the dark sun-darkened skin of his chin. A swordsman in the hire of the Great Kham had bloodied his face, and had paid with his life for scarring him. His shoulders were so wide they could scarcely fit between the lintels of a wide door, ridged with muscles standing out like ropes beneath his sun-burnt skin.

Niall was a mercenary, a sell-sword, but he had a code of sorts. Lylthia had made him a promise last night, or as good as. He would go find her and bring her back to this tavern and throw her down on that rumpled bed. The barbarian chuckled. But he must not gaze into her eyes. No. It might be best to blindfold that one.

Well, he was going after her. Now. No matter where his warboots took him.

He ate sausages and eggs in the common room, making plans in his head. She wanted vengeance on Maylok. The only place she could get that would be in his palace. He, Niall, would go also to that palace and find her and bring Lylthia out of it on a shoulder.

Uneasily, he remembered old Thallia and her prophecy. Demons would carry him off in Angalore, she had said. No matter. Maylok would have to cast a spell on him before he could summon up demons to take him away, and by that time, Maylok would be dead.

He went out into the sunlight and walked the streets of this ancient city, angling his feet always toward the huge pile of masonry standing close to the river's edge, that was the wizard's palace. It was built against the outer wall, and had a wall of its own, but smaller than the city wall, surrounding it and its gardens. Niall stood a long time studying that wall.

He could go over it easily enough. But what would he find when he dropped down onto the other side? He was no fool to go rushing into danger when there was a safe way out of it. Maylok would have guards posted. And, probably, big Commopore hounds trained to drag down any intruder and fang-slay him.

There was a huge oaken door set flush with the cobblestones of the street. Niall studied it for a moment, hitched at his swordbelt, then walked toward it. With the pommel of a dagger, he rapped on the plankings.

After a time the door swung open and two men with naked swords in their hands stood scowling at him. "What want you at the walls of Maylok, stranger?" asked the larger man.

"Money to put in my pouch." Niall grinned and rattled the little leather sack so they could hear his few coins clinking. "I'm told the wizard pays well." His eyes ran over their fleshy bodies. "Men say also that those who work for Maylok eat only thort steaks and pasties, and drink wine instead of water."

"Maylok has enough servants."

"None like me."

The man went to close the door but Niall put out his brawny arm and held the door open, using his eyes on the neat grass and carefully tended bushes that formed these outer gardens. He noted that the men grew angry, but he paid no heed to that, for he was noting the thickness of the walls and surmising that there would be rooms between outer and inner walls.

The other man came to add his muscles to the first, but Niall was a strong man whose full strength had never yet been tested, and he held that door open against both of them.

"Well, if he won't, he won't," he muttered, and released the door.

It banged shut and Niall grinned. He had seen enough. When darkness was upon Angalore he would return. Somehow, he would find a way inside that palace.

He walked around the walls and noted that a big tree grew outside a portion of those parapets. A nimble man could climb that tree, move out along a thick branch. It would be a good jump from the branch to reach the wall, but he could do it.

Whistling, he moved off toward the river gate and through it to the quays where a dozen ships were loading or unloading cargoes. He watched them, savoring the hot sunlight on his back, and fell into converse with two seamen munching on some fruit.

"Your crew works hard," he commented.

"This is Angalore. The sooner out of it, the better."

Niall pondered that. He asked slyly, "Is it because of Maylok?"

"Aye. The mage is like a spider in its web, peering out and taking that which he covets, be it gold or silver or a man and a maid. Right now he may be listening to us."

"I tried to gain employment from him."

"Count yourself lucky you didn't. He'd offer you up as a sacrifice to his demon-gods, in time."

"I think I'll sail with you, then. I'm for Urgrik to the north."

"We lift anchor tomorrow, a little past dawn. Ask for the *Hyssop,* bound for the cold countries. We make a stop at Urgrik."

Niall ate at a seaside tavern, using his ears to feed on words as he did his mouth to savor the kama-fish flavored with leeks and spices. He heard one man tell how he had seen a pretty girl being pushed into the wall-door of Maylok's palace just before dawn, a girl in ragged leather tunic and with black hair almost to her haunches. Six men had hold of her, were forcing her along.

"She's dead by now," someone muttered.

"Too bad. She was a pretty thing."

Niall did not betray himself by the slightest quiver of flesh, but fury was alive inside him. He had liked Lylthia. By the Wargod! She had been a fool, but his flesh had lusted after her. If she'd been sensible and spent the night in his arms, she'd be alive, now. Aye, and happy!

It might be too late to save Lylthia, but maybe he could find a way to avenge her.

He sat on a piling and watched the sun sink, telling himself that he was as much of a fool as Lylthia herself. Old Thallia had warned him that demons would carry him off in Angalore. If he were sensible, he'd walk over to the *Hyssop* right now and get himself a good sleep in a hammock belowdecks, and forget Lylthia.

Still, no one had ever praised his brains.

When the quays were in total darkness outside the faint starlight, Niall began his walk. He was in no hurry, indeed, he was rather reluctant to clamber onto that wall. He could think of better ways to die than to be captured by demons. Still! A man had to do what he felt was right.

The tree was big, but his muscles carried him up the thick bole and in between the heavy branches as though he were a monkey out of the jungles of Poranga. He ran out on the branch he had selected earlier in the day and paused.

The gardens were dark, the wall was empty. Lights were on in the palace. He could see flickering candles and torches through open windows, and once he thought to hear a scream of agony, dulled by distance and the palace walls. He trotted forward, swaying as the branch moved, and leaped.

For an instant he was in the air, then he was dropping down onto the parapet, clinging to its rough stone with both hands and swinging himself onto the wallwalk where he crouched, peering about and listening.

There was no one in sight, neither guards nor watchdogs, that he could discover. It might be a trap, but he had fought his way out of traps before. And if by any chance Lylthia were still alive, then he would bring her out of this pile of stones and carry her with him to Urgrik. His hand loosed Blood-drinker in its scabbard, made certain that his Orravian dagger was ready to his grip, and then slid forward between the merlonshadows.

No sentinel walked these walls, as far as he could tell. Now why was that? Did some awesome fiend patrol these pathways after dark, lurking to attack and perhaps devour—or carry off—some luckless trespasser? It might be Maylok's whim to use demons as his watchdogs. His hand tightened on the daggerhilt as he moved.

At length he came to a doorway set into a tiny shed built against an inner wall. His hand opened that door, he stepped into Stygian darkness and down a flight of worn stone steps. His warboots made no sound, nor was there any clank of swordchain or linkmail, yet the hairs at the base of his neck bristled.

It was too easy!

There should have been an alarm, an attack, before this. The wizard was no simpleton, he must have known that the tales of his ill-gotten treasures would tempt thieves and footpads. They would be protected, by what grim guardian he had no way of knowing.

Men and hounds he did not fear. His steel could handle those. It was the thought of demons which bothered him. Sooner or later he would meet some snuffling cacodemon in this blackness and be forced to fight for his life.

Yet he strode on, down the ancient steps and along a narrow corridor which must run beneath the gardens. From far away he could hear the dripping of water and nearer at hand the click of rats' nails along a stonework floor. Rats? Or—devil imps?

He lifted out Blood-drinker and moved with the blade always before him, as a blind man uses a wooden stick. He saw nothing, the ebon gloom was everywhere, pressing in upon him. And yet—as he turned a corner of the passageway, he beheld a redness up ahead.

It was only a wink of light, shifting, quivering. It seemed like a tiny corner of the Eleven Hells of Emelkartha broken free of the barriers that kept them from this world. Yet it served as a beacon to draw his footsteps forward.

He came into a low-ceilinged chamber, the walls of which were purplish in the radiance of flickering torch-flames set into that stone. A carved and runed altar stood upon a dias reached by stonework steps, and on the flat surface of that shrine to devilry lay a naked woman.

Niall took a step forward, and another. He growled low in his throat. That lifeless body at which he stared belonged to—

Lylthia!

Dead she lay, unmoving, with one arm flung limply over the edge of the altar, her eyes wide and staring upward at the low dome above that was marked with strange and alien signs and sigils. Her black hair was dark and wet, her skin the pallid hue of death itself. No! Even more! Her smooth skin was so white it almost hurt the eyes, as though every last drop of blood had been sucked from her flesh.

Niall glared about him, sword up and ready to thrust, to slay as Lylthia had been slain. Yet there was no foe, no enemy to cleave. It was quiet as a tomb, this charnel room, with only his own breathing to break the stillness.

His eyes went over that face, lovely even now in death. Her lips had lost their redness, her cheeks their tinting. But the traces of beauty lingered, and something inside the Sell-sword sorrowed to its sight. They had reaved her tattered leather tunic from her, her body was nude. As she had come into the world so she had gone from it.

"He'll pay," Niall whispered. "Somehow, I'll find a way to make him pay."

He touched her hand, squeezing the cold flesh just once, then moved on, past the altar to an ironbound door that opened beyond it into another corridor. This passageway was lighted by torches at distant intervals, and his eyes raked it, he saw that it was empty—or was it?

For as he walked he seemed almost to see a blackness in the darker shadows, a blackness that flitted ahead of him, that ran and curved and leaped, seemed almost to—beckon. Niall growled in his throat. He did not like such shadows, that went before him so enticingly.

He followed that shadow, dogged its fluttering steps, for the urge to slay Maylok was strong within him. He must pay the warlock with the same fate he had given little Lylthia. Nothing less would satisfy the barbaric urge to slay that rode him with his every heartbeat.

When he came to a curving stone staircase, he paused, but it seemed that the shadow was still before him, lifting an arm as if to urge him onward. With a grunt, the Sell-sword raced up those steps, his blade ready for instant use—

—and burst into a vast chamber.

He slid to a stop at sight of the lighted bowls about the room, at sight of the pentagram glistening red in blood, within which stood a tall man cowled in purple robe on which were stitched in golden threads the secret symbols of the demon worlds. Rigid stood the necromancer, his face pale and almost skull-like under the cowl that covered his head, a grim smile upon his thin, cruel mouth.

"Welcome, Niall of the Far Travelings. I have waited for you, even since you came through the land gate, two days hence."

"You slew Lylthia. For that you die."

Maylok chuckled. "Do I, Far-traveler? Behold!"

From beyond the blazing bowls men came rushing, big men in chainmail and with swords and axes, maces and warhammers in their hands. They rushed at Niall, and their weapons gleamed redly in the bowl-lights. Niall snarled and went to meet them.

This was why he had been born, to fight, to slay, to wield a sword as though it were a scythe of Death itself. Maybe he was allied to Death, for Death rode where Blood-drinker cut and slashed. With a roar, he fended off a blade and hewed his steel through a neck.

He was in the midst of his attackers, then, whirling, darting, dodging a blow from mace or axe, freeing Blood-drinker to this feast of flesh which had been provided for it. He did not fight as an ordinary man fights, with care and caution, as ready to ward off a blow as he might be to strike one.

Nay! When Niall fought, he sought only to kill. His eyes saw an opening, his arm controlled the sweep of his sword, and when that blade fell, it was already lifting to strike again.

Pantherish were his leaps, lionlike his bellowed challenges. Men fell away before the onslaught of his steel, men died where they faced him or backed away. Yet always the swords and maces hammered at him, though more often than not he avoided their blows.

From his eye-corners, he saw Maylok moving restlessly about the pentagram, crying out encouragement to his guards. Yet there was a palsied fear upon the wizard; never had he seen a man battle as Niall fought now, with a reckless disregard for his own safety, concerned only with slaying all those he could reach with that long blade.

More men rushed from behind the lighted bowls, they hemmed Niall in, they offered their flesh to his blade in order to bring him down. The flat of an axe took him across the side of his head, a mace thumped his swordarm, numbing it.

When he had no more room to swing Blood-drinker, he dropped it and clawed out his Orravian dagger and buried it in chest and throat and belly. His other hand he used to sink iron-strong fingers deep into throatflesh and choke out life from the man he held.

Even his massive muscles tired, after more than three hours of such battling. There were dead men on the floor, and pools of their blood on which his warboots slipped. Once more a mace thumped his arm, again the flat of a blade landed on his skull. He went to a knee, half-conscious, but still he fought. Not until hands caught his arms and held them and someone swung a war-hammer did he go down.

Half-dazed he lay there, held by bleeding, desperate men who panted and sobbed in their tiredness, seeing Maylok as through a rheumy veil approach, to stand above him.

"No man has ever fought like you, Far-traveler," whispered the exultant wizard. "Your blood shall be a strong elixir in my vials and alembics. Take him below to the dungeons and chain him there against my need."

They dragged and half-carried the still-struggling Niall out of the spell-chamber, down the worn steps and into the deep pits below the palace, where the stink of rotting flesh warred with the moans of men and women imprisoned here, kept for the torment and the blood-letting.

To huge chains inset in the stone walls they fastened Niall, his arms apart, so that they seemed almost to be torn from their sockets. He could stand only with difficulty, for those links suspended even his giant frame a little. And then they mocked him.

"The wizard will make you pay for what you've done," one said with a grin, blood running down his gashed face.

"He'll keep you alive a long time, torturing you from day to day, to test your ability to suffer."

"I've known him to cook a man alive, over two weeks, burning a little of him at a time."

"Another man he flayed over the period of a full month, to pay him for a slight."

They hit him with their fists and kicked him with their boots, but he stood stoically, with his eyes wide and glaring. One man carried his dagger and Blooddrinker in his hands, and these he thrust into his scabbards with a mocking laugh.

"I'll leave them here with you, but where you can't reach them. So near and yet out of reach. It may add to your torment, having them so close yet unable to use them."

They went away after a time and left him in the blackness where only a distant torch shed any light. His head drooped, he was feeling the cuts and slashes now, the batterings he had taken from mace and warhammer. Pain was an agony along his flesh and veins, and a raging thirst dried his throat and tongue.

He tugged at the chains, but they were tight-set in stone, and massive. His arms were stretched to their fullest length so he could exert little or no strength. His legs were tired of standing, yet he could not sleep for the manacles about his thick wrists dug their steel into his flesh when he would have relaxed. He stared into the darkness and muttered curses beneath his breath.

He sought to doze but the rats came, grey monsters that stood on their hind legs and sought to bite his knees and thighs, bared above his warboots. These he kicked away, killing some by the force of those kicks, but they remained away for only a short time, being driven by starvation. He heard men scream, and women too, from somewhere off in these pits, and he knew that Maylok was supervising their torture.

His time for that would come, he supposed, and made a wry face. He did not mind a clean death, but torture was repugnant to him. Fury at the wizard burned inside him, and his body shook in his rage so that the chains rattled.

Something touched him, soft as thistledown, so that it seemed not so much a touching as a faint caress. And his tiredness welled up in him so that he hung in his chains and slept. No rats came now to nibble at him, he heard not the screams of dying men and women. Deep were his slumbers, and dreamless.

When he woke, he was refreshed. His wrists hurt him where the manacles had held his sagging body, but there was a renewed vitality in his great muscles and he stood defiantly, as though daring his captors to approach. He had no knowledge of the time, but that distant torch still glowed, though only fitfully, enabling him to see a little better around him.

Once more that thistledown softness touched him and now he glanced sideways, and his flesh crawled for a moment. The shadow was with him!

It was little more than a deeper darkness against the blackness of the dungeon, but he could make it out. Was this some fiend sent by Maylok to bring him some undreamed-of torment? But no. Or if it was, it did nothing but stare at him.

Niall stared back and now—but faintly—he could make out greenish eyes in that umbrageous shape. He shook himself, the chains rattled.

"What are you?" he rasped. "What?"

The shadow did not speak, but stretched out a slim arm at the end of which was a shadow-hand. And at the tips of slim fingers, greenish balls of fire began to glow.

His torture would begin now, the Far-traveler knew. Curse Maylok by all the eleven hells for—

The green balls touched a manacle, not his flesh.

And where the manacle had been was only—rusted powder. That powder fell away, the chain dropped and his mightily thewed left arm was free. Again those green balls moved, to touch the other manacle and Niall stepped away from the stone wall.

"My thanks," he growled. "Whoever you are."

The shadow danced before him as if to lead him away from the dungeon wall. Niall put hands to his swordhilt and his dagger, lifting them half out of their scabbards, and then he went after that flitting shape.

It ran before him, dancing almost in its eagerness, luring him as once before it had beckoned him on. But there was a difference in the shadow-being now; it did not slink but cavorted, spiralled and swayed—more gracefully than any dancing girl he had ever seen. It reminded him almost of that dream he had had, in which Lylthia had danced for him.

The shadow moved and where it went, Niall followed. To a small chamber it led him, and touched the iron bars and locks of its vast oak door with the green balls at the tips of its fingers. Niall put a hand to those plankings and pushed the door inward.

Chests lay piled one atop the other here, with small coffers and caskets above and beside them. The shadow gestured and the Sell-sword lifted the cover of one and then another.

He saw diamonds piled high in one, emeralds in another, golden coins in yet a third. Again the shadow-being waved a hand and Niall filled his money pouch with jewels and golden coins until it overflowed. There were treasures here gathered during Maylok's lifetime and the lifetimes of his father and grandfather, who had been famous sorcerers in their own right. He would have liked to take it all, but knew it was beyond his power to carry.

At the far door, the shadow waited, and finally Niall went with it, running after it as it picked up speed. Through winding passageways and up dusty stairways long forgotten did the shadow-being take him, until they came at last to a walled-up doorway.

With the green balls, the shadow touched those

stones and the stones melted to run in molten slag down onto the floor. Beyond the opening thus made was a dark drapery. This, Niall pushed aside.

He stood on the rim of the necromantic chamber where Maylok could be seen through the smoke of the flaming bowls, head flung back and arms raised high, as he chanted in some forgotten, phylogenetic tongue. He was not aware that Niall was in his necromantic chamber, he was engrossed in his incantation. The shadow danced forward, pointing to Maylok and gesturing the Sell-sword forward.

Niall went at the run, yanking out the Orravian dagger. He would not bother to use his blade on the wizard, deeming him not worth the trouble of lifting Blood-drinker. As he ran, the shadow went with him and now he felt again that thistledown softness of its touch, where it clasped his wrist.

Maylok whipped around, startled by the faint sound of warboots on stone. His eyes opened wide, his lips parted to scream.

Then Niall was over the blood-wet pentagram and raising his dagger for the death stroke. But the shadow was ahead of him, reaching out with its dainty hands for Maylok and the wizard screamed indeed when he saw that graceful blackness reaching out to gather him into its embrace.

Niall could not move. He paused in midstroke, not wanting to harm the shadow—not even knowing if he could—but seeing that shadow now as that of a pretty girl.

"Lylthia," he whispered.

"Not Lylthia, no. But once I was—yes," hissed a voice.

Laughter rang out, cruel and mirthless.

The palace swirled about Niall as he swayed drunkenly inside that pentagram, feeling the floor shift under his warboots, knowing a dizziness induced not by blow of weapon but by some demonaic spell. Faster the palace moved, faster, faster. He could not stand, but reeled and would have fallen but for the cool hand that caught and held him.

He stood in redness.

Beneath him the floor was of scarlet stone, faintly hot. Around him rose gargantuan walls of a brilliant carmine streaked with slashes of deepest ebony, on which were huge strange tapestries and golden vessels. Massive columns of black and vermilion rose upward toward a distant roof half-hidden by redly glowing mists.

A thin high squealing caught his ears. Maylok was grovelling on the warm stone floor, beating at it with his fists and scratching with his nails. His purple cloak and cowl were already smoking, his body writhed as though he were in torment.

"Save me, Far-traveler," he mewled. "Save me and my treasure is yours. All the jewels, all the gold that my forefathers and I have gathered together, shall all be yours. And I—Maylok the Mighty, the wisest wizard in the world, shall be your slave!"

Niall growled, "I ought to kill you, you foul slug."

"Yes!" Maylok screamed, struggling upward to his knees and presenting his scrawney throat. "Slay me! Slay me and take my treasures. Only do me this favor, Niall of the Mighty Arms—kill me, kill me!"

Soft laughter floated through the vast room. It mocked and taunted and when it touched the necromancer he grovelled on the floor.

"Great Emelkartha—spare me," he bleated.

"Too late for mercy, Maylok. Nah, nah. You pay the price."

And Maylok screamed.

In the midst of that screaming, a woman came forward, clad in diaphanous robes of crimson streaked with jet through which Niall could see the flesh tints of her body. Long black hair floated down about her shoulders and her green eyes blazed with fury. On her full mouth was a cold, cruel smile.

"Lylthia," he whispered.

The green eyes slid sideways from the cringing necromancer to touch the Sell-sword, and it seemed to him they softened. "Not Lylthia, no. Not any more. Know me, barbarian, for Emelkartha herself."

Niall said boldly, "too bad. I think I could have loved Lylthia."

Her mouth lost its cruelty, grew softly amorous. "The woman part of me knows that, Niall of the Far Travelings, and—thanks you.

"At first I was angry with you for saving me from Maylok's men. I wanted to be taken by them, to be drained of blood, so that I could become—a shadow being. Yet you did me a favor and for that I am not ungrateful.

"You could pass the pentagram. Not even I could do that, not as Lylthia nor as her shadow. Yet by touching you, your strength drew me along—to catch Maylok in my arms and bring him here to my eleven hells, as men name this domain over which I rule."

She was silent and Niall scanned her features, finding them more beautiful than ever, with broad brow and tiptilted nose and those full lips exerting a sensuous appeal that shook him to his marrow. He licked his lips. Old Thallia had been right. A demon-woman had carried him off the world and into her abode. He wondered if he would ever return.

The green eyes glanced at him slyly.

"Well, Niall? Would you stay with me and be my lover?"

He found himself nodding, and she smiled but shook her head. "Nah, nah, you may not—though a part of me would like to keep you here. This place is not made for—human flesh. It cannot endure the heat and mephitic vapors for very long—without pain."

Maylok screeched and banged his head against the hot floor.

Emelkartha whispered and now eerie shapes to which Niall could not put a name ran from the walls to lay tentacles upon Maylok and lift him to his feet. He was sweating, gasping for breath, trembling as with the ague.

"You made a mock of me, magician," whispered Emelkartha, and how her voice burned the eardrums with its rage. "For that you shall suffer. As you have made your fellow-man suffer, so now shall you, from the first to the last of my eleven hells. You shall be tortured to death, yet shall be reborn after each death so that you may suffer even worse torments. Eleven times shall you die, eleven times shall you be reborn, to begin anew—until the end of Time itself!"

Maylok screamed and screamed. His body contorted and twisted, but he was helpless in those rubbery tentacles that held him. In this manner he was dragged across that hot stone floor toward a distant doorway through which Niall could glimpse blazing fires and upreaching flames.

They drew the wizard through the doorway.

For an instant he seemed to come to a dead stop, with his sandals digging in at the stone floor. Peal after peal of agonized fear burst from his throat when he saw what lay before him. Then he was gone and steam rose up to blot out the sight of what was being done to him.

The demon-woman looked at Niall inquiringly. "You do not approve," she whispered. "Yet Maylok has sinned against the demon world for too long a time, holding us in thrall. Soon—he would have been too strong for me to act against him, for he intended summoning up megademons known to me who would have prevented my disposing of him. His incantations are incomplete, and so my world—and yours—is safe from him, forever."

He nodded, he knew what wickednesses Maylok had done, of girls ravished and tormented, of brave men broken and tortured into mindless hulks, of treasures taken from rightful owners. Maylok deserved these eleven hells.

Shadow of a Demon

There was nothing he, Niall, could do about it, anyhow.

His eyes ran over her body, so much revealed in the black and scarlet transparencies she wore. He sighed, and with that sigh, the woman-demon floated closer, tilting up her head and lifting her bare arms.

Niall caught her in his embrace, held her a moment, and kissed her. He would never forget that kiss. It burned deep into him, seemed to lift him out of his flesh into another state of being where pleasure was almost unendurable. His arms held this lissom woman to him, and something inside him told him that no mortal woman could ever afterward affect him as did this one whom he had known as Lylthia.

"For now—farewell," her voice whispered . . .

She was gone and he stood alone inside the pentagram in the palace of the doomed wizard. A cold wind was blowing through the building, that chilled and refreshed him. He shook himself, touching his swordhilt for reassurance that he still lived, that he was back in his own world.

His heart still thudded with the excitement of that last embrace. Whatever else she was, Emelkartha was a woman, her mouth had whispered to him of indescribable delights in that kiss. He shook his head, telling himself that he had gained a rich treasure in the gold and diamonds in his money pouch, but had lost something worth much more.

"Lylthia," he whispered as he walked through the forsaken halls of the ancient palace. "Lylthia . . ."

Would Emelkartha ever appear to him again—in human form? As—Lylthia? She had the power, certainly, being a woman-demon. But would she? He did not know, all he could do was hope.

He walked out into the gathering dawn and made his way to the wall-gate, unmolested. It was as if, with the wizard's death, his servants had all fled away. Or —been destroyed.

A river breeze had sprung up. He moved along the

street toward the *Hyssop,* which would carry him to Urgrik. Yet there was a sadness in him, despite the wealth in his pouch.

"Lylthia," he whispered once again.

But the seawind caught the name and carried it away.

Pat McIntosh

RING OF BLACK STONE

Either John Martin, editor of Anduril, who has been running these stories in his excellent magazine, or I, who have been reprinting them in each of these Year's Bests, can claim to have discovered Pat McIntosh. This is the third and newest of her off-beat Sword & Sorcery stories about Thula, a girl warrior who is as gorgeous as Red Sonja, and gutsier than Jirel.

When you're talking about stories this good, it doesn't matter if you have to share the credit for their discovery with another. There's a lot of credit to go around.

—L.C.

I came upon them by the last of the daylight, an old woman and a bare legged child filling in a grave before a cold and lonely smithy. Neither moon nor sun being in the sky, I guessed they were burying a married couple, sun-child and moon-daughter; it seemed the proper thing to do, to tether my horse and help.

Once the Passing Words were said, the child and I helped the old woman to her feet. She looked me up and down and glanced, briefly, over my shoulder.

"Bid you thanks for your courtesy," she said, "Will you shelter the night, daughter?"

"A blessing on the roof-tree," I answered formally, "that shelters the stranger."

She smiled crookedly, and turned away towards the house. The child said,

"Are you a girl?"

"She is a war-maid, Melagra," said the old woman, turning back briefly. "She serves the Goddess."

"My name's Thula," I added.

"Does your horse dislike donkeys?" Melagra demanded. I must have looked blank, for she turned on her heel, marched up to Dester and unhitched his reins. "Come and meet the donkey," she said to him. He blew suspiciously at her, but did not offer to bite. I followed her round the house to the stable, and asked as she lit the lantern,

"What happened? Was it a raid from the Eyries?"

"It was the soldiers. They came for Melvia. I hid when I heard the shouting, and they killed Mam and Dad and left Gran for dead and took Melvia away." She thrust a full hay-net at me. "Here. Pulley's there."

"Soldiers don't do things like that," I objected, hauling the net up.

"It was soldiers," she said, her voice rising. Dester tossed his head and snorted, and in the other stall the donkey stirred nervously.

"Was your Gran hurt?" I asked.

"Hit on the head. I'm glad you've come," she said confidingly. "Maybe she won't talk so odd in front of strangers. She's been seeing things for me."

"What sort of things?"

"A man with no face, looking over my shoulder. That sort of thing." She dumped a brimming measure of oats in the manger. Dester thrust his nose in, shouldering me aside. "Gran's a witch," she added.

In the low-raftered kitchen there was lamplight, and the old woman was cooking a meal. She looked around as I came in, bright sharp eyes sizing me up; apart from the eyes she was like any other old women, bent and stringy and hung with the dead leaves of her beauty.

"Melagra, there are blankets in the painted chest," she said. As soon as the door closed behind the child she turned to me.

"Daughter, will you ride into the city with Melagra?" she asked urgently.

"Willingly," I said, "but what about you? You can't stay . . ."

"I will set out," she said, "but I will not reach the city. My end waits me on the road." She reached out, and took my hand in a surprisingly hard grasp. "Daughter . . ."

The door opened. I turned, and Melagra stood there, arms full of blankets. Over her shoulder, clearly as by daylight, I saw a man's face. Red hair hung short over the eyes, long at the sides; and below the eyes, between the heavy locks of hair, a flat expanse of nothing. I jumped, and exclaimed something, and broke the old woman's clasp on my hand. The vision vanished.

"What is it?" said Melagra in a small voice.

"You see it too?" said her grandmother. "A man with no face."

"No, a mask," I said. "From here down, a mask over his face."

"Nearly as bad," muttered Melagra.

"There's a man behind you," said the old woman. I twisted involuntarily to look. "A yellow-eyed king."

"A king . . . ?" I said blankly. "Mother, what does it mean?"

She smiled, a secretive smile, and turned back to the stove.

"It seems to me," she said, "the man for each of you who'll get what you guard most closely."

Melagra snorted.

"No man in a mask's getting anything from me," she said roundly.

Once the child was in bed, I asked the old woman about the raid, and she confirmed my thoughts.

"Great wild men dressed in silks and furs," she said. "One struck me down, and I saw no more, but Ervik would have tried to defend his home, and my daughter, and got them both slain." She sighed. "He was a true smith, and believed cold iron could solve everything. The soldiers must have come and driven them off before they found Melvia. One of the captains saw her at the fair and had a fancy to her. It will be him that took her away."

"Melagra thinks it was the soldiers who killed her parents."

She nodded, and sighed again. There was a silence, until she said suddenly.

"Aye, the child is by far too young. How old are you, daughter?"

"Twenty-one," I said.

"So? I thought you more. No matter, you will do. Melagra will have told you I have the Power?"

"Well," I said, "yes."

"Gran's a witch," she quoted, and laughed shrilly. "She is young, she follows her father's judgment. May he rest in peace. Well, I bear the Power. It was my grandam's, and her grandam's, and in time I meant it for Melagra, but time I do not have. My end comes before we reach the city, and she is too young to take it from me. Yet I must hand it on or my bones will walk with its strength." Another silence. "It is not a great power," she said. "I lack the learning. Healings, plant-blessings, strengthen a halter, make an oven to fire evenly, these I can do. I am no spinner of man-trapping spells." Another silence, which lasted until I thought she was asleep. I shifted position, and she roused with a little jerk. "So, daughter," she continued, "will you take the Power from me?"

"Me?" I said, startled. I had barely been attending. Now, running over what she had said, I saw this as its grounding and design. "Me?" I said again. "But I'm not..."

"You have the strength," she said, "You saw the man who will have Melagra in the end, when you held my hand. You can bear it. Will you?"

"But I'm not the one, surely! Wait and let Melagra..."

"I cannot wait. Since we buried my daughter, I have seen my end coming. It will meet me on the road to the city, and I am glad, for I grieve for the dead. Daughter, will you take the Power and let my bones rest, or must I walk the nights till I find one with the courage to take it from the dead?"

There was another silence. At last, from a dry mouth, "I will take it," I said.

"Then hold out your hands."

I knelt by her and obeyed. She set them palm to palm, her own outside them, and spoke five slow words in a language I did not know. Then she said, "I give the Power I bear, freely given, freely taken, not mine to give."

"I take the Power you bear," I improvised, "freely given, freely taken, not mine to take. You give and I accept."

Her grasp tightened; she closed her eyes. Suddenly the world whirled about me, so that I lost touch with the flags under me, the wooden chair-arm, everything but the dry old hands clasping mine. Then it came straight again; but all was, somehow, different. Brighter, with sharper edges, clearer even by lamplight. As if the windows of my mind had been washed. But the old woman blinked at me with watery eyes.

"I had forgot how dull the world was," she said. After a pause she added, "Three things I must tell you. Remember them well, and pass them on when the time comes, and use them between now and then."

"Well?" I prompted.

"The first is that man's magic and woman's magic are as different as man and woman. Man-spells build, they are mechanical, once begun they are not readily turned aside but only destroyed. They make things, but differently from us. Woman-spells grow things, they turn on loving and hating, and love turning to hate can change a spell in the middle. When they clash, sometimes one wins, sometimes the other. Like men and women." She was silent, seeing something distant. "The Power is from the Lady," she said at length. "Do not use it as she would not wish. You I need not tell that."

"That's two," I said after a moment. She roused again with a jerk.

"Where was I? Aye, I need not tell you that. The third thing is that you will see your end approach, if you have not given the power already. Then you must give it, or you will not rest. Give it to a woman with strength to bear it and wisdom to use it, not to a child, not to one past bearing." She moved the lamp nearer, to peer at my face. "Do you understand these things?"

"I think so," I said.

"If you were certain, you would be wrong," she said. "Good."

"Mother," I said, "what about the other girl? Melvia?"

"My daughter's step-daughter," she said. "She lacks the strength. Go and sleep, lonely one. We will leave early."

Melagra, by daylight, looked like a kitten. She had wide, green eyes and a pointed face, and a hood of untidy dark curls. She was more cheerful than she had been in the evening, and plied me with questions as she harnessed the donkey. I think I scarcely answered; I was distracted by the strange new look of things. Colors were sharper, things were brighter, there were patterns in shapes and movements I had never seen before.

"Gran says there should be two of you," said the child. "You ride in pairs and fight evil under the moon."

I nodded, admiring the long graceful curves of Dester's heavy head.

"Where's your pair, then?"

Reality intruded.

"Dead," I said shortly. There was a silence; then she said.

"Could I be your pair instead? I'd like to do that and have a sword and wear trousers. Does it take long to learn how?"

"You've your Gran and your sister to look after," I pointed out. She scowled, and backed the donkey up against its cart.

Eventually we left. They had very little baggage, and the old woman would take nothing in the cart with her but a blanket to sit on. The rest made a bundle which I tied on Dester's saddle, preferring to lead him. He had struck up a great friendship with the donkey overnight, and plodded happily along beside it, south towards the city, the Old Mountains with the high holds called the Eyries away to our left.

"Why are you going to the city?" I asked.

"To get Melvia back from that man." said Melagra. "The one that did that."

"How do you know it was him that took her?"

"He wanted her."

"He came to ask for her, properly, after the Spring Fair," said the old woman. "But she would have none of him. I think he was too hasty for her."

"She said he was rude," said Melagra. "Father beat her, but she didn't encourage him, whatever he said. I was there, I saw."

"How will you find him?" I asked. She threw me a scathing glance.

"We can ask, can't we?" she said. My heart sank.

We came to a cross-roads, among trees. Melagra halted the donkey and turned her head, listening.

"Horses," she said. I listened, and glanced at Dester, whose ears were pricked.

"At least ten," I guessed. "Coming from straight ahead."

Melagra nodded, and tugged the donkey's head

round and led him into the westward road, as fast as he would go.

"Soldiers," she said. "Coming to make sure we're dead."

The old woman raised her head, and her eyes met mine. I said nothing. We hurried on, until a bend in the road hid us behind the trees; there Melagra stopped, listening. I covered Dester's nose so he would not whinny, and the sound of hooves, muffled by trees, came nearer, grew suddenly louder as they passed the crossroads, and faded into the distance.

"Do we go back to the other road?" I prompted.

"This one's shorter," Melagra said. "The soldiers use the other one because it's paved. Come on," she said to the donkey.

We walked in silence for a while, a mile or two. The old woman appeared to be praying, and Melagra was intent on the road. I began to get a feeling like goose flesh in my mind. I looked around and saw nothing, only the new, clear-edged world, the pair and the donkey before me, the road and the small river beside it, but the uneasiness grew. I dropped back, puzzled, and Dester tossed his head and grumbled, but made no attempt to catch up, which also puzzled me.

The river bent right, and the road followed it, perched between the water and the steep bank. Melagra led the donkey round the curve, under the bank, and slowly, in silence, the entire slope began to move. I cried out, and the first rumbling began; the donkey brayed in terror, and Melagra screamed, and the rumbling was a thunder. Then Dester reared, and tried to make off. He knew about moving cliffs, and disliked what he knew. I got control, after a long sweating minute, only by using all my weight on the reins, and by then it was all over, and a tongue of mixed rock and settling dust lay across the road almost to its edge.

I coaxed Dester forward, and he minced shivering past on the narrow stretch of road that remained, rolling his eyes at the boulders. Beyond them the donkey stood trembling convulsively, Melagra rigid and white-faced beside it.

Behind the donkey were boulders, and one crushed cartwheel. It suddenly dawned on me why the dust under them was wet.

"Mother of mares," I said, and more rock slid down, dust rising as it came. Melagra gasped. I put out my hand to her, and turned to look, and the dust instead of settling hung in the air, swirled and spread, more rising to join it, until we stood in a cloud that stung the eyes and choked the nose.

Then I began to think I saw a face. It was lumpy and uneven, like the faces you see in cliffs and rocks, and it opened a craggy mouth and spoke, in a voice like boulders grinding in a stream-bed.

"I have tasted blood," it said slowly. "For the first time in many frosts I have tasted blood. What do you wish of me?"

I stared. Then I remembered, vaguely, the proper form of address for elementals. I drew breath to use it, and choked on dust.

"You hate," said the voice. "You bear hate as a stone under your heart. Give the ring where you hate and it will do your wishing."

Dust swirled again, and hid the face; something fell on the ground and rolled against Melagra's foot. The dust began, slowly, to settle.

"Mother of mares," I said.

Melagra stooped and lifted the something, pocketed it without a word, and began to cut the donkey free of the shattered cart. After a moment I set to piling more stones on top of the ones that were there, since there was no hope of uncovering what lay below, even using Dester as a draught-horse. He had calmed now, and was standing protectively over his donkey. Melagra, having cut the traces, led the two animals away a few steps and tethered them by putting stones on the donkey's reins; then she came to help me. Still in silence, we finished the task. I knelt for a moment and said the Passing Words, and then said to Melagra,

"What now?"

"The city," she said, "to get Melvia back."

We went on. Looking sideways at the child did nothing to ease my concern for her. Her face was blank and set, like a doll's, and when I spoke she answered only if it was necessary. After a while I asked,

"May I see the thing you picked up?"

She looked at me a moment, then took it out and handed it to me. My palm prickled at its touch. It was a ring, carved out of black stone, smooth and dull, with a pattern of interlaced lines around it. Somehow I was not tempted to try it on; I found it oddly repellent.

"It's magic," I said, recognizing the cause of the prickling. "Sorcery."

"Yes," said Melagra, and took it back.

We walked in silence leading the animals. I was praying for the dead; it seemed to me the living had more need of help, but how do you comfort a doll?

The city was in fact a small garrison town, serving the fort that guards the approaches to the South Pass. Clusters of little houses, two temples (the Sun-Lord's house predictably prosperous), wine-shops, brothels and other essential services, all huddled against the walls of the fort. We made for the market place, and I paused there, looking round, intending to find stabling, food and lodging before anything else; but Melagra marched up to the nearest soldier.

"Where's that Captain?" she demanded.

He stared down at her, puzzlement gathering in his face.

"The dark one," she said impatiently, "The big dark one with a red cloak."

"They'm all have red cloaks, maidie," said the soldier slowly.

"And a gold earring."

"They'm mostly have earrings. Would thee be wishing our Captain Zarkas, maidie? There he'm yonder."

We both turned to look. Two men in red cloaks were approaching, one slight and fair, the other big, well-made, striking rather than handsome, with dark hair and grey eyes and a humorous mouth. I took an instant liking to him.

"That's him," said Melagra. The soldier crashed to attention as his officers came up, and said,

"Party seeking you, Captain, sir!"

Both men returned the salute, and the dark one turned to us enquiringly.

"Good day to you, sister," he said to me. "And what may I do for the Order?"

"Here," said Melagra, and held out the ring. He began to refuse, politely enough. "For you," she added. "Put it on."

"Melagra," I said reprovingly. The Captain, about to speak again, stopped and stared at her.

"Melagra," he repeated. "Melvia's sister?" She nodded.

"By the Knife! Moppet, we thought you were dead, or worse! I've just been out to the smithy looking for you. How did you get here?"

"Walked," said Melagra briefly. "Put the ring on. It's a bridegift," she added, as if inspired. He grinned, a little foolishly, and took it from her. It was a good fit on his middle finger; he turned his hand stiffly to admire it, and said,

"Was anybody else . . . ?"

"The child's grandmother," I said, "but she died on the road."

"I'm sorry to hear it," he said. "I . . . look, Harek, will you excuse me? I must see the ladies home to my wife."

He swept us away before the other man had time to answer, summoning a soldier to see to the beasts, gathering our baggage together. By the time I breathed again we were on the doorstep of one of the little houses, with Melagra and her sister clinging together, and the sister was weeping.

She was a surprise to me. Somehow I had expected a fluffy little blonde, but this was a girl my own height, slender, not pretty but with a bone structure that improves with age. Dark-red hair coiled in the nape of her neck caught the last sunlight as she bent over her sister; and to my strange new way of seeing there was a matching, smouldering glow of resentment coiled in her heart.

"Is there enough to go round?" I asked. "Shall I go out and fetch something? Two extra mouths..."

"We can feed my wife's sister," said the Captain, and Melagra shot him a bright glance from the shelter of the other girl's arm. "And any of your sisterhood gets a welcome at my board, madam." He turned to Melvia, who gazed at him with unfriendly eyes.

"You want Melagra to stay then?" she said.

"Dammit, woman," he said, exasperated, "what have I just said?"

There was a sudden high-pitched humming noise, not loud, and a crack as if a splinter of wood had broken. A strange expression flitted across Zarkas' face; he lifted his hand and stared at it. The middle finger was innocent of ring, whether stone or metal; but about his wrist, fitting too closely to remove, was a band of black stone with an interlaced pattern carved on it. I stared, and turned to Melagra, but she had followed her sister into the house.

"What..." began Zarkas, and manifestly changed his mind. "What chanced at the forge, then sister? I thought they were all dead." He led me into the side room. "I took a detail out this morning to see to things. Must have just missed you. We saw the graves, and my sergeant swore the stove had been used, but..." he grinned, rubbing uneasily at his finger. "Didn't seem a very good start to married life."

"Married?"

"This morning. Seemed the best way to protect her.

She's nervous, what lass wouldn't be, father cut down in front of her eyes, and it makes her edgy. He was dead, right enough?"

"He and his wife both," I said. "Was it a raid from the Eyries?"

"Aye . . . they're getting too confident these days. If we hadn't happened by and driven them off . . . !"

"The child thinks it was your doing."

"Mine?" he said blankly, and dismissed that. "What of the old woman . . . the grandmother?"

"There was a rockfall, about five miles out along the unmade road."

He frowned, then nodded.

"Aye, the Groaning Cliff. Been threatening to go. I'll send a detail out tomorrow to clean up."

We ate in silence. The portions were rather small, for obvious reasons, but there was bread and honey to fill out the corners; once we reached that stage, tired of listening to chewing noises, I said,

"You're not from hereabouts, Captain."

"No more than you," he agreed. "West-aways. Merthilion. Do you know that part?"

I began to draw him out about his home and family. After a time he stopped fingering at the place where the stone ring should be, and talked freely enough. The sisters listened, Melagra with a disquieting glitter in her eyes, Melvia with a slow reluctant interest, beginning perhaps to see him as a person with a past and a future. Then, out above the city, a brazen bell sounded. Zarkas swore, and got hastily to his feet.

"Forgive me, ladies," he said. "Duty calls. Back in an hour or so." He swung his red cloak round his shoulders and reached for his helmet. Melvia, tight-lipped with annoyance again, rose and stood by the door.

"There's only one bed," she said pointedly.

"There are blankets," he said, fastening his chin-strap with one hand.

"And where in this cluttered little . . ."

"Use your head, girl!" he said. "You and I in the..."

There was another high-pitched hum, and a crack like a twig breaking, and his expression flickered. Under his cloak, one hand fell to the other wrist, then moved to the upper arm. I could almost see through the scarlet cloth. He looked down and touched his ringfinger again, frowning, then said more gently,

"Your sister and Mistress Thula must sleep in here. Melagra will make her home with us. If need be we'll get bigger quarters, but until we can get her a bed she must sleep on the floor, because nobody but us is sleeping in our bed. Now be a good girl." He put up his hand and touched her on the cheek, though she jerked away. I could see no stone ring, whether on finger or wrist; but where he had pushed back the tunic sleeve, a corner of bloody bandage showed. "Back in an hour."

The door closed behind him. Melvia stood for a long moment staring at it, and I saw her hand come up to her cheek. Then she turned back into the room.

Once I had assured her that I could perfectly well share with Melagra, we busied ourselves making up a bed. Blankets there were in plenty; the little house was well-stocked with household goods, mostly new. We worked in silence, Melvia angrily, Melagra with the look of a cat about to be fed. I was thinking about Zarkas and the stone ring. The ring which shifted when he spoke sharply to Melvia. Finger to wrist, wrist to upper arm: upper arm to where? And what drove it? Melagra's hatred, perhaps, which burned in her with a cold and sullen fire; the power I bore showed it to me as clearly as the resentment that burned more warmly in her sister. Give the ring where you hate, the face had said, and it will do your wishing. I wondered briefly if I could coax the child to admit his good points, but one attempt, when Melvia went to look for pillows, was greeted with,

"He killed Mam and Dad and he stole Melvia. He's bad."

"He loves your sister, I think," I said.

"He wants her."

I abandoned that approach. She might change her views in time, but time, I feared, we did not have. Later, when Melagra went to the outhouse, I drew breath to speak to her sister, and was forestalled.

"What reason has she to hate him?"

"She thinks he brought the raiders that killed your parents," I said. "She's only a child, and she hid at the first sounds." I looked at her, stiff with anger. "Do you hate him? Can you leave him?"

She shook her head, tight-mouthed.

"We said the words. I thought I was alone, I let him rush me. Now there's Melagra. I don't know what the best thing is!"

"He can support you well," I said, looking at the room. "He must have dowered the place for you . . . all this is new."

She nodded, and Melagra returned. There was a long silence, which in sheer desperation I broke with the nonsense-tale about the boy and the pot of mint. Three tellers is a good number, and although Melagra was reluctant to join in at first, by the end of the tale they were both rocking with laughter, capping each other's descriptions of the people who were stuck to the pot. Melagra had the end-words.

"And with that the sun set," she said, "and they all came unstuck and went home. And if they haven't reached home they must be travelling yet."

"Well told," said Captain Zarkas in the doorway.

Melvia leapt up sharply, and bumped into the table. It shook, and a dish slid off and crashed to the floor. Two of her hairpins, shaken loose by the movement, followed it down.

"Now look what you've done!" she said angrily, and dropped to her knees and began gathering fragments together with shaking fingers. Zarkas strode forward, seized her by the wrist, drew her to her feet.

"Melvia," he said. She raised her eyes and looked at

him, and heavy coils of her hair slipping round her shoulders. I could not see her expression, but he drew a sharp breath. "Is that how you see me, girl?"

She said nothing.

"Come," he said. "We must discuss this. I pray you excuse us," he added in a perfunctory way, hoisted her into his arms and strode into the bedchamber. She was apparently limp with astonishment. The door shut firmly behind them. I looked at Melagra, and she was like a cat that has stolen butter. I looked at the door, and all my new-sharpened senses told me something was wrong. The door was thick, and the two voices came only faintly, but neither was violent.

Then Melvia screamed.

I leapt to my feet, and she screamed again, and again. The rational explanation . . . that Zarkas was exercising his conjugal rights . . . never occurred to me; drawing my knife I ran to the door and flung it open. Melvia was by the hearth, rooted to the floor, screaming and screaming; and on the bed, sprawled as if he had staggered and fallen there, Zarkas lay with his hands to his throat. Between the girl's screams I heard his choked breathing.

"Melagra," I said, "get wine for your sister. And a light."

Unexpectedly, she obeyed. I went to Zarkas and drew his hands from his throat, with some difficulty. Round his neck, just above the shirt collar, was a ring of black stone with a carved pattern of interlaced bands. It was cold to the touch, and my fingers tingled. Magic, said my new-found senses, strong magic, dark magic. Hate directed it, hate powered it, and it was slowly strangling Zarkas. He was going blue, semi-conscious, still struggling feebly with the thing; the wound under the bandage had opened and was spreading scarlet. I judged we had ten minutes at the most to deal with the matter.

"She won't drink it," said Melagra. I looked down at her, and she was staring at the Captain, biting her lip.

Melvia was still screaming. I marched over and boxed her ears, and she stopped, hiccupped a couple of times, and began to cry instead. I tried to give her some wine, but she pulled away from me and flung herself on Zarkas, still weeping.

"Don't die," she wailed, "please don't, oh, please!"

"Thula do something!" said Melagra on a note of rising panic. "Stop the spell, make it go away, Thula do something!"

"Don't you start," I said, taking her hand. Her panic surged through me and abated, and the old woman's words came to me. "Love turning to hate can change a spell in the middle." And contrariwise . . . ?

It was as if I flexed muscles of my mind I never knew were there. I knew exactly what I must do. Hate powered the stone ring, hate guided it; I must replace hate by love.

"Melagra," I said. "You love your sister?" She nodded, looking anxiously from me to the girl on the bed. "Then think about it. Take her hand and think about how you love her and all the good things you've done together. Think about how you want her to be happy."

We joined hands, and I felt the warmth of the child's affection, and gradually, filtering through her, the painful flickering heat of Melvia's brand-new love for her man. I reached out and with my other hand touched the stone ring, and closed my eyes, to shut myself out. There was only love in the circle; Melvia weeping on the Captain's chest, Melagra clutching her sister's hand, Zarkas sobbing for air and still clawing feebly at the ring, all in their own ways loving, loving . . . .

The tingling in my hand increased, and suddenly changed in quality, as if something were drawn out of my finger tips, the same something as came to my other hand where Melagra clutched me. It grew stronger and stronger, and I began to feel that I could not break the circle if I tried. Then a humming began, and a fine vibration under my fingers, and rose higher and higher and began to throb so it hurt my head. Loving, I thought, people who love each other, and the throbbing rose to a sobbing scream that stabbed pain in my ears; and there was a sharp crack, and silence.

I thought for a moment I had gone deaf. Then Zarkas drew a long ragged breath. Melagra fell against me and slid to the floor, weeping quietly and unchildishly, and Melvia said faintly, "Don't die, please don't. I want you so."

"He won't," I said. The ring lay on the quilt beside his ear, finger-sized; I lifted it, and tucked it in an inside pocket. The Temple could deal with it in the morning. Melvia raised her head, and Zarkas opened his eyes and met hers. Five heartbeats they stared.

"Why, Melvia," he said hoarsely, and rolled on his side and kissed her. She returned the kiss, with growing fervor. I knelt and lifted the weeping child and went out into the other room, closing the door carefully behind me.

George R. R. Martin

THE LONELY SONGS OF LAREN DORR

Chances are, if you know Martin's work at all, you know him as a science fiction novelist of the gritty realism school, and would never suspect that he could tune his style to anything as lyrical and delicately spun as this new story. But he obviously has more up his sleeve, or in his bag o' tricks, than he has yet demonstrated.

As the next tale amply demonstrates....

—L.C.

There is a girl who goes between the worlds.

She is grey-eyed and pale of skin, or so the story goes, and her hair is a coal-black waterfall with half-seen hints of red. She wears about her brow a circlet of burnished metal, a dark crown that holds her hair in place and sometimes puts shadows in her eyes. Her name is Sharra; she knows the gates.

The beginning of the story is lost to us, with the memory of the world from which she sprang. The end? The end is not yet, and when it comes we shall not know it.

We have only the middle, or rather a piece of that

middle, the smallest part of the legend, a mere fragment of the quest. A small tale within the greater, of one world where Sharra paused, and of the lonely singer Laren Dorr and how they briefly touched.

One moment there was only the valley, caught in twilight. The setting sun hung fat and violet on the ridge above, and its rays slanted down silently into a dense forest whose trees had shiny black trunks and colorless ghostly leaves. The only sounds were the cries of the mourning-birds coming out for the night, and the swift rush of water in the rocky stream that cut the woods.

Then, through a gate unseen, Sharra came tired and bloodied to the world of Laren Dorr. She wore a plain white dress, now stained and sweaty, and a heavy fur cloak that had been half-ripped from her back. And her left arm, bare and slender, still bled from three long wounds. She appeared by the side of the stream, shaking, and she threw a quick, wary glance about her before she knelt to dress her wounds. The water, for all its swiftness, was a dark and murky green. No way to tell if it was safe, but Sharra was weak and thirsty. She drank, washed her arm as best she could in the strange and doubtful water, and bound her injuries with bandages ripped from her clothes. Then, as the purple sun dipped lower behind the ridge, she crawled away from the water to a sheltered spot among the trees, and fell into exhausted sleep.

She woke to arms around her, strong arms that lifted her easily to carry her somewhere, and she woke struggling. But the arms just tightened, and held her still. "Easy," a mellow voice said, and she saw a face dimly through gathering mist, a man's face, long and somehow gentle. "You are weak," he said, "and night is coming. We must be inside before darkness."

Sharra did not struggle, not then, though she knew she should. She had been struggling a long time, and she was tired. But she looked at him, confused. "Why?"

she asked. Then, not waiting for an answer. "Who are you? Where are we going?"

"To safety," he said.

"Your home?," she asked drowsy.

"No," he said, so soft she could scarcely hear his voice. "No, not home, not ever home. But it will do." She heard splashing then, as if he were carrying her across the stream, and ahead of them on the ridge she glimpsed a gaunt, twisted silhouette, a triple-towered castle etched black against the sun. Odd, she thought, that wasn't there before.

She slept.

When she woke, he was there, watching her. She lay under a pile of soft, warm blankets in a curtained, canopied bed. But the curtains had been drawn back, and her host sat across the room in a great chair draped by shadows. Candlelight flickered in his eyes, and his hands locked together neatly beneath his chin. "Are you feeling better?" he asked, without moving.

She sat up, and noticed she was nude. Swift as suspicion, quicker than thought, her hand went to her head. But the dark crown was still there, in place, untouched, its metal cool against her brow. Relaxing, she leaned back against the pillows and pulled the blankets up to cover herself. "Much better," she said, and as she said it she realized for the first time that her wounds were gone.

The man smiled at her, a sad wistful sort of smile. He had a strong face, with charcoal-colored hair that curled in lazy ringlets and fell down into dark eyes somehow wider than they should be. Even seated, he was tall. And slender. He wore a suit and cape of some soft grey leather, and over that he wore melancholy like a cloak. "Claw marks," he said speculatively, while he smiled. "Claw marks down your arm, and your clothes almost ripped from your back. Someone doesn't like you."

"Something," Sharra said. "A guardian, a guardian

at the gate." She sighed. "There is always a guardian at the gate. The Seven don't like us to move from world to world. Me they like least of all."

His hands unfolded from beneath his chin, and rested on the carved wooden arms of his chair. He nodded, but the wistful smile stayed. "So, then," he said. "You know the Seven, and you know the gates." His eyes strayed to her forehead. "The crown, of course. I should have guessed."

Sharra grinned at him. "You did guess. More than that, you knew. Who are you? What world is this?"

"My world," he said evenly. "I've named it a thousand times, but none of the names ever seem quite right. There was one once, a name I liked, a name that fit. But I've forgotten it. It was a long time ago. *My* name is Laren Dorr, or that was my name, once, when I had use for such a thing. Here and now it seems somewhat silly. But at least I haven't forgotten *it*."

"Your world," Sharra said. "Are you a king, then? A god?"

"Yes," Laren Dorr replied, with an easy laugh. "And more. I'm whatever I choose to be. There is no one around to dispute me."

"What did you do to my wounds?" she asked.

"I healed them." He gave an apologetic shrug. "It's my world. I have certain powers. Not the powers I'd like to have, perhaps, but powers nonetheless."

"Oh." She did not look convinced.

Laren waved an impatient hand. "You think it's impossible. Your crown, of course. Well, that's only half right. I could not harm you with my ah, powers, not while you wear that. But I can help you." He smiled again, and his eyes grew soft and dreamy. "But it doesn't matter. Even if I could I would never harm you, Sharra. Believe that. It has been a long time."

Sharra looked startled. "You know my name. How?"

He stood up, smiling, and came across the room to sit beside her on the bed. And he took her hand before replying, wrapping it softly in his and stroking her with his thumb. "Yes, I know your name. You are Sharra, who moves between the worlds. Centuries ago, when the hills had a different shape and the violet sun burned scarlet at the very beginning of its cycle, they came to me and told me you would come. I hate them, all Seven, and I will always hate them, but that night I welcomed the vision they gave me. They told me only your name, and that you would come here, to my world. And one thing more, But that was enough. It was a promise. A promise of an ending or a start, of a change. And any change is welcome on this world. I've been alone here through a thousand sun-cycles, Sharra, and each cycle lasts for centuries. There are few events to mark the death of time."

Sharra was frowning. She shook her long black hair, and in the dim light of the candles the soft red highlights glowed. "Are they that far ahead of me, then?" she said. "Do they know what will happen?" Her voice was troubled. She looked up at him. "This other thing they told you?"

He squeezed her hand, very gently. "They told me I would love you," Laren said. His voice still sounded sad. "But that was no great prophecy. I could have told them as much. There was a time long ago—I think the sun was yellow then—when I realized that I would love *any* voice that was not an echo of my own."

Sharra woke at dawn, when shafts of bright purple light spilled into her room through a high arched window that had not been there the night before. Clothing had been laid out for her; a loose yellow robe, a jeweled dress of bright crimson, a suit of forest green. She chose the suit, dressed quickly. As she left, she paused to look out the window.

She was in a tower, looking out over crumbling stone battlements and a dusty triangular courtyard. Two other towers, twisted matchstick things with pointed conical spires, rose from the other corners of the triangle. There was a strong wind that whipped the rows of grey pennants set along the walls, but no other motion to be seen.

And, beyond the castle walls, no sign of the valley, none at all. The castle with its courtyard and its crooked towers was set atop a mountain, and far and away, in all directions taller mountains loomed, presenting a panorama of black stone cliffs and jagged rocky walls and shining clean ice steeples that gleamed with a violet sheen. The window was sealed and closed, but the wind *looked* cold.

Her door was open. Sharra moved quickly down a twisting stone staircase, out across the courtyard into the main building, a low wooden structure built against the wall. She passed through countless rooms, some cold and empty save for dust, others richly furnished, before she found Laren Dorr eating breakfast.

There was an empty seat at his side; the table was heavily laden with food and drink. Sharra sat down, and took a hot biscuit, smiling despite herself. Laren smiled back.

"I'm leaving today," she said, in between bites. "I'm sorry, Laren. I must find the gate."

The air of hopeless melancholy had not left him. It never did. "So you said last night," he replied, sighing. "It seems I have waited a long time for nothing."

There was meat, several types of biscuits, fruit, cheese, milk. Sharra filled a plate, face a little downcast, avoiding Laren's eyes. "I'm sorry," she repeated.

"Stay a while," he said. "Only a short time. You can afford it, I would think. Let me show you what I can of my world. Let me sing to you." His eyes, wide and dark and very tired, asked the question.

She hesitated. "Well . . . it takes time to find the gate. Stay with me for a while, then. But Laren, eventually I must go. I have made promises. You understand?"

He smiled, gave a helpless shrug. "Yes. But look, I know where the gate is. I can show you, save you a search. Stay with me, oh, a month. A month as you measure time. Then I'll take you to the gate." He studied her. "You've been hunting a long, long time, Sharra. Perhaps you need a rest."

Slowly, thoughtfully, she ate a piece of fruit, watching him all the time. "Perhaps I do," she said at last, weighing things. "And there will be a guardian, of course. You could help me then. A month . . . that's not so long. I've been on other worlds far longer than a month." She nodded, and a smile spread slowly across her face. "Yes," she said, still nodding. "That would be all right."

He touched her hand lightly. After breakfast, he showed her the world they had given him.

They stood side by side on a small balcony atop the highest of the three towers, Sharra in dark green and Laren tall and soft in grey. They stood without moving, and Laren moved the world around them. He set the castle flying over restless churning seas, where long black serpent-heads peered up out of the water to watch them pass. He moved them to a vast echoing cavern under the earth, all aglow with a soft green light, where dripping stalactites brushed down against the towers and herds of blind white goats moaned outside the battlements. He clapped his hands and smiled, and steam-thick jungle rose around them; trees that climbed each other in rubber ladders to the sky, giant flowers of a dozen different colors, fanged monkeys that chittered from the walls. He clapped again, and the walls were swept clean, and suddenly the courtyard dirt was sand and they were on an endless beach by the shore of a bleak grey ocean, and above the slow wheeling of a great blue bird with tissue-paper wings was the only movement to be seen. He showed her this, and more, and more, and in the end as dusk seemed to threaten in one place after another, he took the castle back to the ridge above the valley. And Sharra looked down on the forest of black-barked trees where he had found her, and heard the mourning-birds whimper and weep among transparent leaves.

"It is not a bad world," she said, turning to him on the balcony.

"No," Laren replied. His hands rested on the cold stone railing, his eyes on the valley below. "Not entirely. I explored it once, on foot, with a sword and a walking stick. There was a joy there, a real excitement. A new mystery behind every hill." He chuckled. "But that, too, was long ago. Now I know what lies behind every hill. Another empty horizon."

He looked at her, and gave his characteristic shrug. "There are worse hells, I suppose. But this is mine."

"Come with me, then," she said. "Find the gate with me, and leave. There are other worlds. Maybe they are less strange and less beautiful, but you will not be alone."

He shrugged again. "You make it sound so easy," he said in a careless voice. "I have found the gate, Sharra. I have tried it a thousand times. The guardian does not stop me. I step through, briefly glimpse some other world, and suddenly I'm back in the courtyard. No. I cannot leave."

She took his hand in hers. "How sad. To be alone so long. I think you must be very strong, Laren. I would go mad in only a handful of years."

He laughed, and there was a bitterness in the way he did it. "Oh, Sharra. I have gone mad a thousand times, also. They cure me, love. They always cure me." Another shrug, and he put his arm around her. The wind was cold and rising. "Come," he said. "We must be inside before full dark."

They went up in the tower to her bedroom, and they sat together on her bed and Laren brought them food; meat burned black on the outside and red within, hot bread, wine. They ate and they talked.

"Why are you here?" she asked him, in between mouthfuls, washing her words down with wine. "How did you offend them? Who were you, before?"

"I hardly remember, except in dreams," he told her. "And the dreams—it has been so long, I can't even recall which ones are truth and which are visions born of my madness." He sighed. "Sometimes I dream I was a king, a great king in a world other than this, and my crime was that I made my people happy. In happiness they turned against the Seven, and the temples fell idle. And I woke one day, within my room, within my castle, and found my servants gone. And when I went outside, my people and my world were also gone, and even the woman who slept beside me.

"But there are other dreams. Often I remember vaguely that I was a god. Well, an almost-god. I had powers, and teachings, and they were not the teachings of the Seven. They were afraid of me, each of them, for I was a match for any of them. But I could not meet all Seven together, and that was what they forced me to do. And then they left me only a small bit of my power, and set me here. It was cruel irony. As a god, I'd taught that people should turn to each other, that they could keep away the darkness by love and laughter and talk. So all these things the Seven took from me.

"And even that is not the worst. For there are other times when I think that I have always been here, that I was born here some endless age ago. And the memories are all false ones, sent to make me hurt the more."

Sharra watched him as he spoke. His eyes were not on her, but far away, full of fog, and dreams and half-dead rememberings. And he spoke very slowly, in a voice that was also like fog, that drifted and curled and hid things, and you knew that there were mysteries there and things brooding just out of sight and far-off lights that you would never reach.

Laren stopped, and his eyes woke up again. "Ah, Sharra," he said. "Be careful how you go. Even your crown will not help you should they move on you directly. And the pale child Bakkalon will tear at you, and Naa-Slas feed upon your pain, and Saagael on your soul."

She shivered, and cut another piece of meat. But it

was cold and tough when she bit into it, and suddenly she noticed that the candles had burned very low. How long had she listened to him speak?

"Wait," he said then, and he rose and went outside, out the door near where the window had been. There was nothing there now but rough grey stone; the windows all changed to solid rock with the last fading of the sun. Laren returned in a few moments, with a softly shining instrument of dark black wood slung around his neck on a leather cord. Sharra had never quite seen its like. It had sixteen strings, each a different color, and all up and down its length brightly-glowing bars of light were inlaid amid the polished wood. When Laren sat, the bottom of the device rested on the floor and the top came to just above his shoulder. He stroked it lightly, speculatively; the lights glowed, and suddenly the room was full of swift-fading music.

"My companion," he said, smiling. He touched it again, and the music rose and died, lost notes without a tune. And he brushed the light-bars and the very air shimmered and changed color.

He began to sing.

I am the lord of loneliness,
Empty my domain . . .

. . . the first words ran, sung low and sweet in Laren's mellow far-off fog voice. The rest of the song—Sharra clutched at it, heard each word and tried to remember, but lost them all. They brushed her, touched her, then melted away, back into the fog, here and gone again so swift that she could not remember quite what they had been. With the words, the music; wistful and melancholy and full of secrets, pulling at her, crying, whispering promises of a thousand tales untold. All around the room the candles flamed up brighter, and globes of light grew and danced and flowed together until the air was full of color.

Words, music, light; Laren Dorr put them all together, and wove for her a vision.

She saw him then as he saw himself in his dreams; a

king, strong and tall and still proud, with hair as black as hers and eyes that snapped. He was dressed all in shimmering white, pants that clung tight and a shirt that ballooned at the sleeves, and a great cloak that moved and curled in the wind like a sheet of solid snow. Around his brow he wore a crown of flashing silver, and a slim, straight sword flashed just as bright at his side. This Laren, this younger Laren, this dream vision, moved without melancholy, moved in a world of sweet ivory minarets and languid blue canals. And the world moved around him, friends and lovers and one special woman whom Laren drew with words and lights of fire, and there was an infinity of easy days and laughter. Then, sudden, abrupt; darkness, he was here.

The music moaned; the lights dimmed; the words grew sad and lost. Sharra saw Laren wake, in a familiar castle now deserted. She saw him search from room to room, and walk outside to face a world he'd never seen. She watched him leave the castle, walk off towards the mists of a far horizon in the hope that those mists were smoke. And on and on he walked, and new horizons fell beneath his feet each day, and the great fat sun waxed red and orange and yellow, but still his world was empty. All the places he had shown her he walked to; all those and more; and finally, lost as ever, wanting home, the castle came to him.

By then his white had faded to dim grey. But still the song went on. Days went, and years, and centuries, and Laren grew tired and mad but never old. The sun shone green and violet and a savage hard blue-white, but with each cycle there was less color in his world. So Laren sang, of endless empty days and nights when music and memory were his only sanity, and his songs made Sharra feel it.

And when the vision faded and the music died and his soft voice melted away for the last time and Laren paused and smiled and looked at her. Sharra found herself trembling.

"Thank you," he said softly, with a shrug. And he took his instrument and left her for the night.

The next day dawned cold and overcast, but Laren took her out into the forests, hunting. Their quarry was a lean white thing, half cat, half gazelle, with too much speed for them to chase easily and too many teeth for them to kill. Sharra did not mind. The hunt was better than the kill. There was a singular, striking joy in that run through the darkling forest, holding a bow she never used and wearing a quiver of black wood arrows cut from the same dour trees that surrounded them. Both of them were bundled up tightly in grey fur, and Laren smiled out at her from under a wolf's-head hood. And the leaves beneath their boots, as clear and fragile as glass, cracked and splintered as they ran.

Afterwards, unblooded but exhausted, they returned to the castle and Laren set out a great feast in the main dining room. They smiled at each other from opposite ends of a table fifty feet long, and Sharra watched the clouds roll by the window behind Laren's head, and later watched the window turn to stone.

"Why does it do that?" she asked. "And why don't you ever go outside at night?"

He shrugged. "Ah. I have reasons. The nights are, well, not good here." He sipped hot spice wine from a great jeweled cup. "The world you came from, where you started—tell me, Sharra, did you have stars?"

She nodded. "Yes. It's been so long, though. But I still remember. The nights were very dark and black, and the stars were little pinpoints of light, hard and cold and far away. You could see patterns sometimes. The men of my world, when they were young, gave names to each of those patterns, and told grand tales about them."

Laren nodded. "I would like your world, I think," he said. "Mine was like that, a little. But our stars were a thousand colors, and they moved, like ghostly lanterns in the night. Sometimes they drew veils around them to hide their light. And then our nights would be all shimmer and gossamer. Often I would go sailing at startime, myself and she whom I loved. Just so we could see the stars together. It was a good time to sing." His voice was growing sad again.

Darkness had crept into the room, darkness and silence, and the food was cold and Sharra could scarce see his face fifty long feet away. So she rose and went to him, and sat lightly on the great table near to his chair. And Laren nodded and smiled, and at once there was a whoosh, and all along the walls torches flared to sudden life in the long dining hall. He offered her more wine, and her fingers lingered on his as she took the glass.

"It was like that for us, too," Sharra said. "If the wind was warm enough, and other men were far away, then we liked to lie together in the open. Kaydar and I." She hesitated, looked at him.

His eyes were searching. "Kaydar?"

"You would have liked him, Laren. And he would have liked you, I think. He was tall and he had red hair and there was a fire in his eyes. Kaydar had powers, as did I, but his were greater. And he had such a will. They took him one night, did not kill him, only took him from me and from our world. I have been hunting for him ever since. I know the gates, I wear the dark crown, and they will not stop me easily."

Laren drank his wine and watched the torchlight on the metal of his goblet. "There are an infinity of worlds, Sharra."

"I have as much time as I require. I do not age, Laren, no more than you do. I will find him."

"Did you love him so much?"

Sharra fought a fond, flickering smile, and lost. "Yes," she said, and now it was her voice that seemed a little lost. "Yes, so much. He made me happy, Laren. We were only together for a short time, but he *did* make me happy. The Seven cannot touch that. It was a joy just to watch him, to feel his arms around me and see the way he smiled."

"Ah," he said, and he did smile, but there was something very beaten in the way he did it. The silence grew very thick.

Finally Sharra turned to him. "But we have wandered a long way from where we started. You still have not told me why your windows seal themselves at night."

"You have come a long way, Sharra. You move between the worlds. Have you seen worlds without stars?"

"Yes. Many, Laren. I have seen a universe where the sun is glowing ember with but a single world, and the skies are vast and vacant by night. I have seen the land of frowning jesters, where there is no sky and the hissing suns burn below the ocean. I have walked the moors of Carradyne, and watched dark sorcerers set fire to a rainbow to light that sunless land."

"This world has no stars," Laren said.

"Does that frighten you so much, that you stay inside?"

"No. But it has something else instead." He looked at her. "Would you see?"

She nodded.

As abruptly as they had lit, the torches all snuffed out. The room swam with blackness. And Sharra shifted on the table to look over Laren's shoulder. Laren did not move. But behind him, the stones of the window fell away like dust and light poured in from outside.

The sky was very dark, but she could see clearly, for against the darkness a shape was moving. Light poured from it, and the dirt in the courtyard and the stones of the battlements and the grey pennants were all bright beneath its glow. Puzzling, Sharra looked up.

Something looked back. It was taller than the mountains and it filled up half the sky, and though it gave off light enough to see the castle by, Sharra knew that it was dark beyond darkness. It had a man-shape, roughly, and it wore a long cape and a cowl, and below that was blackness even fouler than the rest. The only sounds were the Laren's soft breathing and the beating of her heart and distant weeping of a mourning-bird, but in her head Sharra could hear demonic laughter.

The shape in the sky looked down at her, in her, and she felt the cold dark in her soul. Frozen, she could not move her eyes. But the shape did move. It turned, and raised a hand, and then there was something else up there with it, a tiny man-shape with eyes of fire that writhed and screamed and called to her.

Sharra shrieked, and turned away. When she glanced back, there was no window. Only a wall of safe, sure stone, and a row of torches burning, and Laren holding her within strong arms. "It was only a vision," he told her. He pressed her tight against him, and stroked her hair. "I used to test myself at night," he said, more to himself than to her. "But there was no need. They take turns up there, watching me, each of the Seven. I have seen them too often, burning with black light against the clean dark of the sky, and holding those I loved. Now I don't look. I stay inside and sing, and my windows are made of night-stone."

"I feel . . . fouled," she said, still trembling a little.

"Come," he said. "There is water upstairs, you can clean away the cold. And then I'll sing for you." He took her hand, and led her up into the tower.

Sharra took a hot bath while Laren set up his instrument and tuned it in the bedroom. He was ready when she returned, wrapped head to foot in a huge fluffy brown towel. She sat on the bed, drying her hair and waiting.

And Laren gave her visions.

He sang his other dream this time, the one where he was a god and the enemy of the Seven. The music was a savage pounding thing, shot through with lightning and tremors of fear, and the lights melted together to form a scarlet battlefield where a blinding-white Laren fought shadows and the shapes of nightmare. There were seven of them, and they formed a ring around him and darted in and out, stabbing him with lances of absolute black, and Laren answered them with fire and storm. But in the end they overwhelmed him, the light faded, and then the song grew soft and sad again and the vision blurred as lonely dreaming centuries flashed by.

Hardly had the last notes fallen from the air and the final shimmers died then Laren started once again. A new song this time, and one he did not know so well. His fingers, slim and graceful, hesitated and retraced themselves more than once, and his voice was shaky too, for he was making up some of the words as he went along. Sharra knew why. For this time he sang of her, a ballad of her quest. Of burning love and endless searching, of worlds beyond worlds, of dark crowns and waiting guardians that fought with claws and tricks and lies. He took every word that she had spoken, and used each, and transformed each. In the bedroom, glittering panoramas formed where hot white suns burned beneath eternal ocean and hissed in clouds of steam, and men ancient beyond time lit rainbows to keep away the dark. And he sang Kaydar, and he sang him true somehow, he caught and drew the fire that had been Sharra's love and made her believe anew.

But the song ended with a question, the halting finale lingering in the air, echoing, echoing. Both of them waited for the rest, and both knew there was no more. Not yet.

Sharra was crying. "My turn, Laren," she said. Then: "Thank you. For giving Kaydar back to me."

"It was only a song," he said, shrugging. "It's been a long time since I had a new song to sing."

Once again he left her, touching her cheek lightly at the door as she stood there with the towel wrapped around her. Then Sharra locked the door behind him

The Lonely Songs of Laren Dorr

and went from candle to candle, turning light to darkness with a breath. And she threw the towel over a chair and crawled under the blankets and lay a long, long time before drifting off to sleep.

It was still dark when she woke, not knowing why. She opened her eyes and lay quietly and looked around the room, and nothing was there, nothing was changed. Or was there?

And then she saw him, sitting in the chair across the room with his hands locked under his chin, just as he had sat that first time. His eyes steady and unmoving, very wide and dark in a room full of night. He sat very still. "Laren?" she called, softly, still not quite sure the dark form was him.

"Yes," he said. He did not move. "I watched you last night, too, while you slept. I have been alone here for longer than you can ever imagine, and very soon now I will be alone again. Even in sleep, your presence is a wonder."

"Oh, Laren," she said. There was a silence, a pause, a weighing and an unspoken conversation. Then she threw back the blanket, and Laren came to her.

Both of them had seen centuries come and go. A month, a moment; much the same.

The slept together every night, and every night Laren sang his songs while Sharra listened. They talked throughout dark hours, and during the day they swam nude in crystalline waters that caught the purple glory of the sky. They made love on beaches of fine white sand, and they spoke a lot of love.

But nothing changed. And finally the time drew near. On the eve of the night before the day that was end, at twilight, they walked together through the shadowed forest where he'd found her.

Laren had learned to laugh during his month with Sharra, but now he was silent again. He walked slowly, clutched her hand hard in his, and his mood was more grey than the soft silk shirt he wore. Finally, by the side of the valley stream, he sat and pulled her down by his side. They took off their boots and let the water cool their feet. It was a warm evening, with a lonely restless wind and already you could hear the first of the mourning-birds.

"You must go," he said, still holding her hand but never looking at her. It was a statement, not a question.

"Yes," she said, and the melancholy had touched her too, and there were leaden echoes in her voice.

"My words have all left me, Sharra," Laren said. "If I could sing for you a vision now, I would. A vision of a world once empty, made full by us and our children. I could offer that. My world has beauty and wonder and mystery enough, if only there were eyes to see it. And if the nights are evil, well, men have faced dark nights before, on other worlds in other times. I would love you, Sharra, as much as I am able. I would try to make you happy."

"Laren . . . ," she started. But he quieted her with a glance.

"No, I could say that, but I will not. I have no right. Kaydar makes you happy. Only a selfish fool would ask you to give up that happiness to share my misery. Kaydar is all fire and laughter, while I am smoke and song and sadness. I have been alone too long, Sharra. The grey is part of my soul now, and I would not have you darkened. But still . . ."

She took his hand in both of hers, lifted it, and kissed it quickly. Then, releasing him, she lay her head on his unmoving shoulder. "Try to come with me, Laren," she said. "Hold my hand when we pass through the gate, and perhaps the dark crown will protect you."

"I will try anything you ask. But don't ask me to believe that it will work." He sighed. "You have countless worlds ahead of you, Sharra, and I cannot see your ending. But it is not here. That I know. And maybe that is best. I don't know anymore, if I ever did. I remember love vaguely, I think I can recall what it was like, and I remember that it never lasts. Here, with both of us unchanging and immortal, how could we help but to grow bored? Would we hate each other then? I'd not want that." He looked at her then, and smiled an aching melancholy smile. "I think that you had known Kaydar for only a short time, to be so in love with him. Perhaps I'm being devious after all. For in finding Kaydar, you may lose him. The fire will go out some day, my love, and the magic will die. And then you may remember Laren Dorr."

Sharra began to weep, softly. Laren gathered her to him, and kissed her, and whispered a gentle "No." She kissed back, and they held each other worldless.

When at last the purple gloom had darkened to near-black, they put back on their boots and stood. Laren hugged her and smiled.

"I *must* go," Sharra said. "I *must*. But leaving is hard, Laren, you must believe that."

"I do," he said. "I love you *because* you will go, I think. Because you cannot forget Kaydar, and you will not forget the promises you made. You are Sharra, who goes between the worlds, and I think the Seven must fear you far more than any god I might have been. If you were not you, I would not think as much of you."

"Oh. Once you said you would love any voice, that was not any echo of your own."

Laren shrugged. "As I have often said, love, *that* was a very long time ago."

They were back inside the castle before darkness, for a final meal, a final night, a final song. They got no sleep that night, and Laren sang to her again just before dawn. It was not a very good song, though; it was an aimless, rambling thing about a wandering minstrel on some nondescript world. Very little of interest ever happened to the minstrel; Sharra couldn't quite get the point of the song, and Laren sang it listlessly. It seemed an odd farewell, but both of them were troubled.

He left her with the sunrise, promising to change

clothes and meet her in the courtyard. And sure enough, he was waiting when she got there, smiling at her calm and confident. He wore a suit of pure white; pants that clung, a shirt that puffed up at the sleeves, and a great heavy cape that snapped and billowed in the rising wind. But the purple sun stained him with its shadow rays.

Sharra walked out to him and took his hand. She wore tough leather, and there was a knife in her belt, for dealing with the guardian. Her hair, jet black with light-born glints of red and purple, blew as freely as his cape, but the dark crown was in place. "Good-bye, Laren," she said. "I wish I had given you more."

"You have given me enough. In all the centuries that come, in all the sun-cycles that lie ahead. I will remember. I shall measure time by you, Sharra. When the sun rises one day and its color is blue fire. I will look at it and say, 'Yes, this is the first blue sun after Sharra came to me.'"

She nodded. "And I have a new promise. I will find Kaydar, some day. And if I free him, we will come back to you, both of us together, and we will pit my crown and Kaydar's fires against all the darkness of the Seven."

Laren shrugged. "Good. If I'm not here, be sure to leave a message," he said. And then he grinned.

"Now, the gate. You said you would show me the gate."

Laren turned and gestured at the shortest tower, a sooty stone structure Sharra had never been inside. There was a wide wooden door in its base. Laren produced a key.

"Here?" she said, looking puzzled. "In the castle?"

"Here," Laren said. They walked across the courtyard, to the door. Laren inserted the heavy metal key and began to fumble with the lock. While he worked, Sharra took one last look around, and felt the sadness heavy on her soul. The other towers looked bleak and dead, the courtyard was forlorn, and beyond the high icy mountains was only an empty horizon. There was no sound but Laren working at the lock, and no motion but the steady wind that kicked up the courtyard dust and flapped the seven grey pennants that hung along each wall. Sharra shivered with sudden loneliness.

Laren opened the door. No room inside; only a wall of moving fog, a fog without color or sound or light. "Your gate, my lady," the singer said.

Sharra watched it, as she had watched it so many times before. What world was next? she wondered. She never knew. But maybe in the next one, she would find Kaydar.

She felt Laren's hand on her shoulder. "You hesitate," he said, his voice soft.

Sharra's hand went to her knife. "The guardian," she said suddenly. "There is always a guardian." Her eyes darted quickly round the courtyard.

Laren sighed. "Yes. Always. There are some who try to claw you to pieces, and some who try to get you lost, and some who try to trick you into taking the wrong gate. There are some who hold you with weapons some with chains, some with lies. And there is one, at least, who tried to stop you with love. Yet he was true for all that, and he never sang you false."

And with a hopeless, loving shrug, Laren shoved her through the gate.

Did she find him, in the end, her lover with the eyes of fire? Or is she searching still? What guardian did she face next?

When she walks at night, a stranger in a lonely land, does the sky have stars?

I don't know. He doesn't. Maybe even the Seven do not know. They are powerful, yes, but all power is not theirs, and the number of worlds is greater than even they can count.

There is a girl who goes between the worlds, but her path is lost in legend by now. Maybe she is dead, and maybe not. Knowledge moves slowly from world to world, and not all of it is true.

But this we know; in an empty castle below a purple sun, a lonely minstrel waits, and sings of her.

Karl Edward Wagner

TWO SUNS SETTING

Our next author is one of those unusual fellows who, like August Derleth, are as much publishers of note as authors of skill. Karl Wagner has, for some ten years now, been regaling us with swashbuckling sagas of that grim, wandering warrior, Kane. More recently, with his Carcosa Press, he has picked up the torch from Arkham House, determined to continue their good work of preserving the best of the amazing Weird Tales literature in hard covers, and has given us mammoth and handsome omnibusses (omnibi? omnibae?) of the work of Manly Wade Wellman and E. Hoffman Price.

But he's not too busy to still spin an occasional yarn about his brooding, doom-fraught adventurer, as the next story ably demonstrates.

—L.C.

I. Alone with the Night Winds

Sullen red disc, the sun was burying itself beneath a monotonous horizon of rolling gravel waste that stretched behind him miles uncounted—and possibly untrod save by his horse's hooves. Long before the sunlight failed, its warmth was snuffed out in the empty lifelessness of the desert, so that in its last hour the sun shone cheerless as the rising moon. Crimson as it climbed, the full moon seemed a false dawn to mock the dying sun, arriving prematurely, disrespectful as a greedy heir pacing in eager impatience before the master's deathbed. For a space the limitless skies of twilight displayed two rubrous globes low on either horizon, so that Kane mused as to whether his long journey across the desert might not have led him to some strange dusk world where two ancient guns smouldered in the heavens. The region seemed unearthly in its chill desolation—and certainly an aura of unguessable antiquity hung as a grey shadow over each tumbled bit of stone.

Kane had left Carsultyal with no particular destination or goal, other than to ride far beyond that city's influence. There were those who said that Kane was driven from Carsultyal, his power there broken at last by fellow sorcerers jealous of his long held prestige —and alarmed by the bizarrely alien direction his studies had taken in recent years. Kane himself considered his departure more or less voluntary, albeit precipitous, arguing privately that had he really wanted, he could have fended off the attack of his former colleagues—even though he owed allegiance to neither god nor demon from whom he might have sought intercession. Rather, mankind's first great city had grown stagnant over the last century. The spirit of discovery, of renaissance that had drawn him to Carsultyal in its earliest years was burned out now, so that boredom, his nemesis, had overtaken Kane once more. To be sure, he had been restless, his thoughts drawn more and more to the world beyond Carsultyal—lands yet to know the presence of man. But that he returned to his pathless wandering without much forethought could be judged in that Kane had left the city with little more than a few supplies, a double handful of gold coins, a fast horse, and a sword of tempered Carsultyal steel.

Those who sought to seize his relinquished power may have regretted their inheritance, but this minor vindication seemed pointless now.

With dusk, the wind began to rise, a whining chill breath from the mountains whose rusted peaks still burned with the final rays of the sun, now vanished beneath the opposite horizon. Kane shivered and drew his russet cloak closer about his massive shoulders, regretting the loss of warm furs that scavengers now snarled over in Carsultyal. The Herratlonai was a cold, empty waste, where nights dropped to freezing. With the mountain wind, his outfit of green wool shirt, dark leather vest and pants was less than adequate for the night.

The previous day he had eaten the last hoarded chips of dried fruit and jerky—after short rations for a week or more. Water luckily there was yet half a bag; he had filled the skins to bursting before entering the desert, and a waterhole had providentially appeared along the ghost of a trail he followed. Or thought he followed. The gravel waste southeast of Carsultyal's domains was reputed to border on one of the prehuman realms of lost antiquity. There were tales of cities impossibly ancient buried beneath the gravel dunes. Kane had come upon what he hoped might be traces of a forgotten path across the desert to the fabled mountains of the eastern continent. He determined to follow this, and at times he discovered sentinel boulders whose all but effaced heiroglyphs might resemble those glimpsed in books of elder world lore—or might be the deluding artistry of wind and ice. Beyond this tantalization, Kane found nothing further to disrupt the monotonous desolation but stray patches of sparse scrub and gorgeous columns of agatized wood. The grass his mount cropped; for himself Kane had not seen even a lizard in days. Perhaps it had been rash to attempt transverse of a desert whose limits no man had knowledge of, at least without a packtrain of provisions. But Kane had not embarked under the brightest of circumstances, nor had the years dulled his reckless whim. Philosophically he congratulated himself on riding a course no enemy would care to follow.

Then the mountains had broken through the thin haze of the eastern horizon like a row of worn and discolored teeth. Their presence gave some cause for optimism—at least he was across the desert—but this hope was clouded when the late afternoon sun revealed the hills to be merely a more vertical variation on the present terrain. Dry slopes of gravel and crumbling bluffs appeared lifeless except for dark blotches of twisted underbrush. From the talus gleamed iridescent flashes of sunlight, colored then flung back by mammoth slabs of petrified wood, strewn about like a giant's plundered jewel hoard.

But with darkness had also come the startling smell of wood smoke in the mountain wind—a familiar scent uncanny in this stark desolation. Kane brushed smooth the grimy beard that hung like rust over coarse features, thumbed a few blowing strands of red hair back beneath a leather headband sewn with plaques of lapis lazuli—sniffing the night wind of disbelief. His mount paced onward, the night deepened, and against the foot of the mountains ahead beckoned the light of the campfire. No, simply the light of a fire, he mused—there was no reason to be more specific. At this distance it must be a good sized blaze.

He guided his horse closer, picking his way carefully over the gravel in the moonlight. With a twisting ache in his belly, Kane recognized the odor of roasting meat within the smoke, and there was no longer any doubt. Calculatingly he studied the still distant campfire. He had seen no evidence of habitation against the slope, and in the emptiness such would seem an impossibility. Not that it seemed any more probable, but indications were that he had chanced upon some other wanderer. As to who or what might be camped beside the ridge, or what circumstances had brought about his presence, Kane was at loss to conjecture. Nothing was known of those who might dwell beyond the settled northwestern crescent of the Great Southern Continent, and in the dawn world more races than mankind walked the Earth.

Whoever had built the fire, he ate his meat cooked and so could not be hopelessly alien. From the size of the campfire, Kane guessed it was a small party of nomads or savages—likely someone from whatever lay beyond the mountains. The significant point was the roasting meat. Licking dry lips, Kane unfastened his sword from saddle and buckled it across his back, so that the familiar hilt protruded reassuringly over his right shoulder. The scabbard tip he left untied, so that it would pivot freely on its shoulder swivel when he grasped the hilt. Cautiously he approached the campfire.

II. Two Who Met by Firelight

His keen nostrils caught an animal smell, sour beneath the pungency of wood smoke and cooked flesh. At first the crackling firelight screened the shape crouched beyond, so that Kane warily nudged his steed toward another angle of vision to confirm his dawning suspicion. His face tightened upon recognition. Only one man squatted beside the blaze—if a giant might be termed "man".

Kane had seen, had spoken with giants in the course of his wanderings, although in recent decades they were seldom encountered. A proudly aloof, taciturn race he knew them to be. Few in number and scornful of mankind's emerging civilization, they lived a semi-barbaric existence in lands unfrequented by man. True, there abounded gruesome tales of individual giants who terrorized isolated human settlements, but these were outlaws to their own race—or more often the monstrous hybrid ogres.

This particular individual did not appear threatening.

While he obviously had heard the clash of shod hooves on stone, his attitude seemed curious rather than hostile as Kane approached. Not that someone his stature need display an aggressive front at the appearance of a single horse and rider. In comfortable reach lay a hooked axe whose bronze head could serve as ship's anchor. Kane realized that from the other's higher vantage point, his approach had been observed beyond the ring of firelight. Still the giant showed no sinister action. Spitted over sputtering flames turned an entire carcass of what looked to be goat. Hot, succulent meat . . .

Hunger overpowered caution. Poised to wheel and gallop away at the first sign of danger, Kane boldly rode up to the fringe of firelit circle and halted.

"Good evening," he greeted levelly, speaking the language of the giant's race with complete fluency. "Your campfire was visible at some distance. I wondered if I might join you."

The giant grunted and shielded his eyes with a hand larger than a spade. "Well, what's this here? A human who speaks the Old Tongue. Out of nowhere too—and in a land that even ghosts have abandoned. This sort of novelty can't be ignored. Come on into the light, manling. We'll share hospitality of the trail." His voice, though loud as a man's shout, had an even bass timbre.

Kane muttered thanks and dismounted, deciding to gamble on the giant's apparent goodwill. As he stopped before the fire, he and his host exchanged curious inspections. At a bit over six feet and carrying past three hundred pounds of bone, sinew and muscle, Kane was seldom physically overawed. This night he stood alone in the desert before one who could overpower him as if he were a weakling child.

He estimated the giant's height somewhere around fifteen feet. It was difficult to tell since he sat crouched on the ground, knees drawn up, enswathed in a cloak of bearskins like a misshapen hairy tent. Disregarding the matter of size, the giant's appearance was human enough—his proportions were those of a man in his prime, though he seemed somewhat lanky from a slightly disproportionate length of limb. Broadly muscled, his weight must be enormous. He wore rough boots the size of panniers, and under the cloak a crudely stitched tunic and leggings of hide. Calves and arms were matted with coarse bristles. Perhaps too bony to be called craggy, his features were not displeasing; his beard was shaggy, brown hair drawn back in a short braid at the nape. Brown also were his eyes, set wide beneath an intelligent brow.

Looking him over as a man might size up a stray dog, the giant glanced at Kane's face, and gave an interested grunt. He gazed thoughtfully into Kane's cold blue eyes for a moment—something few cared to do. "You're Kane, aren't you?" he commented.

Kane started, then smiled bitterly. "A thousand miles from the cities of man, and a giant calls me by name."

The giant seemed amused. "Oh, you'll have to wander far if you really seek anonymity. We giants have watched the frantic history of your race. We recall when mankind aborted from its womb, pretending to be adult instead of misbegotten fetus. To man these few centuries are time immemorial; to our race a nostalgic yesterday. We remember well the Curse of Kane and still recognize his mark."

"That history is already garbled and distorted," Kane murmured, eyes for a moment focused beyond. "Kane is becoming misty legend in the old homes of man— and lost in obscurity in the new lands. Already I've travelled through lands where men did not know me for who I am."

"And you kept wandering, too—because they soon learned to dread the name of Kane," concluded the giant. "Well, Kane—my name is Dwassllir, and I'm pleased to find a legend joining me at my lonely fire."

Kane shrugged an ironic acknowledgement. "What's

that roasting in your lonely fire?" He looked hungrily at the grease dripping carcass.

"A mountain goat I dropped this afternoon—good game is scarce around here, I've found. Hey, give that spit a nudge, will you?"

Kane heaved the spit to the rarest side. "You going to eat all of it?" he asked bluntly, too hungry for pride.

Dwassllir might well have done so otherwise, but the giant seemed glad for the companionship, and tore off a generous side of ribs that taxed even Kane's voracity. Again the image of stray dog occurred to Kane, but the growling in his belly claimed first place in his thoughts. The goat was tough, stringy, half raw and gamey in taste; it was ecstacy to devour. One eye still watching the giant warily, he gnawed on the ribs with gusto, washing down the greasy flesh with mouthfuls of stale water from Dwassllir's canteen.

With a belch that fanned the flames, Dwassllir stood and stretched—licked his fingers, wiped face with hands, then scrubbed his hands with loose gravel. When the giant was erect, Kane realized that his height was closer to eighteen feet. Leisurely Dwassllir picked over the remains of the goat. "Want anymore?" he inquired. Kane shook his head, still struggling with the ribs. A short tug wrenched loose the remaining hind leg, and the giant settled back with a contented sigh to gnaw the joint.

"Game is hard to run across in this range," he reflected, gesturing with the tattered femur. "Doubt if you'd find anything in that stretch of desert yonder. Likely that horse will be the only meat you'll find until you get into the plains east of here."

"I thought about eating him," Kane conceded. "But on foot I'd stand little chance of crossing this waste."

Dwassllir snorted disparagingly. Because of their enormous size, giants looked upon a horse as only another game animal. "The frailty of your race! Strip man of his crutches, and he's helpless to stand against his world."

"Don't oversimplify," Kane objected. "Mankind will be master of this world. In only a few centuries I've seen our civilization grow from a sterile paradise, from scattered barbaric tribes to a vast and expanding empire of cities, villages and farms. Ours is the fastest rising civilization ever to burst upon this world."

"Only because man has stolen his civilization from the ruins of better races who preceded him. Human civilization is parasitic—a gaudy fungus that owes its vitality to the dead genius upon whose corpse it flourishes!"

"Wiser races, I'll grant you," Kane pointed out. "But it is mankind who has survived, not Earth's elder races. It is a measure of man's resourcefulness that he can salvage from prehuman civilizations knowledge that is invaluable to the advance of his own race. Carsultyal has risen thus from a fishing village to the greatest city in the known world. Her rediscovered knowledge has shaped the emergence of mankind to our present civilization."

Dwassllir snapped the femur explosively and sucked at its marrow. "Civilization! You boast that as man's major accomplishment! It is nothing—only an outgrowth of human weakness! Man is too frail, too unworthy a creature to live within his environment. He must instead prop himself up with his civilization, his learning. My race learned to live in the real world—to merge with our environment. We need no civilization. Man is a cripple who flaunts his infirmity, boasts of his crutches. You retreat into the walls of your civilization because you are too weak to stand before nature as part of the natural environment. Instead of living as partner to nature, man hides behind his civilization, curses and defies true life, distorts his environment to accommodate his own failings. Beware that your environment does not strike back from all your blasphemies, for that day mankind shall be snuffed out like the unnatural freak man is!

"Even you, Kane—you who are reviled as the most

dangerous man of your race. Without your horse, your clothes, your weapons—could you have crossed that desert alive as you have just barely done? One of my race could!

"My race is older than yours. We had grown to maturity while a mad god was playing his idiot game of shaping mankind from the bestial filth that skulked where shadow lay deepest. Had man walked the Earth of my race's youth, his civilization would have protected him no better than an eggshell. That Earth was more feral than this world man knows. My ancestors defied storms, glaciers, catastrophes that would have swept away your cities like dry leaves before the wind! They stood naked before beasts more savage than any man has known—grappled and conquered the sabre-tooth, the great sloth, the cave bear, the wooly mammoth, and other creatures whose strength and ferocity are unknown in this tame age! Could man have survived in that heroic age! I doubt that all his cunning and trickery could have saved him!"

"Perhaps not, but then your race has considerable physical advantage," argued Kane, wondering how wise it might be to provoke the other. "If my stride were long as yours, then I wouldn't need a horse to cross a desert—although I think your disdain might not exist, if there were a steed great enough for a giant to straddle. Nor would I need my sword if I were huge enough to crush a lion as if it were only a jackel. Your boast is founded on the fact that your size makes you physically superior to the dangers of your environment, which is a boast that any large and powerful animal could echo. Who is braver—one of your ancestors who barehanded throttled a cave bear close to him in size, or a man with a spear who kills a tiger many times his superior in physical power?"

He paused, waiting to see if the giant had taken offense. However, Dwassllir was not of volatile temper. Belly full and feet warm, he was in a pleasant mood for fireside debate with his diminutive companion.

"True, yours is an older race, and mankind an arrogant youth," Kane continued. "But what are the accomplishments of your race? If you scorn to build cities, to sail ships, to settle the wilderness, to master the secrets of prehuman knowledge—then what have you achieved? Art, poetry, philosophy, spiritualism—are those fields your race has mastered?"

"Our achievement has been to live at peace with our environment—to live as a part of the natural world, instead of waging war with nature," declared Dwassllir steadily.

"All right then, I'll accept that, Kane persisted. "Perhaps you have found fulfillment in your rather primitive life style. However, the measure of a race's attainments must finally be its ability to flourish within its chosen role. If your race has done this so well, why then do your numbers diminish, while mankind spreads over the Earth? Never has your race been a populous one, and today man encounters giant only rarely. Will your race then fade away with the passing years—until one day the giants will be known only in legend along with the fierce creatures your ancestors fought? What then will survive your passing? What will remain to tell of your vanished glory?"

Dwassllir became sadly pensive, so that Kane regretted having pursued the argument. "You humans seem too content to measure achievement in terms of numbers," he answered. "But I can't make full refutation of your logic. Our numbers have been declining for centuries, and I can't really tell you why. Our lives are long—I'm not as much your junior in years as you may suppose, Kane. We are slow to mate and raise children, but this was always so. Our natural enemies have all passed into extinction or retreated to the most obscure reaches. Our simple medicines are sufficient to nurse us through whatever disease or injury might strike us. No, our deaths have not increased.

"I think our race has grown old, tired. Perhaps we should have followed the giant beasts of the savage past into the realm of shadow. At least our old enemies gave life adventure! It is as if my race has lived beyond its era, and now we perish from boredom. We're like one of your kings who has conquered all his enemies and now has only a dull old age to endure.

"My race rose in a heroic age, Kane! It was truly a day of giants in that era! But that age is dead. Gone are the great beasts. Vanished the elder races whose wars rocked the roots of mountains. Earth has been inherited by the insignificant scavenger. Man crawls about the ruins of the great age, and proclaims himself to be Earth's new master! Perhaps man will survive to accomplish his insolent usurpation—more likely he will destroy himself in seeking to command mysteries the elder races found too awesome for even their powers to control!

"But when the day comes that man will be master of the Earth, my race will hopefully not be present to endure that humiliation! We are a race of heroes who have outlived the age of heroes! Can you blame us if we tire of existence in this age of boastful pigmies!"

Kane fell silent. "I understand your sentiments," he finally said. "But to abandon yourself to despair, to brood upon vanished glory doesn't impress me as heroic."

He stopped, not wishing to deepen the shadow of melancholy that had gathered over their thoughts. "May I ask what brings you to this lost wilderness of dead rock?" he asked, thinking to change subject. "Or do those nameless mountains border on the lands of your people?"

Dwassllir shook himself and tossed an uprooted shrub into the fire. The leaves hissed shrilly, then whipped loose from blackened stems to rise like red stars fading into the night. "What I seek is no secret," he replied. "Although it may seem pointless to you as it has to some of my friends.

"Centuries ago, before this region was stripped barren of soil and hence of life, there were villages of my

Two Suns Setting 111

race along these mountains—which are not nameless, but are called the Antamareesi range. Under these hills lie immense caverns, which my ancestors used for shelter in days before they raised houses, then later mined for the veins of metal they discovered within. The climate was warmer, the land was green, game was plentiful—it was a good region to settle and to look upon in that age.

"Those were the great days! Life in that age was an ever challenging struggle between the savagery of the ancient Earth and the unyielding strength of my race! Can you imagine the tremendous energy of those people! They stood chest to chest against ferociously hostile world, and they conquered whatever enemy they faced! Their gods were Fire and Ice—the implacable opposites that were the ruling forces of their age! And their enemies were not only the forces of nature, or the great beasts—some of the elder races challenged the ascendency of my race as well!

"Perhaps it was their sorcery that left this region lifeless and barren. Our legends tell of battles with strange races and strange weapons in the dawn world—and my ancestors were victorious over these enemies too. The hero of one legendary battle, King Brotemllain, whose name you may know as the greatest king of my race, ruled over these mountains. His body was laid to rest within one of these caverns, and upon his brow remains the ancestral crown of my people—ancient even then, and given to him after death because of the undying greatness of his rule."

Dwassllir was afire now, his momentary depression seared away by intense fervor. He considered Kane thoughtfully, made a decision, and spoke earnestly, "I've been searching for Brotemllain's legendary burial place. And from certain signs, I think I'm about to discover it. I mean to recover his crown! King Brotemllain's crown is emblematic of my race's ancient glory. Although our wars and our kings are all past now, I believe that resurrection of this legendary symbol might unlock some of the old energy and vitality of my people. Perhaps the idea brands me a fool and dreamer as many have scoffed, but I mean to do this thing! Surely this relic from an age of heroes could serve to spark some new flame of glory to my race even in these grey days!

"I wouldn't suggest this to another of your race, Kane—but because you are who you are, I'll offer both an invitation and a challenge. If you'd care to come along with me on this search, Kane, I'd welcome your company. It may be that you will understand my race better if you follow me into the shadow of that age of lost glory."

"Thank you for the invitation—and the challenge," declared Kane solemnly. The venture intrigued him, and the giant seemed to eat well. "I'll be proud to make that journey with you."

III. Dead Giant's Crown

The trees grew less far apart here, though still dwarfed and tortured by the chill breeze. Two days had Kane followed Dwassllir about the crumbling ridges—his horse matching the giant's restless stride. Now on the third day Dwassllir's whoop chorused by a hundred echoes announced the termination of his search.

The discovery seemed unimpressive. They had entered a deep valley and traced a course to its gorgelike head, where Kane glanced uneasily at the boulder strewn slopes enclosing them overhead. At times Dwassllir had eagerly pointed out some rounded monument whose carvings the winds of time had all but obliterated. Again he would pause to examine some unprepossessing mound, where the drifting gravel nestled upon blocks of hewn stone and perhaps a shard of ceramic, a smear of charcoal fragments, or a lump of dried wood so ancient that it seemed more lifeless than the stones.

"There stands the entrance to the tomb of King Brotemllain," Dwassllir proclaimed, and he gestured to a rubble choked patch of darkness that burrowed into the valley wall. The opening had been about twenty-five feet high and half as broad, although several feet were now filled in by debris. Evidence of masonry framed the entrance, along with great chunks of shredded wood, some whose blackened splinters were conglomerate with verdigris—all that remained of portals at last fallen to time itself.

"I'm certain this is the valley described in our legends," the giant rumbled jubilantly. "The passage leads into a vast system of caverns. It was a natural opening my ancestors enlarged to enter a major side branch as it passes close to the surface. Beyond these ruins of the ancient monument should lie the domed natural chamber where Brotemllain's corpse was enthroned for the ages."

Kane frowned at the dark opening doubtfully, a whisper of unease drifting through his thoughts. "I wouldn't count on finding much in there but bats and dust. Time and decay generally devour the leavings of less hallowed thieves. Or does this tomb have its unseen guardians? It would seem unusual with so renowned a tenant and so legendary a treasure, if this tomb were not guarded by some still vigilant spell."

With a shrug Dwassllir dismissed Kane's foreboding. "Unusual for your race, maybe. But this was a shrine most sacred to my race. Besides, who would dare pilfer the grave of a giant. Come on, we'll take torches and see if King Brotemllain still holds court."

While Kane struck fire, the giant scoured about for a supply of resiniferous wood. He returned with a dead tree as thick as Kane's thigh. Taking several shorn branches, Kane accompanied Dwassllir into the cave— the latter wielding a section of trunk.

Their progress was quickly interrupted. Blocking the

passage but for a narrow crevice interposed a jumble of broken rock. A segment of the passage wall had collapsed.

Dwassllir examined the barrier thoughtfully. "It's going to take some time to dig through this," he concluded sourly.

"Assuming your efforts didn't bring down the rest of the mountain, was Kane's ominous comment. "There's a fault in the rock here, or this slide would not have broken through. If the caverns run as extensively as you say, there must be flaws undermining this entire range. The centuries have spread the cracks and further weakened the rock, so it's solid as a rotted tooth. It's a wonder these mountains haven't tumbled flat before now."

Jabbing out his torch, the giant craned his neck to peer along the crevice. "Passage opens up again, and just beyond I think I can make out where it opens into the main cavern." He glowered at the obstruction helplessly for a moment, then gazed down at the man.

"You know, you could squeeze through that crack, Kane," he told him. "You could get past and see what's beyond. If there's nothing to be found, then there's nothing lost. But if this is King Brotemllain's tomb, then you can learn if his crown still lies within."

Kane considered the crevice, face noncommittal. "It can be done," he pronounced. Casually, not wishing to show his nerve less steady than the giant's: "I'll go look for your bones on my own then."

The crack was inches too narrow for one of Kane's massive build, so that his clothing scuffed and flesh scraped as he wriggled through the tightest portion. But the wall had not collapsed in a solid thrust; rather splintered chunks of stone had broken through in a disordered array, and the occlusion was spread like stubby fingers instead of a compact fist. Then his thrusting torch shone clear of the rubble, and Kane edged into unobstructed passageway. Quickly he rebuckled his scabbard across his back, but the bare blade stayed in his left fist.

A short way beyond he found the cavern. A pair of steps too high for human stride completed the passage's gentle descent. Kane lifted the torch and looked about, his senses strained to catch any hint of danger. There was nothing to detect, but the obscure sense of menace persisted. Waving the brand to fan its light, he was unable to discern the cavern's boundaries, although this chamber seemed to extend for hundreds of feet. Stalactites hung from the ceiling far above, making a monstrous multifanged jaw with stalagmite tusks below. "I've just walked down the beast's tongue," mumbled Kane, clambering over the steps. Thin dust sifted over the stone; this cavern was long dead too.

"What do you see, Kane!" roared Dwassllir from the crevice. High above the curtain of bats stirred fitfully.

Despite his familiarity with the giant's deafening tone, Kane started and nervously glanced toward the distant ceiling. The torch flared in his hand as he crossed the chamber, sword poised for whatever laired within the darkness.

Then he froze—a thrill tingling through his body as he gazed at what waited at the torchlight's perimeter.

"Dwassllir!" he shouted, in his excitement heedless of the booming echoes. "He's here! You've found the tomb! King Brotemllain's here on his throne, and his crown rests on his skull!"

Revealed in the torchlight jutted an immense throne of hewn stone, upon which its skeletal king still reposed in sepulchral majesty. In the cool aridity of the cavern, the lich had outlasted centuries. Tatters of desiccated flesh held the skeleton together in leathery articulation. Bare bone gleamed dully through chinks in the clinging mail of muscle and sinew, shrunken to iron-like texture. Thronearms were yet gripped by fingers like gnarled oak roots, while about the base was gathered a mouldering drift of disintegrating furs. The gaunt skull retained sufficient shreds of flesh to half mask its death's head grin with lines of sternness—forming a grimace suggesting laughter muffled by set lips. The eyes were sunken circles of darkness whose shadowy depths eluded Kane's torch. Not so the orbs that brooded from above the brow.

Red as setting suns in the torch-light, a pair of fist sized rubies blazed from King Brotemllain's crown. Kane swore softly, impressed by the wealth he witnessed almost as deeply as he stood in awe of its grisly majesty. The circle of gold could belt a dancing girl's waist, and patterned about the two great stones were another ten or more rough cut gems of walnut size. Ancient treasure from the giant's plutonian harvested hoard.

Thinking of the kingdom encircled in the riches of King Brotemllain's crown, Kane bitterly regretted his shout of discovery. Had he reported the cavern empty, there might have been a chance to smuggle the crown past the giant—or return for it later. But now Dwassllir knew of the crown, and Dwassllir waited at the only exit to the tomb. To attempt to find egress through some hypothetical interpassage into the network of caverns said to run under the mountains would be suicidal—slightly less so than to challenge the giant for possession. Kane ruefully studied the treasure. Unless chance presented for stealthy murder . . .

"Kane!" The giant's bellow concluded his musing. "You all right in there, Kane? Is it really King Brotemllain?"

"Can't be anything else, Dwassllir!" Kane yelled back, echoes garbling his words. "It's just like your legends told! There's a colossal throne of stone in the cavern's center! About twenty feet of mouldy skeleton's sitting on it, and on his skull there's a golden crown with two enormous rubies! Just a minute and I'll climb up and get it for you!"

"No! Leave it there!" Eagerness shook the giant's shout. "I want to see this for myself!" From the barrier sounded groan and rattle of shifting rubble.

"Wait, damn it all!" Kane howled, scrambling back to the passage. "You're going to bring the whole damn mountain down on us! I'll get your crown for you!"

"Leave it! This isn't just a treasure hunt! It's more than just recovering Brotemllain's crown!" puffed the giant, straining to roll back a boulder. "I've dreamed for more years than you can guess of standing before King Brotemllain's throne! Of standing where no giant has entered since the heroic age of my race! Of calling upon his shade for the strength to lead my race back to its lost glory! So I'll stand before King Brotemllain, and I'll lift his crown from his brow with my own hands! And when I return, my people will see and listen and know that the tales of our ancient greatness are history not myth!

"Now come on and help me widen this crevice, will you? You can clear away this smaller stuff. This cavern's stood for millennia; we can risk another few minutes."

Kane cursed and joined him at the barrier—reflecting that it was useless arguing with a fanatical giant. Grimly he hauled back on a boulder jammed against the inner face of the blockage.

A sudden tearing groan and Dwassllir's gasp of dismay gave him barely enough warning. Kane catapulted backward just as the unbalanced rock slide protested their trespass. Like the irresistible fist of doom, the rock shelf burst from the wall and smashed against the opposite side!

Deafened by the concussion, pelted by splintered fragments, Kane twisted frantically to roll clear. He fell in a bruised huddle past the foot of the steps. For a moment of dazed confusion it seemed that the entire cavern rocked and bucked with a crescendo repercussion of the collapsed passageway.

When the last slamming echo had lost its note, the final chunk of cracked stone bounced past, Kane groggily sat up to lick his wounds. Sore, but no bones broken, a long gash down his left shoulder. His sword arm was numb where a rock splinter had struck, and it would need bandaging to staunch the trickle of blood. Relatively unscathed, he decided, considering he had nearly been crushed deader than King Brotemllain.

His sword was still sheathed, but the torch had been lost as he leapt away, and the chamber was as dark as a tomb could get. Kane did not need a torch to learn the worst; the absence of any ray of light told him that. King Brotemllain's tomb was also sealed as thoroughly as any tomb need be.

IV. A Final Coronation

Gloomily he felt his way back along the passage and pushed against the intervening wall of rock. There were boulders as wide as he was tall, and the spaces between were packed solid with lesser rubble. Given slaves and equipment enough, he might clear out another crevice. Dwassllir could perhaps burrow through, but the giant was probably a mangled keystone in the barrier right now.

Burnt pitch stung his groping fingers, and Kane tugged the extinguished torch out from under some debris. Since there seemed little else to do, he sat down and struck a fire. The torch alight once more, the rockslide appeared no less substantial. Angrily Kane kicked at a toppled boulder.

Air fanned the torch flame, however, pointing a yellow beckoning finger back into the burial cavern. Remembering this cave was a branch of a greater plexus, Kane eagerly sought to trace the faint stir of wind.

As he crossed the chamber, Kane saw the effects of the rockslide within the cavern. The sudden grinding force had sent a shudder through the tired stone, so that stalactites had plummeted like crystal lightning bolts from their eternally dark heaven. One had missed spearing Brotemllain by scant yards.

A sighing wind breathed corpse breath through a

gaping pit many yards across at the cavern's one end. The explosive concussions that rocked the stone had not been fantasy of a head blow then. Evidently in the chain reaction shockwave which the slide had drummed the brittle stone, a large section of rock from the high ceiling had struck here. Its impact had driven through the chamber floor to reveal another cavern beneath this one. The network of caves must bore through the mountains like the tortuous course of a feasting worm, thought Kane, peering into the pit.

Wind gusted faintly through the hole, bringing a sick smell of dampness—a stale, unclean animal smell that intrigued Kane. It seemed he could hear the rush of unseen waters. An underground river probably—deep underground it must be too. The wind stole in through rotted chinks in the mountains' shell most likely. At least Kane hoped his deductions were correct.

The floor of this new cavern appeared to be about seventy-five feet below him. The collapsing stone had made a chaotic incline down which progress seemed possible. "I've found another road to Hell," Kane muttered aloud.

A rustle beyond him made him look to its source; then he knew he was on the threshold of Hell. At the edge of light danced a cockroach—incredibly, a bone white cockroach nearly a yard in length. With chitinous concentration, it was nuzzling a dead bat, and it waved its antennae querulously at the offending light. In disbelief Kane tossed a rock in its direction, and the roach scuttled off chuckling into the darkness.

Fascinated, Kane returned to the pit and thrust his torch out over the aperture. Near the incline's base two white furred creatures raised blind eyes to the light and slunk away squealing in fear. And Kane recognized them to be rats the size of jackels.

Understanding came to him. Water, air—the caverns below held life. But an obscenely distorted form of life it was. Probably these out-sized creatures had evolved from cave dwellers who somehow were trapped beneath the surface ages ago—or maybe retreated there from choice when the land became desert. In primeval night, without seasons, without light, they had mutated to grotesque, primitive forms—adapted to the demented savagery of their environment. Falling stone had crushed bats as well as other nameless things, and now the scent of blood was luring the monstrous cave creatures to this area.

And what else dwells below? wondered Kane uneasily. He drew away from the pit, deciding that so certain a path to Hell could rest untrod until all other chances of escape were eliminated. Digging out through the passage even seemed a brighter prospect.

As he returned to the rock fall, he caught the sound of stone grating on stone. For a moment he feared the slide was shifting, but as he watched tensely he saw this was not so. Excitement cutting through despondency, Kane quickly stepped to the barrier and rhythmically pounded against a boulder with a chunk of rock.

After a pause, his tapping was dimly echoed from the opposite side. So the giant had escaped the avalanche! His strength could clear the passage if it were at all possible.

Eagerly Kane began to dig into his side of the barrier. Not daring to contemplate another slide, he strained his powerful back to roll away small boulders, tore his fingers scrabbling doglike through the chipped stone. Luckily, it was a bed of broken rock that had slid into the passage, rather than a solid stone shelf.

Time crawled immeasurably, marked only by the dwindling torch and the deepening excavation. Kane's hands were raw and blistered when a sudden wrenching of stone tore open a patch of daylight. Filtered by distance and dust, the ray of sunlight seemed of blinding brilliance to his eyes.

"Dwassllir!" shouted Kane, peering through the chink in the barrier. A shaft perhaps the size of a man's head had been formed between the angle of two boulders, although several feet of debris yet blocked the passage.

A huge brown eye squinted back at him. "Kane?" The giant sounded pleasantly surprised. "So you dodged the slide, manling! You're as hard to kill as legend tells!"

"Can you get me out of here?"

"Can if I'm going to get myself in!" Dwassllir returned stubbornly. "I think I can prop up these boulders so we can dig out space enough for me to crawl through."

"One of the characteristics of higher life forms is the ability to learn by experience," grumbled Kane, bending his back to dislodge a portion of rubble. But the giant's determination was as unyielding as the rock about them.

Slowly the crevice began to reappear, and with freedom outlined in an ever broadening patch of light, the grueling work seemed less fatiguing. Only a precariously balanced jumble of boulders remained.

But this time warning came too late.

A sudden shriek of rasping stone as Dwassllir recklessly hauled back on one of the piled boulders! Released from pressure, a second slab of rock plunged forward like a catapult missile. Kane yelled and tried to dodge. He had been unbalanced with effort, and even his blurring speed was too slow to evade the tumbling projectile.

Thunder as it struck, the slab caroomed crazily upon the piled boulders, spun about and smashed against the wall where Kane stood. Kane hissed in pain. At the last instant he had twisted behind a sheltering boulder. This had absorbed the impact of the falling slab, but the explosive force had jammed the intervening rock against his thighs, pinning him to the wall.

Blood oozed from torn skin, trickled into his boots. Grimacing in pain as he tried to wriggle free, Kane discovered he had escaped crushed bones by the smallest fraction.

Miraculously, the rest of the pile had held stable. Dwassllir was cautiously poking at the opening. "Kane? Damn! You're harder to kill than a snake! Can you squeeze out of there?"

"I can't!" grunted Kane, straining to slide the rock. "Lot of rock fragments all jammed together—holding it in place! My feet are pinned in!" He cursed and writhed against his pillory, scraping off more skin as the only evident result.

"Well, I'll pull you out as I dig through," boomed Dwassllir reassuringly, and he once more attacked the rockslide.

But Kane heard sounds of grating rock not turned by Dwassllir's hand. From within the burial cavern he could hear a heavy body climbing over loose stone.

Teeth bared in defiant snarl, Kane stared wild eyed into the funeral chamber.

At first he thought the corpse of King Brotemllain had risen on skeletal limbs—for wavering in the darkness he could discern two ruby coals throwing back the torchlight. But the crown had not moved, still made sullen glow above the throne.

These were truly eyes he saw—eyes that held him in a baleful glare. Climbing from the aperture in the cavern floor came a creature from beneath the abyss of night!

Sabre-tooth! Or nightmare spawn of sabre-tooth tiger and stygian darkness! The gargantuan creature that shambled forth from the timeless caverns of night was as demented progeny of its natural forebears as were the other grotesque cave beasts Kane had seen. Rock crunched beneath taloned tread as it stalked from the gaping pit, an albino behemoth more than double the stature of its fearsome ancestor. Dripping jaws yawned hungrily in a cough of challenge—sabre-toothed jaws that could close upon Kane as a cat snaps up a rat.

Lord Tloluvin alone might know what fantastic demons stalked the unlighted caverns that crawled down into his hellish realm, what depraved savagery in their nighted netherworld bred the cave beasts to grotesque giantism. Drawn by the noise and the scent of blood, this monster had left its sunless lair to hunt on the threshold of a land barred to its demonic kin for uncounted centuries.

It sensed its prey.

Unable to squirm free, Kane drew his sword for a hopeless defense. The cave creature had located him—in the darkness its hunting senses must be preternaturally keen—but it hesitated to spring. Seemingly it was confused by the wan rays of sunlight trespassing upon its realm.

The torch lay thrust between rock almost within Kane's reach. By a series of desperate lunges he succeeded in spearing it on his swordtip and drawing it to him. Answering the sabre-tooth's growl, he swung the brand to flaring brilliance. The cat retreated somewhat, still intent on its trapped prey, but uncertain how to cope with this blazing light that seared its all but sightless eyes.

"Dwassllir! Can you break through!" The torch had burned through much of its length, so that the dwindling flame stung Kane's fingers.

The giant groaned with frantic effort. "There's a slab or rock midway I can't shift without bringing down the whole slide! If I had a beam I could use for bracing, I could grub out the boulders holding it up and crawl through! Not enough room through there otherwise!"

The sabre-tooth coughed angrily and advanced a step, stubby tail twitching. Its hunger would soon overwhelm its caution, Kane realized in sick dread, as the cat drew its mammoth bulk into a crouch. In a minute its spring would crush him against the stone.

Eyes blazing feral hatred, Kane steadied his sword. There would be time for only one hopeless thrust as the cat's irresistible spring splintered his chest to pulpy ruin, but Kane meant for his slayer to feel his steel.

"I'll try for his throat when he leaps!" Kane shouted

grimly. "Wound him bad as I'm able! Go back and hunt up a log to brace with, Dwassllir. If my sword thrusts deep enough to cripple, there's a chance you can kill this beast with your axe. Brotemllain's crown waits there for you, and when you return to your people you can tell them the price of its winning!"

Dwassllir was tearing away rubble furiously, though Kane did not risk a glance to note his progress. "Keep the cat back as long as you can, Kane!" His voice came muffled. "It was my doing got you into this, and I'll not abandon you like a slinking coward!"

The torch was sputtering, moments of life remained for both flame and wielder. Came a low rumble of shifting stone, but Kane glared unwaveringly into the cat's wrathful eyes. The tiger started, spat in sudden bafflement. Kane braced himself to meet its deadly lunge, then saw in amazement that the sabre-tooth was edging away.

A flaming length of trunkwood slithered across the stones, propelled by a bass roar from down low. Turning in disbelief, Kane saw Dwassllir's grimy face grinning triumphantly up at him from beneath a jutting shelf of rock.

"Made it, by damn!" the giant bellowed. He grunted breathlessly as he wriggled his colossal frame through the burrow he had dug. "Used my axe to shore up that main slab! She creaked some, but her haft's seasoned hickory, and she'll likely hold till we're out of here!"

At the sudden appearance of a creature rivalling its own awesome bulk, the sabre-tooth had retreated into the darkness of the cavern. Dwassllir shoved his torch further down the passage, then bent to Kane. A heave of his mighty shoulders drew back the imprisoning stone.

Kane pitched forward. Biting his lips against the agony, he slithered out of the crevice to freedom.

"Can you walk, manling?"

Wincing, Kane took a few unsteady strides. "Yeh, though I'd rather ride."

The giant hefted the torch. "I'll see King Brotemllain now." he declared.

"Don't be a fool, Dwassllir!" Kane protested. "Without your axe you're no match for that monster! You haven't driven it off— it's still prowling in the cavern! We'll be lucky to crawl out before it decides to attack!" The giant brushed him aside.

"Look, at least let's draw back and give that cat a chance to leave! We can find timber to shore up the ledge, and free your axe! Then we'll try for the crown!"

"Not enough time!" Dwassllir's face was resolute. "I never really expected that axe to hold. It'll give way any second, and this shaft will be sealed forever! Can't even risk trying to wrench it free! The torch will keep the beast at bay long enough to get the crown. Besides, he won't be the only demon to crawl up from the pit. You don't need to stay though."

Kane swore and limped after him.

"Ha! Sabre-tooth!" roared Dwassllir, scooping up a broken section of stalactite. A growl answered him from the cavern's echoing recesses. "Sabre-tooth! Do you know me! My ancestors were your enemy! We fought your forebears in ages past and made necklaces for our women from your pretty fangs! Hear me, sabre-tooth! Though you're three times the size of your tawny ancestor, I've no fear of you! I am Dwassllir— last true son of the blood of the old kings! I've come for my crown! Hide in your hole, sabre-tooth—or I'll have a white fur cloak to wear with my royal crown!"

The giant's challenge echoed through the cavern, rolled back by the sabre-tooth's angry snarl. Somewhere in the shadows the cat paced stiff legged—but the cacaphony of echoes made its position uncertain. Bats swooped in panic; dust and bits of stone trickled over them. Kane shifted his sword uneasily, not caring to think what silent blow might strike his back.

"King Brotemllain! The legends of my race do not

lie!" breathed Dwassllir in awe. Reverently he stood before the throne of the ages dead hero—his face aglow with vision of ancient glory. Reflected in his eyes was crimson brightness from the ruby crown.

The giant discarded stalactite club, stretched to touch the dead king's crown. With gentle strength he broke it free from its encrusted setting. "Grandsire, your children have need of this . . ."

Avalanche of ivory fanged terror, the sabre-tooth bolted from the darkness! Shattering silence with its killing scream, it leapt for the giant's unprotected back. Off guard, Dwassllir pivoted at the final instant to half evade the cat's full rush. Its crushing impact hurled giant and cave beast against the throne and onto the cavern floor.

Jaws locked in Dwassllir's shoulder, the tiger raked furiously against his back, talons tearing deep gashes. Kane limped in, sword flashing. But his movements were clumsy, and at first slash a blow of the creature's paw spun him away. He fell heavily at the foot of the throne, shook his head dully to clear vision.

Dwassllir howled and lurched to his knees, huge hands clawing desperately to dislodge the murderous fangs. His flailing arm touched the fallen torch, and he seized it instantly, smashed its blazing end into the monster's face. Seared by the blinding heat, the sabretooth released its death grip with an enraged shriek—and the giant's punishing kick flung them apart.

Smoke hung over the cat's gory maw. Gouts of scarlet spurted from the giant's deeply gouged shoulder. "Face to face, sabre-tooth!" roared Dwassllir wildly. "Skulker in shadow! Slinking coward! Dare now to attack your master face to face!"

Even as the tiger crouched to spring, Dwassllir leapt upon it, crippled left arm brandishing the torch. They grappled in midair, and the cavern seemed to quake at their collision. Over and over they rolled, torch flung wide, while Kane groggily tried to regain his feet. The giant struggled grimly to stave off those awful fangs, to writhe atop the sabre-tooth's greater bulk. Fearsome jaws champed on emptiness as they fought, but its slashing claws were goring horrible wounds through the giant's flesh.

Stoically enduring the agony, Dwassllir threw all his leviathan strength into tightening his grip on the cat's head. He bellowed insanely—curses of pain, of fury—locked his teeth in the beast's ear and ripped away its stump with taunting laughter. Life blood poured over his limbs, made a slippery mat of scarlet sodden white fur. Still he howled and jeered, chanted snatches of ancient verse—sagas of his race—pounded the sabretooth's skull against stone.

With a sudden wrench, Dwassllir hauled himself astride the cat's back. "Now die, sabre-tooth!" he roared. "Die knowing defeat as did your scrawny grandsires!"

He dug his knees into the creature's ribs, clamped heels together beneath its belly. The cat tried to roll, to dislodge him—but it could not! Great fists knotted over frothed fangs, arms locked champing jaws apart—Dwassllir bunched his shoulders and heaved backward. Gasping, coughing breath snorted from the cat's nostrils; its struggle was no longer to attack. For the first time in centuries, a sabre-tooth knew fear.

Blood gleamed a rippling pattern across the straining muscles of the giant's broad back. Irresistibly his hold tightened. Inexorably the tiger's spine bowed backward. An abrupt, explosive snap as vertebrae and sinew surrendered!

Laughing, Dwassllir twisted the sabre-tooth's head completely around. He spat into its dying eyes.

"Now then, King Brotemllain's crown!" he gasped, and staggered away from the twitching body. The giant reeled, but stood erect. His fur garments were shredded, dark and sticky. Blood flowed so freely as to shroud the depth and extent of his wounds; flaps of flesh hung ragged, and bone glistened yellow as he moved.

He groaned as he reached the throne and slumped

down with his back braced against it. Kane found his senses clear enough to stand and knelt beside the stricken giant. Deftly his hands explored the other's wounds, sought vainly to staunch the bright spurting blood from the sabre gouges. But Kane was veteran of too many battles not to know his wounds were mortal.

Dwassllir grinned gamely, his face pale beneath splashed gore. "That, Kane, is how my ancestors overcame the great beasts of Earth's dawn."

"No giant ever fought a creature like this," Kane swore, "nor killed it barehanded!"

The giant shruggled weakly. "You think not, manling? But you don't know the legends of our race, Kane. And the legends are truth, I know that now! Fire and Ice! Those were heroic days!"

Kane looked about the cavern, then bent to retrieve a fallen circle of gold. The rubies gleamed like Dwassllir's life blood; the crown was heavy in his hands. And though there was a fortune in his grasp, Kane no longer wanted King Brotemllain's crown.

"This is yours now," he muttered, and placed the crown upon Dwassllir's nodding brow.

The giant's head came erect again, and there was fierce pride in his face—and sadness. "I might have led them back to those lost days of glory! he whispered. Then: "But there'll be another of my race, perhaps —another who will share my vision of the great age!"

He signed for Kane to leave him. Already his eyes looked upon things beyond this lonely cavern in a desolate waste. "That was an age to live in!" he breathed hoarsely. "An age of heroes!"

Kane somberly rose to his feet. "A great race, a heroic age—it's true," he acknowledged softly. "But I think the last of its heroes has passed."

Clark Ashton Smith

THE STAIRS IN THE CRYPT

Of all the many writers who contributed to Weird Tales, it is Clark Ashton Smith who interests me the most. He mastered an intricate, lapidary style begemmed with verbal ornaments (imagine Vathek crossed with Poe), and wrote with suave humor, dry, ironic, subtly morbid—Decadent is the name of the school—producing works like no other American writer this side of Lafcadio Hearn, Edgar Saltus, perhaps, and Poe himself. Since his death there have come to light fragments of unpolished prose, outlines, lists of unused titles and invented names, sketches of story-ideas and plots, none of which he lived to use. So, since 1973, I have been weaving the bits and pieces together, fleshing them out into new stories crafted in as close a style to Smith's as I can create. I like to think he would have approved: occasionally, even I am fairly satisfied with them.

—L.C.

It is told of the necromancer Avalzaunt that he succumbed at length to the inexorable termination of his earthly existence in the Year of the Crimson Spider during the empery of King Phariol of Commoriom.

Upon the occasion of his demise, his disciples, in accordance with the local custom, caused his body to be preserved in a bath of bituminous natron, and interred the mortal remains of their master in a mausoleum prepared according to his dictates in the burying-grounds adjacent to the abbey of Camorba, in the province of Uthnor, in the eastern parts of Hyperborea.

The obsequies made over the catafalque whereupon reposed the mummy of the necromancer were oddly cursory in nature, and the enconium delivered at the interment by the eldest of the apprentices of Avalzaunt, one Mygon, was performed in a niggardly and grudging manner, singularly lacking in that spirit of somber dolence one should have expected from bereaved disciples gathered to mourn their deceased mentor. The truth of the matter was that none of the former students of Avalzaunt had any particular cause to bemoan his demise, for their master had been an exigent and rigorous taskmaster and his cold obduracy had done little to earn him any affection from those who had studied the dubious and repugnant science of necromancy under his harsh and unsympathetic tutelage.

Upon their completion of the requisite solemnities, the acolytes of the necromancer departed for their ancestral abodes in the city of Zanzonga which stood nearby, whilst others eloigned themselves to more distant Cerngoth and Leqquan. As for the negligent Mygon, he repaired to the remote and isolated tower of primordial basalt which rose from a headland overlooking the boreal waters of the eastern main, from which they had all come for the funereal rites. This tower had formerly been the residence of the deceased necromancer but was now, by lawful bequest, devolved upon himself as the seniormost of the apprentices of the late and unlamented mage.

If the pupils of Avalzaunt assumed that they had taken their last farewells of their master, however, it eventuated that in this assumption they were seriously mistaken. For, after some years of repose within the sepulchre, vigor seeped back again into the brittle limbs of the mummified enchanter and sentience gleamed anew in his jellied and sunken eyes. At first the partially-revived lich lay somnolent and unmoving in a numb and mindless stupor, with no conception of its present charnel abode. It knew, in fine, neither what nor where it was, nor aught of the peculiar circumstances of its untimely and unprecedented resurrection.

On this question the philosophers remain divided. One school holds to the theorem that it was the unseemly brevity of the burial rites which prevented the release of the spirit of Avalzaunt from its clay, thus initiating the unnatural revitalization of the cadaver. Others postulate that it was the necromantic powers inherent in Avalzaunt himself which were the sole causative agent in his return to life. After all, they argue, and with some cogence, one who is steeped in the power to effect the resurrection of another should certainly retain, even in death, a residue of that power sufficient to perform a comparable revivification upon oneself. These, however, are queries for a philosophical debate for which the present chronicler lacks both the leisure and the learning to pursue to an unequivocal conclusion.

Suffice it to say that, in the fulness of time, the lich had recovered its faculties to such a degree as to become cognizant of its interment. The unnatural vigor which animated the corpse enabled it to thrust aside the heavy lid of the black marble sarcophagus and the mummy sat up and stared about itself with horrific and indescribable surmise. The withered wreaths of yew and cypress, the decaying draperies of funereal black and purple, the sepulchral décor of the stone chamber wherein it now found itself, and the unmistakable nature of the tomb-furnishings, all served alike to confirm the reanimated cadaver in its initial impressions.

It is difficult for we, the living, to guess at the

thoughts which seethed through the dried and mould-encrusted brain of the lich as it pondered its demise and resurrection. We may hazard it, however, that the spirit of Avalzaunt quailed before none of the morbid and shuddersome trepidations an ordinary mortal would experience upon awakening within such somber and repellent environs. Not from shallow impulse or trivial whim had Avalzaunt in his youth embarked upon a study of the penumbral and atrocious craft of necromancy, but from a fervid and devout fascination with the mysteries of death. In the swollen pallor of a corpse in the advanced stages of decomposition had he ever found a beauty superior to the radiance of health, and in the mephitic vapors of the tomb a perfume headier than the scent of summer gardens.

Oft had he hung in rapturous excitation upon the words which fell, slow and sluggish, one by one, from the worm-fretted lips of deliquescent cadavers, or gaunt and umber mummies, or crumbling liches acrawl with squirming maggots and teetering on the sickening verge of terminal decay. From such, rendered temporarily animate by his necromantic art, it had been his wont to extort the abominable yet thrilling secrets of the tomb. And now he, himself, was become just such a revitalized corpse! The irony of the situation did not elude the subtlety of Avalzaunt.

"Once I yearned to know the terrors of the grave, the kiss of maggots on my tongue, the clammy caress of a rotting shroud against my tepid flesh," soliloquized the cadaver in a croaking whisper from a dry and shrunken throat crusted with the salts of the bitter natron. "I thirsted for the knowledge that glimmers in the pits of mummied eyes, and burned for that wisdom known only to the writhing and insatiable worm. Tirelessly I perused forbidden tomes by the wan and feeble luminance of guttering tapers of corpse-tallow to master the secrets of mortality, so that should ever the nethermost pits disgorge their crawling vermin I might aspire to dominion and empery over the legions of the living dead—among the which I, now, myself, am to be henceforward numbered!"

Thus it may be seen that the mordant humor in its present circumstances was readily perceived by the unblunted wit of the revitalized corpse.

Among the various implements of arcane manufacture which the pupils of Avalzaunt had buried in the crypt beside the mortal remains of their unlamented master there was a burnished speculum of black steel wherein presently the cadaver of Avalzaunt beheld its own repulsive likeness. It was skull-like, that sere and fulvous visage which peered back at the necromancer from the ebon depths of the magic mirror. Avalzaunt had seen such shrunken and decayed lineaments oft aforetime upon prehistoric mummies rifled from the crumbling fanes of civilizations anterior to his own. Seldom, however, had the reanimated lich gazed upon so delightfully decomposed and withered a visage as this bony and wizened horror which was its own face.

The lich next turned its rapt scrutiny on what remained of its lean and leathery body and tested brittle limbs draped in the rags of a rotting shroud, finding these embued with an adamantine and a tireless vigor, albeit they were gaunt and attenuated to a degree which may only be described as skeletal. Whatever the source of the supranormal energy which now animated the corpse of the necromancer, it lent the undead creature a vigor it had never previously enjoyed in life, not even in the longago decades of its juvenescence.

As for the crypt itself, it was sealed from without by pious ceremonials which rendered the portals thereunto inviolable by the mummy in its present mode of existence as one of the living dead. Such precautions were customary in the land of Uthnor, which was the abode of many warlocks and enchanters during the era whereof I write; for it was feared that wizards seldom lie easy in their graves and that, betimes, they are wont to rise up from their deathly somnolence and stalk abroad to wreak a dire and ghastly vengeance upon those who wronged them when they lived. Hence was it only prudent for the timid burghers of Zanzonga, the principal city of this region of Hyperborea, to insist that the tombs of sorcerors be sealed with the Pnakotic pentagram, against which such as the risen Avalzaunt may not trespass without the severest discomfiture.

Thus it was that the mummy of the necromancer was pent within the crypt, helpless to emerge therefrom into the outer world. And there for a time it continued to sojourn: but the animated lich was in no wise discommoded by its enforced confinement, for the bizarre and ponderous architecture of the crypt was of its own devisal, and the building thereof Avalzaunt had himself supervised. Therefore it was that the crypt was spacious and, withal, not lacking in such few and dismal amenities as the reposing chambers of the dead may customarily afford their ghastly habitants. Moreover, the living corpse bethought itself of that secret portal every tomb is known to have, behind the which there doubtless was a hidden stair went down to black, profound, abysmal deeps beneath the earth where vast, malign and potent entities reside. The Old Ones they are called, and among these inimical dwellers in the tenebrous depths there was a certain Nyogtha, a dire divinity whom Avalzaunt had oftentimes celebrated with rites of indescribable obscenity.

This Nyogtha had for his minions the grisly race of Ghouls, those lank and canine-muzzled prowlers among the tombs; and from the favor of Nyogtha the necromancer had in other days won ascendancy over the loping hordes. And so the mummy of Avalzaunt waited patiently within the crypt, knowing that in time all tombs are violated by these shambling predators from the Pit, who had been the faithful servants of Avalzaunt when he had lived, and who might still consent to serve him after death.

Erelong the cadaver heard the shuffle of leathery feet ascending the secret stair from the umplumbed and

The Stairs in the Crypt

gloomy foetor of the abyss, and the fumbling of rotting paws against the hidden portal; and the stale and vitiated air within the vault was, of a sudden, permeated with a disquieting effluvia as of long-sealed graves but newly opened. By these tokens the lich was made aware of the Ghoul-pack that pawed and whined and snuffled hungrily at the door. And when the portal yawned to admit the gaunt, lean-bellied, shuffling herd, the lich rose up before it, lifting thin arms like withered sticks and clawed hands like the stark talons of monstrous birds. The putrid witchfires of a ghastly phosphorescence flared up at the command of the necromancer, and the Ghoul-herd, affrighted, squealed and grovelled before the glare-eyed mummy. At length, having cowed them sufficiently, Avalzaunt elicited from the leader of the pack, a hound-muzzled thing with dull eyes the hue of rancid pus, a fearful and prodigious oath of thralldom.

It was not long thereafter before Avalzaunt had need of this loping herd of grave-robbers. For the necromancer in time became aware of an inner lack which greatly tormented it and which ever remained unassuaged by the supernatural vigor which animated its form. In time this nebulous need resolved itself into a gnawing lack of sustenance, but it was for no mundane nutriment, that acrid and raging thirst which burned within the dry and withered entrails of the lich. Cool water or honey-hearted wine would not suffice to sate that unholy thirst: for it was *human blood* Avalzaunt craved, but why or wherefore, the mummy did not know.

Perchance it was simply that the dessicated tissues of the lich were soaked through with the bituminous salts of the bitter natron wherein it had been immersed, and that it was this acid saltiness which woke so fierce and burning a thirst within its dry and dusty gullet. Or mayhap it was even as antique legends told, that the restless legions of the undead require the imbibement of fresh gore whereby to sustain their unnatural existence on this plane of being. Whatever may have been the cause, the mummy of the dead necromancer yearned for the foaming crimson fluid which flows so prodigally through the veins of the living as it had never thirsted for even the rarest of wines from terrene vinyards when it had lived. And so Avalzaunt evoked the lean and hungry Ghouls before its bier. They proffered unto the necromancer electrum chalices brimming with black and gelid gore drained from the tissues of corpses; but the cold, thick, coagulated blood did naught to slake the thirst that seared the throat of the mummy. It longed for fresh blood, crimson and hot and foam-beaded, and it vowed that erelong it would drink deep thereof, again and again and yet again.

Thereafter the shambling herd roamed by night far afield in dire obedience to the mummy's will. And so it came to pass that the former disciples of the necromancer had cause to regret the negligent and over-hasty burial of their unlamented mentor. For it was upon the acolytes of the dead necromancer whom the Ghoul-horde preyed. And the first of all their victims was that unregenerate and niggardly Mygon who still dwelt in the sea-affronting tower which once had been the demesne of the necromancer. When, with the diurnal light, his servants came to rouse him from his slumbers, they found a blanched and oddly-shrunken corpse amidst the disorder of the bedclothes, which were torn and trampled and besmirched with black mire and grave-mould. Naught of the nature of the nocturnal visitants to the chamber of the unfortunate Mygon could his horror-stricken servants discern from the fixed staring of his glazed and sightless eyes; but from the drained and empty veins of the corpse, and its preternatural pallor, they guessed it that he had fallen victim to some abominable and prowling vampire in the night.

Again and again thereafter the Ghoul-herd went forth by the secret stairs within the crypt of Avalzaunt, down to those deeps far beneath the crust of the earth where they and their brethren had anciently tunneled out a warren of fetid passageways connecting tomb and burial-ground and the vaults beneath castle, temple, tower and town. After nine such grisly atrocities had befallen, some vague intimation of the truth dawned upon the ecclesiarchs of Zanzonga, for it became increasingly obvious that only the former apprentices of the dead necromancer, Avalzaunt, suffered from the depredations of the unknown vampire creatures. In time the priests of Zanzonga ventured forth to scrutinize the crypt of the deceased enchanter, but found it still sealed, its door of heavy lead intact, and the Pnakotic pentagram affixed thereto undisturbed and unbroken. The night-prowling monsters who drained their hapless victims dry of blood, whoever or whatever they might prove to be, had naught to do with Avalzaunt, surely; for the necromancer, they said, slept still within his sealed and shutten crypt. This pronunciamento given forth, they returned to the temple of Shimba, in Zanzonga, pleasantly satisfied with themselves for the swift and thorough fulfillment of their mission. Not one of them so much as suspected, of course, the very existence of the stairs in the crypt, whereby Avalzaunt and his Ghouls emerged in the gloaming to hunt down the unwary and abominably to feast.

And from this vile nocturnal feasting the sere and withered mummy lost its aforetime gauntness, and it waxed sleek and plump and swollen, for that it now gorged heavily each night on rich, bubbling gore; and, as is well known to those of the unsqueamish who ponder upon such morbidities, the undead neither digest nor eliminate the foul and loathly sustenance whereon they feed.

Erelong the now bloated and corpulent lich had exhausted the list of its former apprentices, for not one remained unvisited by the shamblers from the Pit. Then it was that the insatiable Avalzaunt bethought him of the monks of Camorba whose abbey lay close by, nigh unto the very burial-ground wherein it was supposed he slept in the fetid solitude of his crypt. These monks were of an order which worshipped Shimba, god of the shepherds, and this drowsy, rustic little godling demanded but little of his celebrants; wherefore they were an idle, fat, complacent lot much given to the fleshly pleasures. 'Twas said they feasted on the princeliest of viands, drank naught but the richest of vintages, and dined hugely on the juiciest and most succulent haunches of rare, dripping meat; by reason thereof they were rosy and rotund and brimming with hot blood. At the very thought of the fat, bubbling fluid that went rivering through their soft, lusty flesh, the undead necromancer grew faint and famished: and he vowed that very night to lead his loping tomb-hounds against the abbey of Camorba.

Night fell, thick with turgid vapors. A humped and gibbous moon floated above the vernal hills of Uthnor. Thirlain, abbot of Camorba, was closeted with the abbey accounts, seated behind a desk lavishly inlaid with carven plaques of mastodonic ivory, as the moon ascended towards the zenith. Rumor had not exaggerated his corpulence, for, of all the monks of Camorba, the abbot was the most round and rubicund and rosy; hence it was from the fat jugular that pulsed in his soft throat that the necromancer had sworn to slake his febrile and unwholesome thirst.

In one plump hand Thirlain held a sheaf of documents appertaining to the accounts of the abbey, the which were scribed upon crisp papyrus made from calamites; the pudgy fingers of the other hand toyed idly with a silver paperknife which had been a gift from the high priest of Shimba in Zanzonga, and which was sanctified with the blessings of that patriarch.

Thus it was that, when the long becurtained windows behind the desk burst asunder before the whining, eager pack of hungry Ghouls, and the swollen and hideously bloated figure of the mad-eyed cadaver

which led the tomb-hounds came lurching toward the
abbot where he sat, Thirlain, shrieking with panic fear,
blindly and impulsively thrust that small blunt silver
knife into the distended paunch of the lumbering
corpse as it flung itself upon him. What occurred in
sequel to that instinctive and, ordinarily, ineffectual
blow is still a matter of the theological debate among
the ecclesiarchs of Zanzonga, who no longer sleep so
smugly in their beds.

For the bloated and swollen paunch of the walking
corpse burst open like an immense and rotten fruit,
spewing forth such stupendous quantities of black and
putrid blood that the silken robes of the abbot were
drenched in an instant. In sooth, so voluminous was
the deluge of cold, coagulated gore, that the thick carpets
were saturated with stinking fluids, which sprayed
and squirted in all directions as the stricken cadaver
staggered about in its throes. The vile liquid splashed
hither and yon in such floods that even the damask
wall-coverings were saturated, and, in no time at all, the
entire chamber was awash with putrescent gore to such
an extent that the very floor was become a lake of
foulness. The liquescent vileness poured out into the
hallways and the corridors beyond when at length the
other monks, roused by the shriekings of their horror-
smitten abbot, rose from cot and pallet and came
bursting in to behold the ghastly abbatial chamber floating
in a lake of noisome slime and Thirlain himself
crouched pale and gibbering atop his ivory desk, pointing
one palsied hand at the thin and lean and leathery
rind of dried and dessicated flesh that was all which
remained of Avalzaunt the necromancer, once the vile
fluids his mummy retained had burst forth in a grisly
deluge, and drained him dry.

This horrendous episode was hushed up and only
distorted rumors of the nightmare ever leaked beyond
the abbey walls. But the burghers of Zanzonga marveled
for a season over the swift and inexplicable
resignation from his fat and cozy sinecure of the com-

placent and pleasure-loving Thirlain, who departed that very dawn on a barefoot pilgrimage to the remotest of holy shrines far-famed for its wonder-working relics, which was situate amidst the most hostile and inaccessible of wildernesses. Thereafter the chastened abbot entered a dour monastic order of stern flagellants, famed for their strict adherence to a grim code of the utmost severity, wherein the all but hysteric austerities of the zealous Thirlain, together with his over-rigorous chastisements of the flesh, made him an object of amazement and wonder among even the harshest and most obdurate of his brethren. No longer plump and soft and self-indulgent, he grew lean and sallow from a bleak diet of mouldy crusts and stale water, and died not long thereafter in the odor of sanctity and was promptly declared venerable and beatific by the Grand Patriarch of Commoriom, and his relics now command excessive prices from the dealers in such ecclesiastical memorabilia. As for the remains of the necromancer, they were burnt on the hearth of the abbey at Camorba and were reduced to a pinch of bitter ash which was hastily scattered to the winds. And it is said of the spirit of the unfortunate Avalzaunt, that at last it found rest in whatever far and fabulous bourn is the final haven of perturbed and restless spirits.

Raul Garcia Capella

THE GOBLIN BLADE

Ray Capella began, in Amra, writing Sword & Sorcery yarns set in Conan's own world and period, but in which the doughty Cimmerian makes no appearance. They were good stories.

Now, however, his apprenticeship done, he has begun to write his own tales, set in lands of his own invention. I am happy to see him take that extra step (although, as one who has imitated everyone from ERB and REH to CAS and on, I can hardly gripe at imitation: it is not only the sincerest form of flattery, but the school in which almost all fiction-smiths begin). It is a giant step, and he has taken it well, as the following story, published here for the first time, proves.

—L.C.

1. Siege and Skullduggery

The live rope floated upwards, parallel to the seawall of Castle Skernach. Neither of the two men clinging to its knots dared look to the boat that bobbed on an anchor line, fifty meters below them. The sea slashed at the rocks in the shadows there, checked in its attempt to swallow both them and their craft.

The rope's free end bent like a questing reptile into a crenelation. Briot and Dalmask did not let go until they were well between the merlons. From that point, the struggle at the castle's eastern bastion sounded like the clash of a million iron-clad scorpions. The cries of men, dying or triumphant, counterpointed it. The sea-breeze was tainted with the smell of blood, the waning sunlight was filled with dust-motes from the battle.

"Me of all people—why me?" Dalmask said. He watched the long rope coil at his feet of its own accord and become limp, its spell finished. "I am no warrior! I wasn't meant to—"

He yelped. A sentry was coming round the turret towards them. Briot wore his eyepatch on the left and had barely turned in that direction when the soldier opened his mouth to sound an alarm.

Dalmask waved his long fingers at the man, saying a word under his breath. The guard worked mouth and throat, but no sound came out. However, he simultaneously raised his spear and ran at them.

Briot ducked under the point, managing to knock it upwards. The sword now at the end of his short arm rammed home, just below the armpit and past the edge of the sentry's cuirass. As Dalmask's conjuration had been brief, the warrior toppled with a groan and a clatter, dragging Briot forward.

"There must have been a dozen witches or sorcerers they could have picked from," whined Dalmask, dropping onto the floor of the tower proper behind his companion. "So I ask you, why—"

"Shut up!" Briot cursed. He was tugging at his weapon. "Help me—get this—out!"

Although it had pierced the heart, the blade had wedged between a rib and the top strap of their antagonist's armor. The warlock advanced timidly. His robe had loosened from where he had hitched it on his belt, just before their ascent, and now it tangled over the corpse's feet. Dalmask promptly fell, nearly braining himself against the inner turret wall. The sound of steps on the tower stairs reached their ears.

Abandoning his sword, Briot wheeled, picked up the spear and raced off for the head of the stairwell. He arrived there in time to employ his advantage, catching the second warrior in the throat as the fellow's head emerged into sunlight. Briot jumped down the intervening steps as the guard sagged.

Fortunately, his victim was slender enough, and he was able to lower the body onto the steps without much noise. He stood a few moments in tense silence, listening to the hubbub from the floors below.

Laying the corpse's spear aside, he drew the man's sword, wet it with blood and curled stiffening fingers around the hilt. At first glance, it could look as if the dead men had reeled away from each other after a deadly personal battle. Which might serve in covering his and the warlock's tracks if the sentries were found.

When he returned after Dalmask, he found the latter had cut the strap on the first guard's cuirass with his own little dagger, freeing his sword.

"Give me that." Briot took the warlock's blade. Before the other could raise an outcry, he had slit the man's hem and torn a large piece around the robe's bottom, exposing Dalmask's thin legs. He wiped his own weapon, saying: "Now *that* should save you from further blundering.

"It might interest you to know," he added, as they ventured down the narrow stairway, "that you were the only choice Count Webba had. King Dumian approves not of sorcery and there are few practitioners in this country. You should be thankful they returned your belongings and let you out of the dungeons."

"I had no business in that dungeon to begin with—" Dalmask started, stopped. His shorter companion had placed a thick hand over his mouth. The sounds from below were now louder.

The stairs led to a gallery which overlooked a long,

high-ceilinged guardroom. Briot descended the last few steps on all fours, approaching the balustrade on his knees to peer at the activity below.

Presently, a resounding *kerraaashh* announced the mangonels' assault on Skernach's southern walls. Although he had expected it, Briot jumped in place, feeling the vibrations that ran through the great keep. He felt a bump at his elbow, discovered Dalmask had followed and was cradling his head as if tower and castle were collapsing around them.

Briot grinned to himself when a voice from below alerted everyone of a breach at the southern parapets. Pikeman and warlock gazed down while the enemy soldiers filed out, still strapping on weapons and headgear.

Briot scuttled downstairs as soon as the place was empty. He climbed back up the wooden ladder burdened with helmets, cuirasses and a sky-blue cloak. Dalmask held up a hand.

"Stop! I've suffered enough indignities! I shall *not* play the buffoon in some common warrior's accoutrements! I refuse to—"

"Refuse my left eyeball," Briot cut in. "Disguised, we've a chance of getting out of this alive. If we're to die, however, it's likely you'll go sooner if you traipse around like *that*. Besides, yours is no common warrior's garb. Only this lieutenant's helm can cover your long head. Certainly the cloak that goes with it is too long for me!"

He wasted no time with his own disguise and was soon helping his reluctant ally. He then led Dalmask around a corner of the gallery to a massive wooden door. The warlock resumed his complaining while the soldier drew the bolts.

"I told you before I'd no business in prison any more than I've any here," Dalmask repeated, "A man of my station and abilities should not be used thus, just because of a misunders—"

"By Tia's purple pubes!" Briot exploded. He grabbed

The Goblin Blade

at and shook the taller man by the cloak-collar. "You were caught red-handed, pilfering from Count Webba's mausoleum! You thought a menial like me wouldn't know of it, eh? Well, I *do!* By our laws, you should be dead, instead of earning your freedom whilst punishing my ears in the midst of a dangerous task! *Now* —lean on me as if you were wounded and keep quiet! I'll take care of the rest!"

He half-propelled the warlock through the doorway with his last words. They emerged onto a thin span that arced above a terrace, a strip of garden and a fosse-full of spikes. This ended at a gate, high on the central donjon, twenty meters to their right front. Skernach was a largish keep, supposedly unassailable on two sides because of the sea-cliffs it perched upon. Three more causeways connected the outer ramparts to the inner structure, and yet that fortress still seemed isolated, aloof from the drama that reddened its outer ramparts.

A squad had been assigned to guard the gate Briot and Dalmask approached, probably as a battle precaution. Soldiers fidgetted with their weapons there, gazing past lesser rooftops and courtyards to the bristling walls at the intruders' left and left-front. Now and then one would exchange shouts with the men bustling through the alleys below, while another might duck an arrow that sailed that far into the enclosure with power expended. After the comparable quiet within the northwest tower, the din outside was like a palpable obstacle.

When they were halfway across, Dalmask suddenly collapsed like a stuffed doll, dragging his partner and tormentor to his knees. Briot grimaced; the warlock was neither wounded nor terrified.

"You've cursed and pushed me about enough, you!" Dalmask gritted, clutching at Briot's shell cuirass, "What I do or say next can ruin this enterprise and leave us impaled within that fosse—"

"Wh—what's this? Why, I'll kill you here—"

"The devil you will! You'll die then, accomplishing

nothing. Now promise—as soon as we get off this thing you'll tell me our specific mission. I'm sick and weak from using my powers without knowing our goal! I know not how much energy I must hoard. Promise!"

"Well fry my balls! I promise." Briot straightened, helping the other man up. His one eye glared at the magician with both anger and grudging respect. The confrontation had taken less than a minute. The squad leader approaching from the opposite end had not reached them.

"News—from outside," Briot yelled to the approaching sergeant. He had one arm around Dalmask, but his free hand made a salute which he had learned was used only by the enemy's couriers. The man acknowledged it, wide-eyed, while Briot continued with feigned effort: "The lieutenant's wounded—but he must—deliver the message—himself. The high command expects him—"

The squad leader turned and preceded them, as he could offer little help on the narrow span. Once he had opened the gate, however, Dalmask had to refuse the two men he offered with a wave of a hand. Briot said: "You may need them at their regular duty, sergeant. We'll make it."

As soon as they rounded a corner of the empty hall inside, the one-eyed man broke into a run, pulling the warlock along.

"What in the five hells—" panted Dalmask, "You promised—"

"Not *now*," Briot whispered, jogging on, "Consider this: Where does a courier from these troops' main host gain entrance? Why would he, wounded and all, climb up the seaward tower to bring in a report? When they start thinking, they may get curious. And then —hush . . ."

He slowed to a walk. They were at a cross-corridor, hung with yellow draperies and carpeted in black. Five meters to their right, an enemy colonel bent over a table near a wide doorway, flanked by two guards.

The Goblin Blade

The officer looked up as they crossed the hall into a roughly triangular weapons-room beyond. An archway opposite them led to a gallery which obviously followed the inner donjon wall, but the pikeman turned right, past a spear stand. He elbowed Dalmask, pointed at a crossbow rack and made grabbing motions, then knelt in front of a panel hung with shields.

A voice reached them from the carpeted hallway: "Lieutenant?"

Briot cursed under his breath, feeling along the wall's base. Abruptly, the panel tilted inwards at the top. The bottom edge, swinging outwards, caught the advancing warlock's right shin. Dalmask stifled a yelp, on the brink of dropping crossbow and bolts. There was a rustle of steps from the hall.

Briot hissed, dodging under the tilting wall-section as it pivoted higher. Dalmask followed. In another moment, both men stood in the hidden doorway. The panel swung back, closed. The colonel's second call was cut off in mid-word.

2. Dialogues in the Dark

"Their turning that antechamber into an auxiliary supply-room is a stroke of luck," said Briot softly. "Give me those. Now here—hold that end of my scabbard. There's two turns ahead; I don't want to lose you in the dark."

"Can we talk? Won't they hear us?"

"There might be echoes if we speak loudly. Otherwise, there's little danger. We're surrounded by stone half a meter thick at the thinnest juncture." Briot chuckled. "You seem to have a reserve for guts when at the end of your patience. You startled me back there, on the span."

"You'd showed you were apprised of my crime and obviously I could no longer cajole for better treatment. Tit for tat. 'Tis your turn to tell me how you know

Skernach so well. It bespeaks greater rank. What were you ere you became a pikeman?"

"Captain of an elite private guard for Castle Skernach." Briot was candid. "Unfortunately, I chose to use these passageways for my own ends, so I *have* truly been a pikeman for a time. Here's where the stairway begins. Steep, but there's little danger of losing our wa—*ouch!* Stay off my heels—remember you've longer legs!"

They climbed in silence; the warlock saved his breath. After a few minutes, however, he prodded: "Was the woman involved punished also?"

"Nay, she was of noble blood, and—*how did you know?*" Briot slowed. Then he snorted: "Ah, one would think you'd used your powers then, when you're but making a shrewd guess. Well yes, there *was* a lady involved. Further up a ways I lost an eye, slew a man —and all the time, it had been but a lark for her . . ."

They continued upwards through blackness. Then, as if he had not paused, Briot spoke on: "Luckily, Count Webba's a wise man, who knows the—um, vagaries of love. My act was self-defense but considering whose life I took, he would've been justified in executing me. Instead, he demoted me. *She* left Julna. For greater conquests, no doubt. We all forgot her . . ."

Dalmask smiled in the dark at that, but said nothing. They came to a landing, the pikeman signalling a halt. The warlock sat on the cold stone beside him with a grateful sigh. He whispered: "I suppose now you'll have a chance to regain all you lost?"

"More than that, not counting the eye. Consider: the Conqueror marched on Julna and took this castle just three weeks ago; tomorrow, thanks to Count Webba, King Dumian may have it back. If our mission succeeds, it may even be mine, a week hence—"

At that point, Dalmask forgot how difficult it was to steer the other to his promise. He interrupted: "Nonsense! You people are resisting *Tormahan*'s might, you fool! There hasn't been a barbarian leader like him in

The Goblin Blade

all of Ocba's history! Think you your kinglet can hold off a horde that's overrun a whole continent and visited yours for a mere skirmish? When the Conqueror himself learns Julna's stood up to him, he'll crush this and the neighboring countries the way a child treads on an ant!"

"When?" the other started, with what was almost a whoop. Briot clapped a hand to his own mouth. Dalmask would have had his answer if he had seen his companion's convulsed face then. Briot rose with a sound of mingled fury and laughter in his throat. He hissed: "Follow me!"

"You promised—" Dalmask was too late. His guide raced up the steep ascent, breathing through bared teeth. The warlock toiled after him, two steps at a time. His heart was hammering, legs trembling under him when they finally reached their goal. Having had no warning, Dalmask ran into the smaller man. They teetered on the stairs.

Briot threw himself against one wall, braced a bent foot on the opposite one. One hand shot out, succeeded in grasping the warlock's forearm. They regained their balance.

The pikeman shrugged the incident off with a curse; it was unimportant now. Loosening his hold, he handed Dalmask the crossbow and strained at something overhead.

The stairwell was suddenly flooded with reddish sunlight. Both men were temporarily blinded and simultaneously shocked by the roar from outside. Grabbing the weapon, Briot hoisted himself up with a noncommittal: "Wait."

In spite of the din, Dalmask only did so for a few minutes. Then he followed, to find himself on a curving, crenelated parapet that apparently ran completely around the main donjon tower. From outside, it had resembled a decorative cornice, but its inner width could accommodate and conceal seated archers.

Gazing through the small embrasures, the magician

found he had a terrifying bird's view of the battle. The setting sun cast the inner keep's shadow on the turmoil far below, but moving highlights on helms, blades and trappings etched out fury and destruction in doll-sized detail. A haze stung the eyes; the babble was deafening.

He crawled along, to find Briot a-crouch over a vertical opening. This was evidently for pouring oil or whatever on any attackers upon the corresponding span at that point. Briot was firing with difficulty into the melee directly below. He shot a venomous look at the warlock, who then crawled back to the hidden exit.

Dropping gingerly through the hole, Dalmask huddled in a corner, hands clapped to ears. The last thing he was to see in that sunset was Briot's triumphant one-eyed leer when the warrior returned, bow in hand. The trapdoor swung up, plunging them into comforting darkness and relative quiet.

"They had no time to guess where the bolts were coming from," Briot chortled. "The bodies kept the gate ajar—our men are in. We'll be taking the donjon tonight, floor by floor."

"Is our mission then accomplished?" There was an edge to Dalmask's tone "That is, of course, until word reaches Tormahan—"

"Have you not guessed by now?" Briot cut in, "Tormahan knows. Truly, did you think we came but to get me up there? Our chief task is to get The Sword."

"*The* Sword? You mean—the Lightsword?"

"Of course! *He'll* be trapped in here, marshalling a handful, waiting to hold out 'til reinforcements arrive. But he has to rest sometime—and then our moment will come—"

"He's here, then! *Tormahan!*" It was a suspicion Dalmask's mind had refused to face. "Here in Castle Skernach . . ."

The warlock's voice trailed off. Unable to see his companion, Briot did not understand what was happening to him. He blurted out the rest: "Naturally he's here—he's never without the Lightsword, right? When I said the Conqueror had taken Skernach, I didn't just mean his forces!

"Tormahan's always in the thick of campaign or battle; he thrives on it. And having taken the Southern continent, he wasn't content to bask in peace. He crossed the isthmus with his scouting forces and came on northeast.

"Don't you see? In so doing, he made his first tactical error. *We've cut him off from his damned horde!* That's why Count Webba had to take a chance on us. Saddled by King Dumian's edict against sorcery, he had no time to send for a wizard from elsewhere in Korpad. Here was Tormahan, at Castle Skernach—there our Julnan army at hand; me with the castle's secrets. And you in a local dungeon. A desperate gamble, and we must make ... Dalmask, what in. ..."

The pikeman's words were a faraway echo. In the enveloping murk, the warlock sat with eyes rolled up into his head, clutching his knees and shuddering. Remembering.

The forges of Lonoch, his birthplace, where the scant metal was turned into weapons for trade outside the mountain region. The violent tribal gatherings he and others had preferred to leave behind. And then, the tide that rode out of the crags to pillage for sustenance owed them by the lake cities.

It had become a horde that had not distinguished between the guilty and the innocent, adding bloodletting to vengeance. A ruthless, mystery-shrouded leader had risen to gather the reins of power. And Dalmask, one of the million casualties to wanton destruction, had lost his second apprenticeship.

He had starved in a ditch for days, then joined the barbarian train, with death as an alternative. He had entertained and served warriors, fearful to reveal greater powers and be enlisted into a darker trade.

The growing host marched out of Lonoch to take

Riame. Then into Madiria, where he had seen a city's people turned into living pyramids of bone and flesh outside its burning gates. That had been years ago, but its sight was carved into his memory. By then he had been an officer's aide, who learned much by keeping his counsel. Twice he had seen Tormahan the Conqueror himself. He would not soon forget that, either.

When the horde had turned west, on the now-legendary invasion of the Saffron Escarpment, Dalmask hid. He had managed to stay behind, trekked east. As a wizard's majordomo, he had boarded ship at a small Madirian port, bound for the far isles of Mofac, and thence Korpad. Away from a land that would soon be all Tormahan's. Away from fear and chaos. . . .

The magician's helmet clicked against stone. A hand was shaking his shoulder gently. The voice was saying: "What's amiss? Dalmask! You can't be asleep?"

"No. I'll be along. Right behind you."

"What in Tia's Game is wrong?"

"Never mind. Lead the way. It is cold here." The hand of fate had touched him, and he was chilled.

Neither armies, jungles, drought or storm had checked Tormahan's progress. Wizard-kings beyond the Saffron Escarpment had fallen before him. And now—now a daring count in a back-water kingdom had chosen a simple warlock, who could scarce hobble down a stairway, to stand against such might.

"Knowing little of your loyalties, Webba instructed me not to reveal much until you were committed to do all you could for our purposes," Briot concluded, "Your price out of this, you see."

"I have already reasoned *that* out, my one-eyed friend," Dalmask's voice sank. "But if 'doing my all' requires blasting *him* with a thunderbolt or such-like, you're sadly mistaken. I wield no such power."

"No, no, Tormahan we need as hostage against his legions. If he doesn't disappear, as he did that other time he was cornered, in Western Iria. 'Tis his sword we're here to steal. He's nothing without it, right? We've heard he sleeps only three hours a night. And even that would be enough. Now—here's the landing again. Sit a spell."

Briot helped the magician sit, handed him a packet: "Here, eat something while I reconnoiter. Feel that? I'm leaving my helmet there—don't knock it down the stairs. Wait."

With a slither and a rush of musty air, another trapdoor opened. Dim light made a rectangle in the gloom. For a moment, the pikeman stood, watching the enervated warlock eat the hardtack ration mechanically.

Briot found his unwilling partner had been transformed in the preceding minutes. He preferred the wretched but competent bungler to this suddenly-old man, who seemed complacent in the face of death.

3. The Conqueror Unconquerable

Briot tiptoed into a tiny secret alcove off the landing, turned a corner. To his right, the wall he now faced was slotted with spyholes. He placed his eye to one, cursed softly. Coffers and tables lay upended on the floor of the room beyond. Torn curtains hung awry, the bed on the dais was unmade. From the dust and smell, it was apparent the chamber was unused, had been in that condition since the taking of Castle Skernach by the Conqueror.

It was told their enemy spent his evenings reading battle histories or picking his generals' brains when not in the midst of campaign plans or battles. But—if one were to believe the rumors—where did he spend those three hours' rest? Did the man not have a place for private moments?

Briot pivoted on a heel. His mouth fell open. The hair on his forearms and scalp tingled, and he moved back a step. A long, pale head, crowned with a nimbus of grey locks, was floating towards him out of the half-lit corridor.

"Master's bedroom?" said the head, tilting to peer through a peephole. "Don't expect Tormahan to use it. Have you not heard he sleeps in his campaign headquarters?"

"Glawk," Briot unstuck the tongue from the top of his palate. He flushed: *"Damn you!* You near scared my arse off! And 'tis a good thing the room's like that! Sounds filter through—we'd have been discovered. Are you telling me *he* never rests? Has he not attended orgies 'midst kingly allies? He must needs sleep it off . . ."

"It is said that for *him,* the same three hours suffice. And none may distrub him, then." Dalmask's head bobbed to look from another angle. He too had removed his headgear, but the cloak covered him to the neck, contributing to the previous illusion. "He is not an ordinary—"

The portal on the opposite wall of the chamber beyond swung wide with a crash that drowned out the warlock's whisper. It was his turn to back against the hidden corridor's stone wall, eyes wide with terror.

The figure at the threshold was a glittering, implacable tower. It filled the doorway in width and height, stooping to bring its complex, barbaric helmet into the room. Instantly, the bedchamber seemed to dwindle in proportion; it was not built to house such a huge, ominous presence, whose identity was unmistakable.

Three strides brought the big man to the middle of the floor, oblivious of what stood in his way. Debris crunched under his weight or was pushed aside. His breath was audible, like that of some great carnivore. The wide-bladed sword in his left hand shone bright wherever blood did not darken it.

Briot ogled the gore-spattered yellow armor from his hiding place. In a world where men were usually content to carry metal foils for weapons, to wear shell-studded leather tunics or cuirasses fashioned from bone or wood, this giant used a king's ransom for protection. Ocba was poor in metal, but Tormahan could afford to wear linked iron for armor. Was the shining sword what legend held it to be, or did the man's invincibility lie in size and accoutrements?

And how could a man this size escape so easily? In the Labyrinth Forest of Western Iria, the Conqueror had been lured from his main host, his personal guard slain. Surrounded, Tormahan had battled singlehanded atop a knoll, until midnight. He had been shielded by rock on two sides, protected on a third by the heaped bodies of friend and foe. After a pause in the fighting, enemy bowmen had climbed up to him —to find he had vanished.

Gone, although no wizard, live or dead, had been near him. No trace of that towering body among the corpses, which were in turn ringed by his adversaries. Hours later he had reappeared, rallying a scattered troop, holding his ground until his forces came to the rescue. How? Gazing at the legendary figure now, Briot could see why the barbarian inspired such awe. Dalmask obviously knew and believed all the legends.

The massive head turned. The pikeman shrank back as that owlish mask formed by the helm's cheek-and-nose plates seemed to glare directly at him.

But Tormahan had not really seen him, nor guessed the secret of the wall-frieze carved on his side. He was listening to the clangor of battle on the floors below. With a sudden movement, the colossus was back at the doorway. The dripping sword left a trail as he ducked to stand outside again.

Briot had to shove the magician, force him through the passageway. When the stone sighed shut behind them at the landing, he panted: "What in Lyos's name is wrong with you? Are you *that* fearful of him?"

"Yes. I was loath to make noise. I've no magic that can harm him, or protect us from him."

"Might that unwillingness to try your magic not be fear, also? Remember his invincibility has never been truly put to the test." Briot put as much conviction behind his words as he could muster, having had his doubts. "He's up here because he must be trapped. I'll wager they're fighting for the stairs. We must watch, lest he find some way—Damn! I've got to make sure the Count *has* taken all the floors."

"Go if you must. I will watch."

"Leave you—in there? If you bungle, if you make a sound—"

"I die; what could b-be simpler?"

Briot had little choice. Most of the officers, Webba's included, did not know Dalmask and would likely kill him. He had to rely on the warlock's terror. Again, he worked the mechanism, holding his breath. The other man crawled out of sight, the stairway plunged into darkness. He started downstairs.

Dalmask found a slit low on the partition and sat cross-legged in the passageway, knees and toes braced against the wall. From an angle he could see Tormahan had been joined by half a dozen men, just beyond the entrance across the room. Two were wounded; these stumbled inside to sit or lie amid the shambles on the floor.

The massive door was left ajar. There was much running and yelling outside. Time stretched tautly on, while Dalmask gripped his thin knees to ease their cramped position. His eyeballs felt dry and hot, as if he had not blinked for hours.

Abruptly, the door was thrown back. Four armed men careened in, each nursing bad wounds. Only one stood alert, facing the threshold. He went down first, bowled over by Tormahan, who stormed into the chamber shortly afterwards.

Once, twice, thrice, he struck. The warriors in red-and-yellow went down, slain by their own leader.

The room swam in a haze of violence before the magician's eyes; corpses littered the floor. One of the men who had previously entered had died; he saw the other rise to his knees, hefting an axe. Tormahan approached him deliberately. The warrior's amazement was shattered by a blow that tore into face and skull.

The Conqueror then sauntered imperturbably to the bed, sat on its edge. He removed his helmet. Dalmask could see part of the yellow-white mane, the spattered, impassive, rock-hard features, the jewel-bright eyes.

There was a rustle of sound beside Dalmask, who turned his head with a wrench that hurt his neck-muscles. Briot was edging towards him across the passageway. He grimaced; it was well he had not been startled by the man's approach. Dalmask might have jumped, and they would be dead meat.

Briot rose to peer out of their hiding-place and glanced down with a scowl. He whispered—but too loudly and carelessly—"What the devil! Where's he gone?"

"*Shhh!*" Dalmask was frantic. The sounds of battle outside the room might not have drowned out Briot's words. He immediately looked back through his peephole.

Tormahan was not in the bedchamber.

4. Sword Sorcery

"Vos take you!" Briot was bending over the older man, hands curled like talons, "We've taken all the floors; we're on that main hallway! He *had* to be here; he's nowhere else! Didn't you watch? *Where is he?*"

Dalmask had not moved from the slit. He grabbed at Briot one-handed, propelled the other's face to another point of light.

As both men watched, there was a ghostly swirl of movement near the sword that leaned by the edge of the bed, on the dais beyond. For an instant, Tormahan —or a tenuous mirror-image—stood there, glaring at the wall that hid them. Then the menace on his face turned to impotence as he vanished again, like dissipating smoke.

"Wh—what." Briot started. "Did you s-see..."

"I saw." Dalmask struck his forehead with a palm. *"I see."*

The magician untangled himself from his position, rising with a groan. He rubbed his face, leaning on the stone. "How does one gain access to the chamber?"

"What? B-but Tormahan, he—He or his ghost is there—"

"No, my one-eyed friend. Tell me, is it midnight?"

"It should be. I wanted to find Webba and nearly got killed doing so. It took time. What difference—"

The pikeman was automatically working another hidden counterweight. Where the "L" of alcove and passageway met, a segment of wall pivoted, forming a narrow entrance. Dalmask paused there, face glistening with perspiration. The place reeked with the smell of death—and something worse.

Even the less-sensitive Briot could feel Tormahan's presence. Although the giant had disappeared, it was as if he hovered nearby, unseen. Ready to pounce and destroy them both.

"Briot—do you trust me?" The warlock was crossing the room like a man walking through water.

"Aye. I do, now."

"There are two things Webba must do to overcome Tormahan. You must convince him of them, understand?"

"Yes, Dalmask, but is not Tormahan—?"

"Listen closely: Convince Webba we have the Conqueror, but that a major spell must be worked to overcome his might. In order for this to be accomplished, Castle Skernach must be emptied at once. Webba must make certain no troops remain; his or the invaders'. Understand?"

"But why? What did we see?"

The magician placed a heavy hand on his ally's shoulder. "You saw. You saw him vanish. He will return, as he does each night. In three hours; this is why 'tis said he retires for that long. So all must be done quickly. And perhaps, if I am right, we can stay his power."

"And what if Webba—"

"He must. 'Tis a theory we must all risk. And there's something to what you said: Tormahan thrives on battle and conquest. If Webba's to defeat him *there must be no conflict.* Go—go quickly!"

The one-eyed man retreated. Suspicion struggled with awe across his face. Then his expression hardened; he had decided. He turned, raced out the door, sword in hand.

Dalmask picked up the Conqueror's weapon from the bed. He wiped it on the coverlet, his hands trembling. Then, with a thump, Briot reappeared at the doorway. Dalmask dropped the sword.

"The other task," the pikeman puffed, breathless, "What is it?"

"O mother of men!" the warlock reeled, fists raised. And with unnatural calm, added: "Yes. Have a man carry an empty receptacle—a weapons' chest will do; one of the long ones—to the tower we first climbed. It must be long enough to hold a sword; it must be heavy and have a locking device or lock. Now go."

Briot went. With a shudder, Dalmask sank to his knees.

On the floor beside him was the Lightsword, near it one of the dead men's blades. As both were relatively clean, they were exactly alike. Of course, he reflected: the Lightsword shone only when bloody, and in Tormahan's hand. The Conqueror had equipped his officers with weapons resembling his own, for his hideaway lay in anonymity. Thus, the previous escape Briot had reminded him of earlier. Dalmask knew of the invincible leader's exploits even better than the Julnans. But who might have guessed his secret?

His eyes searched the room and verified the theory. One axeman and five swordsmen. But there were six broadswords. What was it the pikeman had said? "Tormahan is nothing without his sword." Indeed.

To be entirely certain, Dalmask wrapped both similar blades in the cloak, tying them securely. He paced the cluttered, blood-spattered room, waiting for the sounds of war and confusion to die. Finally, he started downstairs.

He made his way through the donjon, clambering over wreckage and skirting corpses. Logic told him where the correct span would be and he found it. As he started across it, an arrow sliced the air in front of him.

The magician sat down abruptly with a curse. This bowman might be some hidden invader who would not surrender, or one of Webba's more suspicious troopers, for the keep was not yet wholly emptied. Guttering torches cast grotesque shadows everywhere. The wounded were still being trundled out through the alleys below. How long had it been now?

"Very well." He sighed. He had known it would not be simple.

He rose and ran. He had to hurdle the dead that blocked the span, his body bent. He stopped to lever a carcass over the parapet near the tower gate.

There was a hum, and a second arrow ripped into his right side.

Dalmask swayed, his face set. He went through the gateway. He fell at the foot of the spiral stairway, but kept his arms stiff, avoided doing further damage to himself. Sprawling there, he recited a cantrip, eyes glued to the fingers of one hand. It took over a minute, but the pain receded.

A shriek from outside interrupted his concentration. Savagely, he hoped the bowman had found death. The warlock closed his eyes. Holding the pain at bay, he broke the shaft that protruded from his rib-cage. Using the bundled swords, a nearby wall, he regained his feet.

Halfway to the top of the tower, he sank onto a step.

The Goblin Blade 161

It was useless; he could climb no more. Footsteps told him someone had heard his moan. He waited.

"What in the five hells?" It was Briot. The pikeman was dragging a narrow but heavy weapons' chest. A moustached, middle-aged man who looked elegant even in chipped and bloody armor came after him, torch in hand. It was Webba, his iron-grey mane bare.

Briot opened the chest to Dalmask's motion. As the warlock lowered his burden into it, he saw the portruding arrow-shaft and emitted another curse.

"The Lightsword?" the Count asked. At Dalmask's nod, he added: "We mustn't let *that* out of our sight. Now, about Tormahan—"

"You must take this upstairs and drop it into the cove; it must be deep there," said the warlock as the lid snapped shut. He spoke a few low words, his hands on the locking device. His face was grey when he turned to them: "Is it three hours past midnight? If it is, and *he's* not reappeared, I'm correct. Away from a climate of conflict, he is weaker. In the depths, he will be helpless."

" 'Tis not three hours yet, but never mind," Briot put in, "We must get you a physician."

"Aye," the Count agreed, "I'll stay with him, Briot. However, Dalmask, we can't drop the Lightsword into—"

"Fools, can't you hear me?" Placing his back against the curving wall, Dalmask pushed himself erect. "I asked for the castle to be emptied to weaken Tormahan's strength after the three hours, in the event—Do you think me delirious?"

"No, but I do not understand what Briot told me of Tormahan's disappearance; neither does he!" The Count reached to help him. "This sword, however—"

"Tormahan is sealed in here!" Dalmask slapped the chest. "I used a simple locking spell, aye, but anything connected to the weapon must be contained by it!

"Don't you understand? The Conqueror is not human. Just as some wizards' familiars, or the thralls of ring, temple or lamp, Tormahan *is a djinn!* Somehow, some time ago, the spell that bound him to his master's will was broken. Perhaps the error was made when he was invoked; no matter.

"Whatever the reason, Tormahan is loose all but three hours a day, during which he must be in his own plane. But he can only live and thrive 'pon Ocba *as long as the sword is in use*. Therefore, *he himself uses it!* 'Tis why he must always seek battle and strife."

"By the gods, do you know what you're saying?" Webba mused: "If you're right, when we're rid of the sword—where's the Conqueror? We'll have no hostage against an invasion! What will happen to Julna if we do this?"

"What will happen to *all of Ocba* if you do not?" Dalmask almost shouted. "Use high-ranking prisoners for hostages; claim Tormahan's death. No one seems to know his true nature amongst his horde; he could not afford that. I will die soon; I've no time or spell to bind him to our will. *Will* you bicker with me now? We speak of the fate of a world!"

Without waiting for an order from his superior, Briot hefted the chest, levered it onto his shoulder with a grunt. He started up the steps.

Dalmask smiled. He felt nothing, now. He would have fallen down the steps, but Count Webba held him up. One-handed, Webba stuck the torch in a wall-bracket, then picked up the magician bodily.

When they were at the top of the stairs, a splash reached their ears, a sound that mingled with the roar of the waves below.

" 'Tis done. That chest was heavy enough," said Briot. Behind his dark silhouette, a sea wind had scattered the stench of battle. Skernach was a faery castle under the great blue crescent of Ocba's moon.

"Some day, ere I die, I'll have someone go down and attach a line to that chest," Webba said. "When midnight comes that day, I'll melt the thing down and sink the remains in a stone sarcophagus once more."

"That would be perfect, eh Dalmask?" Briot went to crouch over the warlock's thin form.

"He cannot hear you." The Count sighed. After a pause: "He was a remarkable man, this fellow-skulker of yours."

"You have no idea, sire. You have no idea." Briot made one wordless sound after that. He looked away from Court Webba, to the silent keep beyond the parapet.

C. J. Cherryh

THE DARK KING

In the last several years, a half-dozen-or-so new fantasy writers have made their debut with impressive first novels—Tanith Lee, Richard Adams, Patricia A. McKillip, John Crowley, Sanders Anne Laubenthal—and most of them are women. To the list we must now add Miss Cherryh, whose Gate of Ivrel *at least ties this year's honors-list for best new novel. Hers is an impressive first novel, and she is a young and very attractive woman: I know these facts, because I read her book at a sitting, and met her over the Labor Day weekend in Kansas City.*

Not only is this next story a fine job, but it appears here in print for the first time. And if that isn't enough, it happens to be the first and only short story she has ever written. Some people just naturally start at the top ...

—L.C.

Death walked the marketplace of Corinth.

He paused in the bazaars, looked with pleased eyes on the teeming throngs of men, laughed gently at the antics of children. He had the shape, at the time, of a dusty man in brown rags, staff in hand. He was indeed a traveller: he had been that morning to Syria to attend a famous general; to India to visit a sage; in Egypt to attend an assassination. He had a thousand, thousand servants besides, did Death, going and coming at his orders, although they were all fragments of himself. He was, at this moment, in the marketplace; and in a hut in Germany; and in an alleyway in Rome: all himself, all seeing with his eyes, all minute reflections of his own being.

He laughed gently at a child, who looked up into his face and smiled, and the laughter faded as a mother snatched him away, shuddering as she scolded him about strangers. He turned his face from the lame young beggar at the steps, who looked at him; he gave him only a coin, and the beggar took it and gazed after him anxiously.

The palace lay ahead, up the steps. The guards there came to attention, but seeing only a poor traveller, rested their spears and let him pass: it was the custom in the land that all strangers were welcome in the palace, to sit at the end of the table and receive charity, for travellers were few and news scant.

And Death would sit at the king's table this night, drawn by that sense that led him toward his appointed tasks.

He was no stranger here. He knew his way, found familiar the gaily painted halls, that led to the king's own hall, where a wedding feast was in progress. He had visited here only a year ago, to lead away the old king. His servants had made many a call here, attending this and that; and through their eyes he was well-familiar with every corridor of this palace, as with most places across the wide face of the earth.

But the servants saw him only with dull human sight, and shrugged in disdain at his rags, and saw him to the lowest seat, hardly interrupting the gaity. There was a helping of food for him, and drink; he took them, savoring the things of earth, and listened to the minstrel's songs, pleased by such; but none spoke to him and he spoke to no one, save that he gazed up to the high table, where sat the young king.

He had not known until then,—until the king met his eyes with that pale and sighted look the dead have—what had drawn him here. Death looked again to the king's left, where the young queen sat, his bride; and around the room, where sat the courtiers, unseeing. Only when he met the king's eyes did he know that he was known, and that not wholly. The king was young: he did not have the familiarity of the old toward him.

The meal was done; the wine was brought, and the king drank first, of the king's cup, wrought in gold; and passed to the queen. Servants passed round the wine-bowls, and filled cups to the brim for the merry drinking to follow, for it was holiday.

And the king's eyes turned constantly and fearfully upon Death, whose traveller's clothes perhaps seemed less brown than black, whose face less tanned than shadowy: the dying have a sense the living do not.

"Traveller," said the king at last, in a voice strong and firm, "it is the custom that our guests be fed, and then give us their name and the news of their travels, if it be their pleasure. We do not insist, but this is the custom."

Death rose, and time stopped, and all in the hall were still: wine hung half-poured, lips in mid-word, a fly that had come in the open window stopped as a point in the air, the very fire a monument of flame.

"Lord Sisyphos, I am Death," he said softly, casting off his disguise and appearing as he is, Sleep's dark twin, a handsome and gentle god. "Come," he said. "Come."

The soul shuddered within Sisyphos' mortal body, clung fast with the tenacious strength of youth. Sisyphos looked about him at the hall, at the gold and the wealth, and he touched the hand of his beautiful young queen, who in no wise could feel his touch, nor sense anything that passed: her motion was stopped in rising, her eyes, blue as summer skies, shining open, her hair like wheat fields in August,—beautiful, beautiful Merope.

Sisyphos' hand trembled. He turned a tearful face to Death.

"She cannot see you," Death said. "Come away now."

"It is not fair," Sisyphos protested.

"You are fortunate," said Death, "to have possessed all these good things, and never to have seen them fade. Come away now, and let go."

"I love her," Sisyphos wept.

"She will come in her own time," said Death.

Sisyphos ran his hand over the lovely cheek of Merope, whose eyes did not blink, whose hair did not stir. He planted a kiss on her cheek, and looked again at Death.

"One word," he pleaded. "Lord, one word with her."

Death's heart melted, for like his brother he is a kindly god. "A moment, then," he said.

The room began to move again. The fly buzzed; the flames leapt, the hum of conversation resumed.

And Merope touched her husband's hand, and blinked, wondering, as her husband leaned close and whispered in her ear. Her summer-sky eyes widened, filled with tears; she shook her head, and he whispered more.

Death averted his face as the woman wept with her husband and a hush fell upon the gathering. But a moment more, and he lifted his staff, and the room stopped once more.

"It is time," he said.

"My lord," said the king, surrendering.

And this time the soul stepped cleanly from the body, and looked about, a little bewildered yet. Death took him by the hand, and with his staff parted that curtain that lies twixt world and world.

"Oh," said Sisyphos, shuddering at the dark.

But Death put his arm about the young king and walked with him, comforting him for a time.

And then Death withdrew to his own privacy, for he had long distracted himself, and his other eyes and hands were paralyzed, wanting their direction. He sat on his throne in the netherworld and gazed on the grey meanderings of Styx and the balefire of Phlegethon, and in the meantime his other selves were attending a shipwreck in the Mediterranean and a dying kitten in Alexandria.

He, brother of Sleep, does not sleep, and is everywhere.

But after the world had turned for the third time and Death, once more rested, was on the far shore of Styx, about to fare out toward the land of Africa (there was an old woman there who had called him) a sad ghost tugged at his sleeve. He looked down into the tearful face of Sisyphos.

"Still unhappy?" he asked the soul. "I am sorry for you, Sisyphos, but really, if you would only leave the riverside and cross over . . . there are meadows there, old friends, why, I've no doubt your parents and grandparents are longing to see you. Your wife will come in her own good time; and time passes very quickly here if you wish it to. You are still entangled with the earth; that is your misery."

"I cannot help it," wept the young king. "My wife will not set me free."

"What, not yet?" exclaimed Death, shocked and dismayed.

"No funeral rites," mourned the ghost, stretching forth a hand toward the grey, slow-moving river, where the ferryman plied his boat. "No coin, no farewell. I am still tied there, unburied, a prisoner. O lord, give me leave to go haunt the place until my wife gives me decent burial."

"That is the law," Death admitted, taking pity on

him, thinking on the woman with the summer sky in her eyes and hair like August wheat. Cruel, he thought, so cruel, for all she was so beautiful. "Go," he said, "Sisyphos, and secure your proper burial. There is the way."

He parted the curtain between worlds for him, and showed him Corinth; and straightway he sped by another path, for the African woman cried out in pain, and called his name, and he came quickly, in pity.

But the ghost of Sisyphos smiled as it walked the marketplace by night, and walked up the steps. Guards shivered as it passed, and straightened a little, and the torches in the hallway fluttered.

And there in the hall, on a bed of shields, lay his body in royal state; and near it, her golden hair unbound and her sky-blue eyes red with weeping, knelt Merope.

Laughing, he touched her shoulder, but she looked up not seeing; and with a touch on his own body, he lay down, and lifted himself up, smiling at her.

"Lord!" she cried, and he hugged her as he stood in his own body once more. Tears became wild laughter.

And servants shuddered at the pair, the clever king and his brave bride, who had made this pact while Death waited at their side, that she would not, whatever betided, bury him.

"Admit no strangers," he bade the servants then.

And he with his bride went up the stairs to the bedchamber, where blue dolphins danced on the walls, and torches burned right gaily in the night.

There was a war in China, that raged up and down the banks of the Yangtze, that burned villages and cities, elevated some lords and ruined others. Death and a thousand of his servants were busy there.

There was a plague in India, that on hot winds ran the streets of cities, killing first the beasts and then the men, that cried out in agony; and Death, whose name is heard in Hell, came quickly there, bringing his servants with him.

There was war in Germany, than ran across the forests and the river and spilled bloodily into Gaul, as year after year the fightings continued.

Death, who does not sleep, was seldom in his castle, but much about the roads of Europe and the hills of Asia, and walking here and there in the persons of his thousand, thousand servants.

But in the passing years he found himself again in the marketplace of a certain city, and the children stared at him in horror, and people drew away from him.

"How is this?" he asked, remembering another welcome he had had in Corinth, when a child had smiled at him.

"Go away," said a merchant. "The king does not favor strangers in this city."

"This is ill hospitality," said Death, offended, "and against the law of the gods."

But when they gathered stones, he went, sorrowing, from the gates, where a beggar sat, wizened and miserable. He turned his face from that one, who looked on him with longing, and gave him a coin.

And then he stepped (for the steps of Death are wide) from the gateway to the palace door, where the guards came to abrupt attention. And his aspect now was that of a king in black robes, with a golden band about his dusky brow, and fires smouldered in his eyes.

The guards shrank from him, weapons untouched, and he passed silently into the hall, angry and curious too, what the custom was in this city that barred travellers.

The torches flared in dark as he went, shadow enveloping him and flowing over the gay tiles of octopi and flying-fishes, along the walls of dancers and gardens. He heard the sounds of revelry.

A shadow fell upon the last table, that was the unused place of guests. A torch went out, and laughing men and women fell silent and turned their heads to see what passed there, seeing nothing.

Only the king rose from his place, and the wide-eyed queen beside him. He was older now, with white dusting the dark of his hair; and the first touch of frost was on the wheaten-haired queen, the pinch that kills the flush in the cheeks and makes little cracklings beside the eyes. She lifted her hand to her lips and stopped, as everything stopped, save only Sisyphos.

"Sisyphos," said Death with a frown that dimmed the frozen fires.

Sisyphos' hand touched his wife's arm, trembled there, an older hand, and his eyes filled with tears.

"You see I loved her so," said Sisyphos, "I could not leave her."

And Death, forever mateless, grieved, and his anger faded. "You gained the years you wanted, Man," he said. "Be content. Come." For he remembered the young queen that had been, and was sorry that the touch of age had come on her: mortals; he pitied them, who were prey to Age.

But the soul resisted him, strong and determined, and would not let go. "Come," he said, angered now. "Come. Forty years you have stolen. You have had the best of me. Now come."

And with a swoop that obscured the very hearthfire he came, and reached out his hand.

But quicker than the reach of Death was Sisyphos, whipping round his hands his golden belt, and moly was entwined therein, and asphodel. Death cried out at the treachery, and the spell was broken, and the queen cried out at the shadow. The fires went out, and men shrieked in terror.

They were brave men that, with the king, bore that shadow into the nether reaches of the palace, that was cut deep in the rock, deep cellars and storage places for wine and oil. And here they used iron chains, that wrung painful moans from Death, and here they left him.

Somewhere in Spain an old man called, and Death could not answer; in anguish, Death wept. In Corinth's very streets a dog lay crushed by a passing cart, and its yelping tortured the ears of passers-by, and tore at the heart of Death.

Disease and old age ran the world, afflicting thousands, who lingered, calling on Death to no avail.

Insects and beasts bred and multiplied, none dying, and were fed upon and torn and did not die, but lay moaning piteously; and plants and grasses grew up thick, not seeding, through the stones, and when they were cut, did not wither, but continued to grow, until the streets of cities began to be overgrown and beasts wandered out of the fields, confused and crowded by their own young.

Wars were without death, and the wounded kept fighting and the horridly maimed and the diseased walked the world crying out in agony, until there was no place that was free of horrors.

And Death heard all the cries and the prayers, and, helpless, wept.

The very vermin in the basements of the palace multiplied, while Death lay bound and impotent; and fed upon the grain, and devoured everything, leaving the people to starve. Famine stalked the streets, and wasted men, and Disease followed raving in his wake, laughing and tearing at men and beasts.

But Death could not stir.

And at last the gods, looking down on the chaos that was earth, bestirred themselves and began to inquire what passed, for every ill was let loose on earth, and men suffered too much to attend to sacrifices.

The wisest of them knew at once what had been withheld from the world, for wherever men called on Death, he did not come. They searched the depths of earth and sea for him, who never visited the higher realms; and made inquiry among the snake-bodied children of Night, his cousins, but none had seen him.

Then from the still, shadowed quiet of Sleep crept

The Dark King

the least of Night's children, a Dream, that wound its serpent-way to the wisest of gods and whispered, timidly, "Sisyphos."

And the gods turned their all-seeing eyes on the city of Corinth, on the man named Sisyphos, on a mourning shadow in the cellars of Corinth's palace. They frowned, and earthquake shook the ground.

And quake after quake rocked at the city, until pillars tottered, and people cowered in fear, and Sisyphos turned knowing eyes on his queen, and kissed her tearfully and took a key.

It was fearful to enter that dark place, with the quakes rumbling and shuddering at the floor, to approach that knot of shadow that huddled in the corner, wherein baleful and angry eyes watched: he had to remember that Death is a serpent-child, and it was a serpent-shape that seemed imprisoned there, earth-wise and ancient, and unlike his twin, cold.

"Give me ten years," Sisyphos tried to bargain with him, endlessly trying.

But Death said nothing, and the floor shuddered, and great cracks ran through the masonry, portending the fall of the palace. Sisyphos shivered, and thought of his queen; and then he fitted the key to the lock, and took the bonds away.

Death stood up, a swirling shadow, and cold breathed from him as Sisyphos cowered to the floor, trembling.

But it was the dark-faced, gentle king who touched him on the shoulder and whispered in his ear: "Brave Sisyphos, come along."

And Sisyphos arose, forgetting his body that lay in the crumbling cellar, and stepped with the dark king out into the marketplace, out into a wilderness that began to die wherever the shadow fell; grass, insects, all withered and went to dust, leaving only bright, young growth; a dog's wails ceased; children's voices began to be heard; and when at last they passed the gates of Corinth, Death paused by the forlorn beggar. Death took his hand gently, and the old man shivered, and smiled, and that immortal part shook free, rising up. The soul blinked, stretched, found it easy to walk with them, on feet that were not lame.

They strode down the shore to the river, where thousands of rustling ghosts were gathering, and the ferryman was hastening to his abandoned post.

It was nine full turnings later that Death gathered to him the summer-eyed queen, and three after that before her gentle ghost appeared before his throne on the far side of the river.

He smiled to see her. She smiled, a knowing and mischievous smile. She was young again. August bloomed in her hair, a glory in the dark of Hell. Far away were the meadows of asphodel, the jagged peaks that were the haunt of the children of Night. She was beginning her journey.

"Come," said Death, and took her hand, and led her with his thousand-league strides across the meadow and beyond to the dark mountains.

There was a trail, much winding, upon a mountainside; and high upon it toiled a strong young king, covered in sweat, who heaved a stone along. Vast it was, and heavy, but he was determined, and patient. He heaved it up another hand's breadth, and braced himself to catch his breath and try again.

"He can be free, you know," whispered Death in the young queen's ear, "once he sets it on yonder pinnacle."

And gently Death set her on the roadside, saw the young king turn, wonder in his eyes, the stone forgotten. It crashed rumbling down the trail, bounding and rebounding, to shatter on the floor of the Pit and send echoes reverberating the length and breadth of Hell. A moment Sisyphos stared after it in dismay; then with a laugh that outrang the echoes, opened his arms to the young queen Merope.

Death smiled, and turned away, with thousand-league strides crossing the plains of Hell until he reached his throne. And remembering duty, he extended himself again into his thousand, thousand shapes, and sighed.

Lin Carter

BLACK MOONLIGHT

I have been intimately involved with the fortunes of Thongor the Mighty throughout my entire career. He was the hero of my first book—the first one that sold, that is—and by now I feel a bit superstitious about the valiant Valkarthan. I don't want to ever stop writing about him, if only on the possibility that if I ever wrap his series up, I may stop selling fiction and have to go back selling canned beans for an ad agency again.

In recent years I have gone back before the beginning of the Lemurian books, to chronicle some of Thongor's earlier adventures before ever Jeled Malkh threw that cup of wine in his face and started him on the road to the Empire of the Sun and me on my way to a million and a half words of fiction.

Here is the latest, from the days when he was one of the pirates of Tarakus.

—L.C.

CHAPTER ONE

Uncharted Seas

The red sun sank in a sheet of flame over the dark waters of Yashengzeb Chun the Southern Sea. It blazed fiercely, igniting the western sky, and against the flame the jungle isle of Zosk loomed up: shaggy, black, mysterious.

Since noon the pirate galley *Black Hawk* had stood against the wind, lying off the wide lagoon where billows drove snowy foam against a curve of tawny beach. Now a chill wind arose with the coming of night. It rattled the fronded tree-ferns and cycads that stood like a green wall beyond the curve of wet sand; it caught and boomed the scarlet sails of the lean, rakish black galley, and the gusting breeze sent waves slapping against the sharp dragon-prow.

The guests were dank with wet and chill. On the foredeck of the galley the first mate shivered to the wind's bite, and drew his heavy boat cloak more closely about him. He was a tall, massive Zangabali with heavy, stubbled jaws and a shaven pate. Gold hoops glittered in his ears as he shivered to the keen breeze. It was late in Shamath, the first month of autumn, with a hint of winter on the wind's edge.

A dark shape loomed against the crimson sky; turning, Chelim nodded to his Captain. "No signal yet; the lad's lost," he grunted heavily.

The Captain of the *Black Hawk* said nothing. The dank wind caught and spread his black cloak, like dark wings on the wind. Beneath the cloak he was half-naked, his bronze body thewed like a young gladiator. Black and thick as a *vandar*'s mane, his unshorn hair blew from broad shoulders, framing his stern, impassive face, strong-jawed, clean-shaven, grimly expressionless. Under scowling black brows his strange gold eyes blazed with sullen, lion-like fires. Few city-bred men could meet the glare of those somber, burning eyes; fewer still could stand before him in battle. Despite the chill night-wind, his superb body was clad only in a Lemurian war-harness of belted straps, with a heavy ornate girdle about his lean hips and a scarlet cloth about his loins. He was a Barbarian from the wintry Northlands beyond the Mountains of Mommur, and to him the night was sultry.

To the pirates of Tarakus, to his fellow Captains of the Red Brotherhood, he was Khongrim of the *Black Hawk*. But his name was Thongor.

"Lost, or slain," he growled in a deep voice. "Gorm knows what beasts lair in those jungles. And there may be savages. . . . I have heard the Captains tell strange tales of such isles."

"I, too," muttered the mate, and if he shivered a little, mayhap it was the cold edge of the wind. But these were uncharted seas, and yonder isle was marked on no chart. Few ever dared sail this deep into the unknown west: the fat merchants of Thurdis or Tsargol clung to the coasts of Kovia or Ptartha, and the corsairs preyed only where there were rich cities to loot and plunder.

But Thongor of the *Black Hawk* would venture down the red throat of hell itself for such a treasure as the jungle isle of Zosk held hidden, if old, whispered legends be true. Somewhere in the dark mass of trackless jungle lay a fortune in pearls, a treasure-trove of the rare flame pearls of Cadorna, worth a kingdom's price in the thieves' bazaar at Tarakus. And the Captain of the *Black Hawk* meant to claim that treasure at sword's point, if needs be. Since noon the corsair craft had sounded the jungle isle, finding this lagoon, and sending ashore a volunteer to scout for hostile savages. Reckless young Kanthar Kan had won the toss of the dice. Hours since they should have glimpsed his signal, as arranged. What unexpected doom had befallen the gay, laughing young swordsman? They could wait on him no longer.

Thongor tossed back his mane impatiently.

"Chelim, take us in and let go the anchor. Trice up all sail. Fulvio!"

"Aye, Cap'n?" A scrawny, wizened little rogue detached himself from the wheel and snapped to alertness.

"Pick a landing party, and see them well-armed. Lower the longboat when ready. We're going in."

CHAPTER TWO

Death by Fear

A quarter-hour later the longboat was swung over the side on squealing winches. Fulvio's landing party swarmed down the lines to take places in the thwarts —a motley crew of ruffians they looked, ragtail scrapings of the gutters of half the citics of the West. There was a fat, moon-faced Kovian with cold eyes and a placid smile, and a notched cutlass in his sash; swarthy-hued, black-thatched Turanians, a villainous and foul-mouthed lot, with gaudy kerchiefs knotted about their brows and gems flashing on dirty fingers; even a few tawny-skinned, almond-eyed men of Cadorna, who cursed their mates in singsong, soft voices, fingering dagger-hilts. Some were marked with slave-brands and some bore the sign of outlawry; all were scarred with sword-cuts from many battles on land and sea. A villainous lot, but loyal to the death, and gallant fighting-men who would follow wherever Thongor led, and serve him to the last drop of red blood.

The longboat pulled away from the lean black hull of the galley and glided in on silent oars. They ran the boat up on the wet beach and sprang out, seaboots crunching in slick sand, dragging the hull further up the strand where the waves could not reach. It was nearly dark as they entered the dense wall of foliage; the moon had not yet risen, and the dying coals of sunset glimmered on their naked cutlasses and flashed in their eyes as they glanced about uneasily.

The jungle was thick and black and still. *Too* still! The jungle aisles should have rung to the roar of hunting *vandars*, the screech of river-*poa*. But all was silent as death.

Thongor sensed the wrongness in the heavy air from the first. His pirates were city-bred men, their senses dulled from the stench and clamor of the back-alleys that had spawned them. But he had the keen, sharp-honed senses of the wilderness-born—the cruel wastes of the frozen North had cradled him, and his was the hair-trigger sensitivity of the true savage. To have survived in the bitter land of his native Valkarth, he had learned to taste the breeze like a hunting cat, to listen to every whisper, to read the night like a stalking beast.

Once they had wormed through the dense wall of trees, the chill wind died. Blackness lay about them, heavy with the stench of rotting leaves, sour mud, thick with the heady perfume of jungle flowers. And there was something else on the air, as well.

There was the smell of death . . .

His strange gold eyes searching the gloom to every side, his great Valkarthan broadsword naked in his hand, Thongor took the lead, prowling through the black jungle as silent as a cat. A quarter of an hour later they found the body.

It was Fulvio who came upon it first. The scrawny, one-eyed little rogue almost stumbled across it in the impenetrable gloom. His squawk of alarm brought Thongor shouldering through the heavy bushes. The body lay sprawled half under a towering *jannibar* tree. They dragged it into the open and the bosun, a grizzled old Thurdan named Thad Novis, unhooded the lantern he carried, lighting the man's face with the dim beam of candle-flame.

It was Kanthar Kan!

"Gods, Cap'n, I nigh stepped on him in the dark, and me blind as a *xuth!*" Fulvio whined, shivering. The other men crowded around, muttering. One stifled a cry of surprise as the lantern lit the face of the young swordsman.

Thongor said nothing, but his jaws set grimly. There was no mark on the swordsman's body, no cut or wound to be found. But he was stone-dead; and the expression stamped on his face was horrible to view— hideous beyond thought.

His eyes started half out of his skull, frozen in a goggle-eyed stare of incredulous horror. His lips were peeled back from his teeth in a ghastly grin. His features were distorted in a grimace of utter horror that sent a chill up the spine to look upon.

Thad Novis ran his hands gently over the cooling corpse, finding nothing. He raised grim eyes to the questioning gaze of his Captain.

" 'Tis devilish weird," he said in a low voice. "Like the lad died of sheer fright. Not a mark on him, anywhere."

The men muttered at that, casting uneasy glances at the black jungle that crowded silently to every side. Some fingered protective amulets or small images of carved stone that dangled about their necks on chains or leathern thongs.

Thongor took up the lantern and went to search the ground where Kanthar Kan was found. The lantern-beam disclosed something even more mysterious than a man who died from fear alone. Kanthar Kan had drawn three words in the bare earth with his fingers before death had claimed him—and they had another mystery to solve.

"*Beware . . . Black Moonlight,*" he read in a grim voice.

"Cap'n, let's go back to the ship an' wait for day,"

Fulvio whined. "Gods know what that means, but I don't like the sound of it!"

"Nor I," admitted Thongor. "But we go forward, nonetheless."

They shouldered further into the black jungle, leaving the corpse behind. There would be time enough later to lay their dead comrade to rest, if they lived. Gallant, gay young Kanthar Kan would laugh no more: and the mysterious doom that had struck him down in the black jungles of the isle of Zosk lay somewhere ahead of them, brooding in the silence of the night.

CHAPTER THREE

The Warning on the Monolith

The moon had risen over the edge of the world, the great golden Moon of old Lemuria, flooding the jungle with its silken light. It was easier, now, cutting through the dense foliage with cutlass and scimitar and blunt-tipped Chushan *kunwars*. But they were growing weary by this time, tired of the fetid reek of rotting vegetation, the bite of insects. Tangled vines caught their feet, tripping them; they slipped in slick mud, cursing, grumbling at thorn-edged leaves that raked bare arms and drew blood.

By moonrise they had come as far as they could go. Here the jungle fell away in a stinking marsh of black mud and rotting stumps; snakes thick as a man's thigh slithered fluidly over fallen tree trunks, and the track of monstrous *poa* were visible on the mud-banks.

Thongor gave the signal for a rest-halt. The men sprawled wearily about, wiping sweaty brows with dirty rags, gulping lukewarm wine from skin bottles, glad of a chance to rest aching legs. But the Valkarthan needed no respite: his iron thews seemed invulnerable to fatigue and he could go forward far more swiftly alone. Leaving scrawny little Fulvio in charge, he moved out to the east, skirting the swamp, searching the thick brush with every sense at the alert.

He found the thing by moonlight. A great shaft of grey, lichen-covered stone, thrusting out of the wet earth at a steep angle. The roots of a giant *lotifer* tree had netted the stone pillar, tilting it awry. The clear gold moonlight lit the mold-encrusted monolith sharply.

Thongor paused. Then men *did* inhabit this strange isle of death and nameless, shadowy horror—or had once dwelt here; for the inscription on the stone was in an antique mode of glyphic writing. With the blade of his dagger, he scraped away the crust of lichens, laying bare the deep-craven hieroglyphs. The language of the inscription was known to him from his travels, for once, years before, in a ruined, deserted city in the desert country of the north, he had seen such glyphs. The young Valkarthan was unschooled, but his adventurous career had carried him into strange corners of the Lemurian continent, and he had acquired shards of odd and curious knowledge along the way.

The inscription sent a chill up his spine as he read it by moonlight.

The stone god walks when the Black Moon shines.

His hackles stirred; a tingle of preternatural uneasiness prickled at the nape of his neck, as if he sensed the touch of unseen eyes on his back. He half turned, the steel blade of his great sword, Sarkozan, flashing in his hand; then, with a wry grin twisting his lips, he restrained himself. No puling boy, he, to start and pale at a few words cut on a stone pillar! It took more than an ancient warning to strike fear into the heart of Thongor of the *Black Hawk*—Khongrim of the Red Brotherhood, the terror of the Southern Sea!

He went forward again, but this time with greater care than before, and keeping well to the shadows. Some hand long ages dead had cut that warning of the Black Moon on the mould-crusted monolith; but something very alive had struck down gay, reckless Kanthar Kan to death. And he, too, had warned of the mysterious peril with his last strength, digging numb fingers in the wet earth to warn his shipmates when they came on his track ...

Thongor glided through the underbrush like a stalking *vandar*.

What was the curse that haunted this weird isle of treasure and nameless terror?

He would learn the answer sooner than even he could dream!

CHAPTER FOUR

The City of Death

The cold wastes of the Northlands had spawned him, but since he had come down across the Mountains of Mommur five years before, the jungle-girt cities of Kovia and Chush and Ptartha had been his home. So the Valkarthan was no stranger to the tropic wilderness wherethrough he moved silently and swiftly, yet with great care. A mere youth, he had joined a pack of bandits in wild Chush, rising to chieftain the band ere long. He and his legion of cut-throats had been the bane of the fat-bellied merchants of Shembis, whose jungle caravans they had raided time and gain, until the vengeful prince of that city, Arzang Pome, had hunted them down.

Then he and the survivors of his band had been sold on the block like animals. Arzang Pome had chained the Valkarthan and his bandits to the oars of the slave-galleys of Shembis, and long did they toil under the singing whips in the blazing sun while the hated Dolphin banner floated lazily overhead and the perfumed merchant-captain who was their master sipped cold wine and fondled his wench under striped awnings while they broke their backs at the oars. Then one hot night they rose with naked hands and broken oars to slay and slay in red, roaring rage—stealing the very galley on which they had slaved—and off to the high seas, to join the fierce corsairs of Tarakus the Pirate City, and to learn a new trade. But piracy was close akin to banditry, and thus Thongor and his comrades had risen in the past two years to a high rank amid the corsair fleet. It was the dying whisper of an old veteran sailor they had rescued from execution in Cadorna had put them on the track of the fabulous treasure of the isle of Zosk, deep in the uncharted wastes of the sea. Somewhere in those black jungles a fortune in flame pearls lay hid—"in the place of the great stones," the old sailor had said.

And then he came upon it, stark and cold and dead in the flood of the golden Moon.

The young Barbarian came to a sudden halt there at the edge of the jungle. He stared ahead, his blood racing with the thrill of discovery. Was *this* the 'place of the great stones' whereof the dying sailor had spoken?

A few yards from where he crouched in the thick brush, the jungle dwindled away to a rocky plain. The ground fell away beyond, in an immense, circular valley like a vast bowl cut in the rock. Tumbled stone slabs lay about; broken spires of rock loomed and tilted, for all the world like the shattered pillars of some dead, ruined city of time's dawn. Here and there, tremendous blocks of stone lay tumbled, as if scattered about by the careless hands of playful giants.

Thongor searched the wilderness of broken, scattered stone with thoughtful eyes. Surely, this must be the place the old sailor had whispered of. But was it a thing of nature, or the work of men? The monolith he had come upon in the jungle had been cut and set by human hands . . . and the regularity of these stones were haunted by an uncanny suggestion of human purpose and worksmanship.

He went down into the valley and prowled the silent avenues of somber desolation. No sign of life alerted his keen senses. If men had ever dwelt here, they were long vanished. No smoke of cooking fires ascended the moonlit sky, no footstep echoed down the empty avenues of tumbled stone, no human rubbish caught his searching gaze, not a shard of broken pottery, a discarded rag, or the ashes of a dead fire. It was like a city of death, this waste of broken rock: like the gaunt bones of a dead metropolis, eerie and silent and empty in the wash of moonlight, and if aught wandered here it was ghosts of the long-dead past.

Amidst the trackless ruin, he came upon the pool whereof the old sailor had spoken. A motionless disc of dark waters, impenetrable to the eye, ringed about with a lip of stone. This surely was the work of men, for the pool formed a perfect circle and the stone marge was cut and dressed and smoothed by skill and not by nature.

Amidst the pool, a stone pillar rose against a tropic sky filled with blazing stars. It was like the monolith he had found in the jungle, and yet different, too. For thirty feet the stone pillar loomed up in the moonlight, tall and straight as an obelisk, but rough-hewn and jagged, and it bore no glyphs that he could see. All about the motionless pool stretched a plaza of tumbled, uneven stone slabs. Thongor crossed the plaza with silent tread and knelt by the edge of the pool, dipping one hand within.

The water was cold and foul, bescummed and stagnant, but his hand came up filled with dripping pearls. Slick and moony were they, with a sullen glow of fire in their sheen and rondure. Flame pearls of Cadorna— he knew them at a glance—of superb and perfect water and extraordinary size!

He held a satrap's ransom in his hand. And the wealth of a dozen emperors slept still beneath the dark waters. A smile lit his somber features. The buccaneer scooped up handful after handful of flame pearls from the black pool, admiring their glistening fire in the cold moonlight. Entranced, he stared down at the wet pearls in his hand. They glowed like little moons.

Then a deep-chested snarl reached his ear—the scrape of calloused bare feet on dry stone. He sprang to his feet, thrusting the dripping handful of pearls in the top of his swash seaboots, and turned.

And then the savages were upon him, a herd of snarling naked beast-men, broken tusks bared and bloodlust burning in their slitted eyes. The very earth spewed them up: from dark lairs under the tilted slabs of the plaza they came. Troglodytes—cave-dwellers! He knew then why he had found no token of human habitation in all these acres of immemorial desolation.

And they were upon him, heavy bodies hurled at his back, hard paws clutching his arms, fangs snapping at his very throat.

CHAPTER FIVE

Red Steel!

The young buccaneer shook the hairy-pelted savages from him as the kingly *vandar* of the jungle shakes off a pack of dogs. He drove his booted heel deep in the belly of one snarling foe: the beast-thing grunted, folded, and fell.

Then the great broadsword, Sarkozan, was free of its scabbard and singing its cold and eerie song of death as it cut the wind. There were old runes acid-etched down the length of the long, deep blade, and the great gem set in the pommel blazed like an angry eye. The broadsword flashed, a brilliant steel mirror in the Moon, as Thongor whipped it high over his head and brought it whistling down to bite through brain and bone and meat. The clean steel glittered once and when he drew it back it was washed with red.

For a time he held them, sweeping the great sword

in a tireless arc. They feared the cold flash of the edged steel as a witch fears silver. He held them at bay, but they came at him in twos and threes, bounding like jackals, fangs snapping hungrily for his flesh. The Valkarthan at first thought them savages, then beasts, finally men. They went naked like brutes, but walked upright like men. They had hulking, anthropoid bodies, sloping ape-like shoulders, and long arms, knotted with bulging sinews, that hung dangling to their knees. Their heads were bullet-like, sunken deep in massive shoulders, hidden in a tangle of filthy, matted hair through which slitted eyes gleamed redly with mad fires.

But their thick torsos and bowed legs bore but a sparse pelt. The hide that showed bare between patches of stringy fur was the hue of dirty amber and their blazing eyes were aslant, as far as he could judge. The young buccaneer knew but one nation in all Lemuria with tawny amber skin and slanted eyes,—the men of ancient Cadorna, westernmost of all the cities of Lemuria. Could these snarling, shambling, loping beast-things be the degenerate remnants of a lost Cadornyana colony, forgotten for ages?

Perhaps. But he had no time to puzzle it out now. He was too busy merely staying alive. They came at him like mad dogs and he cut them down with singing red steel till they heaped the stone margin of the pool with their gore-splashed bodies. Eight, ten, a dozen he slaughtered, but it was only a matter of time until they swarmed over him, battered him down, dragged him to earth under the sheer weight of their numbers.

Now he wished he had not come down alone into the great bowl-like valley, but had gone back to camp as he should have done. O, to have a stout dozen of his brawling buccaneers at his back, with dirk and cutlass and scimitar! But it was too late for recriminations now. He fought on, but now even his iron thews ached with weariness and the breath rasped in his dry throat. He blinked against the red mist that thickened before his gaze.

Then one of the loping beast-things, perhaps less sunk in the red murk of savagery than its fellows, closer to the light of reason and manhood, saw in its cunning that it could not reach the hated man-thing through that wall of red and singing steel. So it squatted on the broken pave, plucked up a heavy shard of rock in one hairy paw, and flung it at Thongor with all the coiled strength of that ape-like arm.

It caught the Valkarthan on the brow—a stunning blow. He lurched, staggered, fighting for consciousness, and the red sword sagged in suddenly nerveless fingers and fell, ringing against the stone pavement of the plaza like a stricken gong.

Then they had him at last. A thick-set body slammed into him, chest and belly, and drove him from his feet. In a flash the burly beast-thing was worrying at his throat. Thongor jammed one forearm under the creature's jaw and held the snapping fang away from his jugular. Fetid, stinking hot breath blew in his face. The naked, furry body was rank in his nostrils. Thick-fingered paws closed about his throat, throttling him. He grunted as another heavy body slammed on top of him, and another, until he was buried under a pack of snarling, clawing beast-things.

His mind dimmed as he fought for breath. A haze thickened before his eyes; his lungs were afire; his heart labored within his breast. He fought for air and fought with ebbing strength to hold those snapping tusks away from his throat.

Then a sharp, imperious voice called out from somewhere beyond the heap of beast-things. Thongor could not make out the words, for they were in a tongue unknown to him. But the crushing weight that pressed him against the broken stone slabs lessened and the iron grip loosened from about his neck. He gulped air into starved lungs as strong hands dragged him to his feet and bound his wrists behind his back with tight leathern thongs that bit into numb flesh. Many men would have despaired then, taken captive by the shambling horde that infested the ancient ruins.

It was not the way of Thongor to despair, but he stared into a grim future, knowing that his life could now be counted in hours; perhaps, in minutes.

CHAPTER SIX

Night Fears

It was the grizzled old Thurdan warrior, Thad Novis, who was the first to become uneasy over Thongor's prolonged absence. The old warrior had been a stalwart of Jorn's Raiders when the boy Thongor had first joined the pack of bandits he would later chieftain. From the first, the older warrior had felt a paternal stirring in his breast as he saw the grim courage and iron strength and utter fearlessness the Barbarian boy displayed. Thad Novis had followed his young leader from banditry into slavery, and from thence to a life of lawlessness and adventure on the high seas. His dogged loyalty had never wavered; now he prowled the perimeter of the camp, baffled and obscurely worried, peering into the moon-washed jungle with searching eyes.

At length he sought out scrawny little Fulvio, who sprawled lazily against a log, nursing a fat wine-skin.

"Hell's blood, man, what ails you?" Fulvio whined. "The chief can take care o' himself better nor any of us. Wait here, said he, and wait here we does. He'll come back, in his good time. Sit—rest—take some wine!"

The older man shook his head determinedly.

" 'Tis not like the lad to be gone so long," he growled. "He meant to scout a path around this swamp, not explore the stinking isle himself. Somewhat has taken him, I know . . . mayhap the same Thing that took poor Kanthar Kan . . ."

The words hung there in the air. Fulvio licked thin lips with a pointed tongue, and shivered as to a sudden gust of cold. Deep in his heart, the wizened little one-eyed rogue knew the stolid, loyal Thurdan spoke the truth. But the whining little Fulvio was reluctant to stir from this place of safety to plunge into the unknown and silent depths of the waiting jungle.

Fear and loyalty wrestled within Fulvio's scrawny breast. Self-love and the greed for gold were the only passions the little gutter-rat had ever known. But he, too, worshipped Thongor and went in awe of the mighty Barbarian. Thongor was what he could perhaps have been, had he been nourished in the wintry wild among strong stalwart men and noble-hearted courageous women; but Fate had given him a sniveling beggar for a father and a sluttish shrew for a mother, and the stinking back-alleys of the slums of Pelorm for his home.

Fulvio was cowardly at heart, and vicious as only the cowardly can be. But in his heart, where fear wrestled with loyalty, he idolized the strong young buccaneer Captain. And, for once, loyalty won out against a lifetime of twisted selfishness.

Spitting vile curses, little Fulvio scrambled to his feet and snarled at the sprawled men of the landing-party.

"On your feet, you yellow-gutted whelps! We be movin' out, Gods help us. The Cap'n should of been back by now; somewhat may have happened to 'im." He fixed the stolid old Thurdan with a venomous eye. "Gorm help ye, grizzled old dog, if the Cap'n be not in need of us!"

Thad Novis said nothing. Incapable of feeling the cold sick gnaw of fear himself, he never knew what spark of true heroism he had stirred to fire in Fulvio's breast.

They fanned out when they hit the jungle, keeping well in earshot of each other. Blackness closed about little Fulvio like a clammy hand. Sweating and cursing foully under his breath, the little rogue limped along, lashing out at tangling vines and thorny branches with his cutlass as he went. It was one thing to follow such a man as Thongor into the black yawning maw of unknown peril; it was quite another thing to do it on your own volition.

The jungle thickened about them, entangled boughs shutting out the rich floods of moonlight. Clumping along through wet darkness, Fulvio thought of the slithering, befanged things that mayhap lurked all about him in the night. He envisioned the landslide-rush of the *deodath,* the dreaded dragon-cat of the jungle countries. Cold dew dripped down his scrawny neck—or was it the numbing kiss of the *fathla,* the ghastly blood-sucking tree-leeches of Chush and Kovia? A heavy vine swung overhead—or was it the horrible, man-crushing coils of the *oph,* the horned serpent of the tropic depths?

Night-fears preyed upon him, nibbling away at the edges of his courage, sapping his resolution. But the little one-eyed rogue limped forward without pause, cursing himself for a foolhardy, reckless madman every long step of the way.

They came to the stony monolith Thongor had discovered earlier, and paused, eyeing its enigmatic glyphs with shuddering apprehension. Dread shapes of night and terror were known to haunt old ruined cities—ghouls and *morgulacs,* as Lemurian legend named vampires, and prowling ghosts of the dead that could not rest.

Thad Novis hefted his heavy scimitar restlessly.

"Which way?" he asked.

Fulvio gnawed his under-lip, glancing dubiously about. Here the jungle aisle parted, one lane wandering deep into the jungle's black heart, the other striking away due east. In was in that direction Thongor had headed an hour before, but Fulvio could not know that.

"Which way, Fulvio?" puffed a fat, moon-faced Kovian named Qualb. The other crowded near.

Fulvio said nothing, chewing his lip in a torment of indecision. Which way? One path led to Thongor, who might even now be face to face with death; the other route led far from his peril, and if they followed it they would become lost in the black jungles of Zosk. *Which way?*

CHAPTER SEVEN

The Black Moon

The beast-men staked Thongor out to die. They drove four pegs into the earth between the riven slabs of the plaza and bound his wrists and ankles to them with tough thongs. Spread-eagled, his sinews stretched to the limit of endurance, even the Valkarthan's steely strength could not free him of his bonds.

Jaws set grimly, Thongor waited for death.

The leader of the horde of shambling degenerates paid his captive no attention. With the rapt, blind gaze of a fanatic or a madman he stared without blinking up into the cold fire of the golden Moon. He was unlike the loping horde of grunting savages he ruled: tall, slim, gaunt to the point of emaciation, his lean frame wrapped in tattered, filthy rags of what had once been the gorgeous ceremonial robes of an ancient priest.

He stood atop a block of stone, staring beyond the black pool and the rough-hewn pylon of rock to the soaring Moon. His hair was a tangle of matted witch locks as it fell about the starved skull of his face. His eyes burned through the tangle like sick green fires. He was priest-king of the hulking, naked brutes, the last of a time-forgotten line. But he was only slightly more *man* than they. Beneath the gorgeous, filthy tatters his gaunt body was naked and unwashed. His feet were bare and black with filth. His grime-crusted hands, gaunt like terrible claws, clutched a rod of sleek black *nebium,* atop which a smoky crystal pulsed like a dying coal.

Thongor had seen black rods like his before, and he knew them for Rods of Power. He also knew the black, unholy sorcery men wrought with such relics of ancient wisdom, and his lips pressed together until they paled.

With Thongor securely bound, the shambling beast-men withdrew grunting, squatting in a semi-circle behind the priest and the sacrifice. And the ceremony began ...

Scattered rags of cloud fled before the Moon, scattering its light in wandering shafts of cold fire that flickered eerily here and there over this weird scene of stony desolation. The wizard began talking to the half-hid Moon in guttural, clotted sounds that hardly sounded like human speech. The blood ran cold in Thongor's veins as he heard the strange, coughing sounds. He knew *that* tongue from of old; it was the Chaos Litany. The Dragon Kings of age-lost and legend-drowned Hyperborea had learned it from the black gods of madness who ruled beyond the stars. Human lips were never meant to frame such sounds, and to hear them spoken by a man was blasphemy against humankind.

The alien speech droned on, and suddenly a thrill of superstitious awe ran through Thongor. For the shifting, flickering rays were changing hue. He stared up, scalp prickling with chill premonition. *And the Moon turned to blood*.

Shafts of weird crimson light wandered about the scene of primal desolation. It was uncanny—horrible! The Moon glared down at him like the red, burning eye of some maddened god.

Behind him somewhere, the beast-things groaned

and whimpered, grovelling before this awesome display of supernatural power. On the stone block, the wizard stood like a stone carven image, rapt in unholy ecstacy, as the abominable litant spewed from his writhing lips.

Then Thongor sensed a tension in the air. Nature seemed to hold its breath, awaiting some dark miracle of evil. An aura of force tingled along the nerves of the young buccaneer.

And the sky, which had been velvet-black, flushed with cold, dead white radiance!

As the heavens reversed their coloration, the very stars did so as well. Now, through weirdly-colored ragged clouds the stars burned like black diamonds. The scene was such a mingling of incredible terror and wonder, that it wrung a cry from Thongor's grim lips. *"Gorm!"* he groaned, calling upon the god of his savage homeland. And it was as much a prayer as a curse.

And then the Moon turned black, and even the gods could not help him now ...

CHAPTER EIGHT

It Walks By Moonlight

From a disc of evil crimson, the Moon's brilliant fires curdled, darkened, became utter blackness like a pool of ink. Weird, weird, to watch a Black Moon blaze in a sky of dead white flame! In his wildest nightmares, the Barbarian had never dreamed of a spectacle so awesome and unreal.

But the ultimate abomination was yet to come.

For still a ragged drift of torn and tattered cloudlets hung before the orb of ebon fire, scattering its rays. The shafts of dark light floated here and there about the plaza, blackening the crumbled stones which else lay bathed in the strange, sourceless luminescence of the glowing sky.

Now, shaft after shaft of black moonlight flashed across that massive pillar of dark, jagged stone that loomed from amidst the pool. And as the uncanny negation of light blackened the rugged monolith, it began to—*change!*

It softened, slid and clotted like hot candlewax; it was as if the kiss of the black rays awoke the dormant spirit within the stone pillar, which struggled to regain its lost shape. As Thongor watched in unbelieving amazement, the stone flowed like wax, melting and reshaping itself in the dark radiance. The pillar cleft at the base; two shards split from its flanks; a rough sphere melted into being at its crest. The new shape the monolith assumed under the weird influence of the moon-rays bore a loathsome yet haunting familiarity. It was like a botched, obscene caricature of Man—a hideous, twisted, distorted semblance—but a semblance, nonetheless!

The melting stone solidified now. Like a grotesque idol hewn by a glibbering madman, the stone thing stood amidst the dark pool. And lived!

And—*walked!*

One stone limb thrust forward, lurching. At the knee—or where the knee would have been, had the stone thing possessed one—rough stone rubbed against stone with an indescribably horrible *grating* sound. Then, jerkily, the other leg thrust forth dripping from the dark pool. The misshapen paw that was the thing's foot or hoof crunched on the stone pave, which squealed under its many tons of ponderous weight.

Behind the spread-eagled buccaneer, the beast-men moaned and babbled in an ecstacy of fear and gloating anticipation. And globules of cold sweat burst forth on Thongor's brow: he knew now the death decreed for him. *He was to be trampled to red slime beneath the stone paws of the walking god!*

But it was not the way of Thongor to lie supinely,

Black Moonlight

waiting for death. Savage rage surged up within him, crushing out his cold fear. Black fury boiled in his veins. His brows contorted in a spasm of berserk, fighting wrath. Suddenly he split the air with a bellow of inarticulate anger. The roar of a cornered *vandar* burst from his snarling lips. And down his widestretched arms great thews swelled in a vain attempt to wrench his arms free. Mighty bands of solid muscle stood forth in knife-edge relief on his magnificent chest. His face blackened with effort as he threw every ounce of iron strength his splendid physique possessed into one colossal surge of power—

And failed!

Though he tore his wrists raw, the leathern thongs held and the deep-driven stakes did not budge. Again and again he threw the coiled strength of back and arm and shoulder in a terrific effort to burst his bonds. His deep-chested roar of challenge made the night hideous: booming echoes bounced from rock to rock. But naught sufficed to free him from this death-trap. And step by ponderous, shuffling step the weirdly-animated stone thing advanced upon him. Its blind, ghastly caricature of a face stared stonily down at him now from what seemed a tremendous height. Another instant—another slow, dragging scrape of stone against stone, and it would be upon him.

Then—somewhere behind him, beyond the edges of his vision—*riot!*

The beast-men exploded into squeals of pain. The ring of blades—the patter of many running feet. A spear went whizzing over his prostrate form to clatter off the pitted breast of the now-immobile stone thing. Slowly, hideously, the blind featureless face of jagged rock twisted to as if to stare beyond Thongor to the source of the inexplicable interruption. Due to a trick of light and shade, the mask of stone bore a momentarily quizzical expression.

Then, from behind Thongor, a hand grabbed at

his arm and a steel dagger-blade flashed downward toward his flesh!

CHAPTER NINE

Night of Hell

The flashing blade slashed through the thongs that bound his wrist. The leather snapped and his arm was free. He looked up, relief flooding his features, to see the plump, anxious face of the moon-faced Kovian, Qualb, as he bent puffing to cut free Thongor's other arm.

"Damn your hide," Thongor growled, "I thought you lazy dogs would never come!"

"Bless me, Cap'n, an' we might not yet be here, lost in this cursed maze of tumbled stone, had it not been for you a-yellin' like to wake the dead!" Qualb wheezed, chuckling, as he slashed the thongs that bound his feet. "Once ol' Thad Novis heard that bellowing, he knew 'twas you, and we came straight!"

Thongor staggered to his feet, grunting at the pain of circulation gnawing at his numb flesh. His hands were black and swollen, almost useless, like blunt paws. But the heavy seaboots had protected his legs from the worse punishment, and he could stand.

He turned, taking in the situation with one swift, all-encompassing glance. His stout band of rogues were cutting the shambling savages to ribbons. In another few moments, the beast-herd would break and flee for their subterranean burrows—

A screech of fury!

The gaunt wizard, his uncanny trance broken, stood atop the great rock, glaring down at them with mad eyes of scarlet wrath. One starved, skeletal arm brandished aloft the Rod of Power. From writhing lips burst forth again that hellish litany of black ensorcellment.

And the stone thing moved again!

Slabs squeaked under its shifting weight as it lurched forward, heavy clubbed arms raised threateningly. And directly in its path, Thongor's gallant little band of buccaneers stood holding off the horde of grunting savages. A few more sliding steps and the walking idol would be among them! Feet like boulders would crush and slay, trampling the men down as a man might snuff out the lives of crawling insects under his heel!

There was no time to shout the warning—no time even to think! Thongor was triggered into a rush of instant action by some instinctive thing quicker and simpler than thought itself—the killing fury of a maddened beast. A growl of challenge burst from his lips, which writhed back from his white teeth in a fighting grin. And he exploded into action—

One fantastic, superhuman bound carried him to the crest of the towering rock whereon the warlock stood, arms lifted in imprecation. Thongor was upon the crazed witch-man before anyone even saw it. His hands were still numb and useless, but they were calloused and hard and heavy. With the back of one he clubbed the warlock across the mouth and knocked him to his knees, spitting broken teeth and dribbling blood. With the other numb paw Thongor ripped the crystal-tipped wand from his hand—then kicked him full in the face, hurling him backwards off the rock to thud sprawling and astounded on the pavement below.

Directly in the path of the stone monster!

Dribbling blood and the foam of maniacal rage, the warlock staggered to his feet, eyes burning like hell-moons through tangled locks. Then his fury ebbed—his swarthy features paled milky-white—his eyes goggled in unbelieving horror—*for his own god was about to trample him down underfoot!*

Thongor whirled, poised, and flung the *nebium*

wand like a javelin! Straight and true it hurtled against the pitted breast of the walking thing it had roused to a hideous travesty of life. The flashing crystal struck the stone breast first—and exploded in a dazzle of diamond dust.

And the Black Moon died. . . .

Swift as waking from a dream, the haunting spell of evil magic faded from the night.

The uncanny, incandescent heavens dimmed—darkened!

The evil Moon glowed red—then bright, pure gold again. No more did black stars blaze in an enchanted sky: now the familiar stars of old twinkled down from dark and friendly heavens once again.

There came a creak of stone rasping against stone. The lurching, dragging thing froze into immobility as the evil spell which had for a time flogged it to a ghastly semblance of life perished with the splintering of the crystal. And the stone god became . . . only a thing of stone.

But when the spell that had animated it was broken, it had been off-balance, lurching forward to trample Thongor's embattled pirates. Now, like an avalanche, it came crashing down to smash asunder against the pave. The thunder of tons of stone against stone was deafening. But even above the clangor of the fallen image, as it shattered into a thousand crumbling bits against the floor of the pavement, one sharp, agonizing screech of unbelieving horror pierced the thunder-clap of noise.

It was the gaunt warlock. The wizard-priest of the troglodytes had been directly in the path of his toppling god. Tons of falling rock buried him from sight and his last cry was cut short.

Then the beast-men broke and fled, shambling whimpering for their holes, while Thongor's weary pirates rested panting on their encrimsoned swords and watched them go. Their spirit was broken; but then few men can endure to stand and watch the death of their god. And they were not quite men.

In the ringing silence, Thongor sagged, relaxing, and began to rub feeling back into his hurting hands. He was grey with rock-dust from brow to heel, and devilishly thirsty, but he was alive and whole.

And this night of hell was over!

CHAPTER TEN

High Seas

Dawn burst flaming up over the edges of the world and drove away the shadows of the night.

With dawn came a quick, freshening breeze that caught and boomed in the scarlet sails of the lean black galley. Taut rigging thrummed like a great harp in the rising wind. The deck swayed and the prow rose sharply.

Wrapped in a warm cloak, Thongor leaned against the rail, pouring cold red wine down his gullet. When he came up for air, bald, glum-faced Chelim was at his side.

"The burial-party be all aboard now," the Zangabali grunted heavily. "Kanthar Kan sleeps with his fathers now—or drinks the morning cup in the Hall of Heroes, if the priests tell it true."

"Aye," Thongor nodded. "And is that why you've such a long face? He died like a man, writing a warning to his shipmates with his last dregs of strength. There's naught to mourn in a brave man's death. Pray Gorm we all meet our end so gallantly!"

The first mate rubbed bestubbled cheeks, his expression sour.

" 'Tis not that, Cap'n—but this cursed voyage, come to naught! All this way, and lose a good man, and for what? No treasure . . . only black jungles, stinking savages, and sorcery to boot. Mayhap we'll greet a fat merchantman on our way home to Tarakus and lighten his cargo a mite, but I cannot help but wish it had been..."

His words trailed off. His eyes widened and a look of blank stupefaction passed over his face, giving him a singularly ludicrous expression. For without a word, face solemn, Thongor had bent and dug one hand deep in his high sea-boots, and brought up a handful of glistening ruddy pearls. And another. And another!

"The brutes surprised me at the pool, just as I was admiring their pretty pearls," the young buccaneer explained. "I just had time to stuff a few handsful in my boots—devilish uncomfortable, things to walk about on, pearls are. But there should be enough pretties here to warm the heart of the coldest trader in the thieves' bazaar back in Tarakus ... and enough to split among the crew so that any that want can retire to a life of ease, after this voyage."

The look of astonishment passed from Chelim's face and was replaced by a wondering, beaming grin.

"Hoy, Fulvio, lads, come here!" he boomed. "See what the Cap'n fetched back from that cursed city ... lad," he said frankly, "my heart goes out to you: with a pack of howling savages just leapin' on your back, you take time enough to shove a prince's ransom down your boots before turning to fight for your life. Now *that's* what I call thinking like a born pirate!"

Dog-tired from the night's perils and exertions, the crew ambled over to the rail to find out why their Captain and first mate were whooping with laughter in so odd a manner. Needless to say, once the cause of the hilarity was made clear to them, their hearts lifted at one glimpse of the fabulous flame pearls of Cadorna.

A pirate, like a man who follows any other trade, likes to turn a tidy profit from a day's toil. And not long thereafter, as the lordly Sun ascended the clear blue sky, the pirate galley *Black Hawk* drew up her dripping anchor, turned about into the wind, and pointed her dragon prow to the high seas, and sailed away to a host of new adventures . . .

But that's *another* story.

Gary Myers

THE SNOUT IN THE ALCOVE

I don't want to hear anybody griping about my printing too many of Gary Myers' stories; keep your opinions to yourself. It is as impossible for me to reject anything from his pen as it is for me to walk past a fifty dollar bill in the street without picking it up or to say, "no, thanks," when somebody offers to buy me a martini.

Quasi-Lovecraftian, semi-Dunsanian, deliciously Myersian, I find his yarns completely irresistible. So you may expect to find stories such as this next (which appears here in print for the first time) in just about anything I edit.

So shut up about me printing Gary Myers. Or go edit your own anthology; see if I care.

—L.C.

I awoke from an evil dream into a strange alcove. A pointed arch was curtained with a tapestry. A lamp like the full moon depended from above. So dim was the lamp, and so gloomy the tapestry, that the rays of the one could light but feebly the design of the other.

Thinking to find in this design some clue to my whereabouts in space and time, I was turning out my pockets in a vain quest of matches, when the curtains suddenly parted to admit a snout—a snout palely luminous and cloudily transparent—a snout in the shape of a long grey cone tapering to a clump of wriggling pinkish tentacles.

I threw myself down on my face.

Pulled to my feet by many pairs of reassuringly human hands, I found myself in a circle of seven old men in long white robes and beards, who menaced me with ankh-headed wooden staves and harangued me in a language I did not know. They took me behind the curtains into a circular room lit entirely by braziers in which irons were heating. Some of the things I saw in this room I recognized as many of the more standard appliances of human torture: There was a bed of knives of such glittering sharpness as it pained the eye to look upon. But most were too queerly proportioned to be meant for the discomfort of any human being.

When I saw that we were approaching one of the latter, I knew that these old men could be none other than the venerable priests of the Elder Ones, and that this dungeon could exist only in the dreamlands that surround our world. And therefore I made the Elder Sign, which is the mighty shibboleth of these dreamlands, where by the ability to make it are men distinguishable from daemons.

Then the priests of the Elder Ones begged my pardon for not having known me at once; but when you found a man in the curtained alcove where you looked to find a daemon, what were you to think? And they deduced from my outlandish clothing that I had but lately arrived from the waking world.

So I told them of my eleven previous visits to the dreamlands—but not of my vow that the eleventh should be the last, because of a much-whispered prophecy whose truth I could no longer doubt. For this prophecy was, that presently the benign Elder Ones would be deposed by infinity's Other Gods, who would drag the world down a black spiral vortex to the central void where the daemon sultan Azathoth gnaws hungrily in the dark; and that this doom would be prefigured horribly in the second coming of the crawling chaos Nyarlathotep. And I wished to spare the priests any reminder of this prophecy, for I knew that they had no waking world to flee to when it should be fulfilled.

When I had finished, they volunteered the information that I had dreamed myself into the Temple of the Elder Ones at Ulthar. And when I asked how so holy a place could have become the haunt of daemons, they told me that they had summoned the daemon, that the interrogation of daemons was one of their procedures for verifying supernatural rumors. So I asked what supernatural rumors they were trying to verify. They answered, one that announced the impending fulfillment of a fundamental prophecy of their faith.

And perhaps my face betrayed to them my understanding of more than their words were meant to convey, for then they hoped for me that, as I had dreamed my way into the dreamlands, I should be able to dream my way out again when the need arose. But if I would learn more, they said, I must go to their patriarch in his room at the top of the temple.

So I took my leave of those good old men, and climbed, at their direction, the spiral stair around the wall of the circular room, sidling up the narrow stair with my back to the knobby wall, watching the braziers below me wheel and dwindle until they looked for all the world like stars in a well. And all the while I prayed to the Elder Ones that the priests would quickly find their daemon, that it was not following me up the stair as I feared. I climbed a little faster after that, until I began to fear that the daemon had preceded me and was even now awaiting me in the darkness above, and then I climbed slower than ever. And then I remembered that the daemonic snout was luminous; and if it drew near I would see and avoid it; and if I could avoid it in no other way, I could jump: for it was better to jump to certain death than to be taken alive by the snout.

But my fears were not realized then, and I continued to climb until I felt a wooden door with metal bosses in the wall at my back, and heard a low murmur of human voices behind it. With my ear to the door I could distinguish three voices, and all belonged to ancient men.

"For three months," said the first voice, "has come to Celephais no ship out of cloud-fashioned Serannian where the sea meets the sky. For two months has come no caravan over the Tanarian Hills from Drinen in the East; and the last did not return to Drinen, but took ship westward over the Cerenarian Sea to Hlanith on the estuary of the river Oukranos. One month ago a sea of darkness rolled out of the East by night, even to the shoulders of the Tanarian Hills, and did not roll back at dawn. The darkness wailed with the voices of lost souls, and we of Celephais lit watch-fires on the heights lest the rising flood roll over them and drown the land of Ooth-Nargai in its darkness and wailing. And when I took ship for Hlanith, a red-robed stranger was preaching heresy in the bazaar, and no man there but feared to lay hands on him."

"Many ships," said the second voice, "came to Hlanith from the East in the month that is past, and poured into the streets of Hlanith an endless stream of tight-lipped mariners who started at every shadow. And many more ships were turned away to seek out other ports. And then for a while no more ships came. But four nights ago a last ship rowed out of the East, and she glowed eerily in the dark and smelled of the sea as no ship ever smelled of it before. We of Hlanith repelled her with long poles which sank deep into her spongy sides. On the next night she came again, and again we repelled her. And as the galley bore me up the Oukranos toward Thran, the strange ship was rowing into the harbor for the third time, with a red-robed stranger standing like an iron figurehead in the prow."

"We of Thran," said the third voice, "awoke but yestermorn to find the water of Oukranos brackish and the flotsam of Hlanith awash against the marble wharves of Thran. And yestereve at the hour of dusk a red-robed stranger was stopped by the sentry before the eastern gate, until he should have told three dreams beyond belief and proved himself a dreamer worthy to pass the hundred gates of Thran. And what dreams he told to the sentry, I did not hear; but they who did hear fled screaming out of the northern and western and southern gates, and then we who did not hear fled also. And yesternight at midnight we looked eastward from the jasper terraces of Kiran, and saw the thousand gilded spires of Thran melt beneath the gibbous moon."

Here the door swung open inward, and I stood blinking in the light as three priests filed past me onto the stair. They were robed and bearded like the seven below, but their staves were gilded and their heads were crowned with golden poppies. And as they passed they severally blessed me in the names of the Elder Ones, but their faces as they blessed me were white and drawn with nameless terrors. I watched them descend into the darkness below, and then I turned and entered the room they had left.

A canopied four-poster loomed in a circle of tall candles that the glass fronts of the surrounding bookcases mirrored obscurely. An old priest half lay, half sat on the counterpane, supported by many pillows. And I would have guessed that this was the patriarch I sought, by the amazing length of his snowy beard alone, or by the signs of an alien zodiac embroidered in silver upon his night-black robe. But I knew him at once by the weariness in his wrinkled face and the wisdom in his faded eyes: The aching weariness of a man fully three and a half centuries old, the troubled wisdom of an old disciple of Barzai the Wise. And I knelt at the bedside of the patriarch Atal and reverently kissed his wizened hand.

Very briefly I recounted my awakening in the alcove, my vision of the snout, and my subsequent conversation with the priests. The old priest listened in silence to the end and solemnly nodded his venerable head. The simultaneous arrival of the daemon and myself was not wholly a coincidence, he allowed. The children of darkness were never drawn from their native pit but through holes in space, and who could tell what other beings these ubiquitous holes might draw, from what other spheres or planes of existence? It might be that I, as an experienced dreamer, was particularly susceptible to the influence of such holes, and so he deplored the inconvenience that the opening of this one might inadvertently have caused me.

But since it might well be otherwise, he continued, as that I was sent by the Elder Ones to be their chosen instrument, he now proposed that I accompany him upon a quest that he planned shortly to undertake. For the report of the second coming of the crawling chaos Nyarlathotep had lately been confirmed beyond any doubt, and it only remained to be seen whether man could contrive to prevent the doom of the world, even as the Elder Ones had done when they and the world were young and only the Other Gods were old.

But before he would disclose the object of his quest, he would have me declare what I knew of infinity's Other Gods. So I said I knew only what all men knew: that the Other Gods were the prankish servitors of the Elder Ones; and that they had been disembodied by the Elder Ones to punish them for their prankishness; and that only the eternal vigilance of the Elder Ones, as symbolized in their Elder Sign, warded the prankishness of the Other Gods away from the habitations of man. But I saw from his face that this was the wrong answer.

So then I admitted to knowing what it was unlawful for any but a priest of the Elder Ones to know: "The

Other Gods are the ultimate gods, who came to earth in a dim age of chaos before the Elder Ones were born. The Other Gods were born in the black spiral vortex where time began, and they died when the cycle of eternity bore them too far from the primal chaos. But they will live again when the cycle of eternity bears them into the black spiral vortex where time will end, where the world and the stars will be devoured by the boundless daemon sultan whose name no lips dare speak aloud.

"And the corollary is also true, that time will end when the Other Gods return. But when the young Elder Ones came down from the stars in their ships of cloud, they found the horrible dead bodies of the Other Gods and knew what they portended. And they wove potent spells between the bodies and the souls of the Other Gods, binding the bodies beneath the ground and banishing the souls beyond the orbit of the moon. And the first coming of the crawling chaos Nyarlathotep, the soul and messenger of the Other Gods, was thwarted by the spells of the Elder Ones.

"But too much of eternity has weakened those spells, and the terrible souls of the Other Gods have lowered like dark clouds upon even the lesser peaks of earth. And the senile Elder Ones, their spells long forgotten, have withdrawn into their onyx fortress atop unknown Kadath in the cold waste, there selfishly to prepare their last defense, or fatalistically to await the doom they have no longer any power to avert. And if the Elder Ones themselves despair, then where is there any hope for man?"

It lay, said Atal, in something that Barzai the Wise had told his young disciple on the eve of their ill-fated ascent of forbidden Hatheg-Kla, over three centuries ago. The worshippers of the Elder Ones knew that the Elder Ones had created man, and the priests of the Elder Ones knew that he had evolved unsupervised from the source and prototype of all earthly life, which the Elder Ones had created and the elder records named

Ubbo-Sathla. But what even the priests did not know, for only Barzai had been able to decode those frightful parts of the moldy Pnakotic Manuscripts which were too ancient to be read, was that when the Elder Ones were tired of creating life, they had left their inconceivable wisdom, written on mighty tablets of star-quarried stone, in the keeping of Ubbo-Sathla. And it was Ubbo-Sathla that the furry pre-humans had worshipped and the later Hyperboreans had vilified by the name of Abhoth, the father and mother of all cosmic uncleanliness, which had laired beneath the mountain Voormithadreth on the continent Hyperborea in the prehistory of the waking world. And it might be that the spells wherewith the Elder Ones had averted the doom of the world were preserved by Abhoth beneath the mountain Voormithadreth. And this being the hope of Atal, his quest was to fetch them hither.

Here the old priest arose and shuffled, leaning heavily upon the unadorned staff of office that had lain beside him on the counterpane, to a spot before the bookcases opposite the door. He rapped feebly with his staff three times upon the marble floor. And directly in front of him, two tall bookcases swung outward like French windows, opening onto a rectangular patch of the night sky strewn thickly with brilliant stars.

The fear of the unknown, he resumed, was worse than all other fears but one, because the unknown might prove to be the worst thing in all the universe. The priests of the Elder Ones were more deeply learned in the elder mysteries than I, and they knew, as I could not, what the worst thing in the universe was like, and that we stood in a fair way to encounter it. But the worst that I could fear was the unknown. And my fear might not unman me, as theirs certainly would them, because the fear of the unknown was not as bad as the fear of the worst thing in the universe.

So saying, he plucked out of his beard a little silver whistle on a chain, and blew it silently. As he returned it to its hiding place I glimpsed it only briefly, but I saw and recognized the singular stamp it bore, the hieroglyphic abomination of horns and wings and claws and a curling tail. Then a distant caterwauling arose, and then some stars on the sill began to be blotted out—I thought by a dense cloud of bats, for the stars still blinked within its shifting outline, but its center was opaque. Larger and larger grew the cloud, until all the stars were blotted out, until the frenzied caterwauling had to compete with a loud drumming as of many pairs of great, leathery wings. A dank, evil-smelling wind blew in through the window in fitful gusts, beating down the candle flames and causing the beard of Atal to fly and his robe to belly behind him. Then he turned to me with a bony finger laid across his bearded lips, and motioned me to extinguish the candles.

But when the last candle was before me, and I leaned forward to blow it out, I saw something emerge from the darkness behind it—something palely luminous and cloudily transparent—something in the shape of a long, grey cone tapering to a clump of wriggling pinkish tentacles.

But as I watched, the pale luminescence grew paler, and the cloudy transparency clearer, until there remained only my own leering face mirrored obscurely in the glass front of a bookcase.

I blew out the last candle.

Charles R. Saunders

THE POOL OF THE MOON

I feel about Chuck Saunders the same way I feel about Pat McIntosh: maybe I wasn't the first to discover him, but I was the first to give him bookroom. Imaro, the black warrior of prehistoric Africa, may be only a "chocolate-covered Conan" as one of his unkinder critics quipped, but I find this interesting blend of Howard's hero with Burroughs' Tarzanish setting quite a clever idea. How Phil Farmer or I failed to think of it first sure beats me. But I'm glad somebody thought of it, and had the skill to spin some decent yarns out of the notion!

—L.C.

The great Soudanic war-horse strained mightily as Imaro urged it to greater speed. Galloping through the rocky country that led to the Gwaridi-Milima Mountains, the black warrior was a formidable figure; a giant of a man clad only in loincloth, boots, and cloak of tawny lion skin. A string of beast-teeth circled his thick neck and his hair grew wooly and untamed. His weapons were a broadsword of Meroitic steel and a huge, double-bladed Bornu battle-axe that hung from a thong at the side of his saddle. He rode as if something were pursuing him.

After an abrupt turn, Imaro reined in his magnificent mount. A sheer scarp of barren rock rose like a wall before him. The rocky barrier was broken only by a narrow declivity. Imaro was urging his horse toward the opening when he heard the shout of voices and the clash of arms drifting from its other side. Upon hearing these sounds, Imaro looked about for an alternative route. There was none; unscalable heights rose from either side of the trail.

Cursing venomously, the Ilyassai barbarian realized that he had no choice other than riding ahead into the fighting. He was not afraid of battle; far from it! He was only angry that he might be delayed in his flight from the squadron of Bornu soldiers pursuing him. He did not know how persistent the men of Bornu were, but he did not want to increase their chances of catching him. By now he was as angry as a rogue elephant and probably more dangerous. Whatever the conflict ahead was, Imaro would make a volatile addition to it.

Into the declivity he plunged. For several yards it was narrow; abruptly it widened into a sizeable valley. Imaro immediately reined in his steed, for his hard black eyes had espied a strange scene.

A lone black woman stood at bay, beleagured by five men. Ragged of garment and desperate of mein, these men could only be hill-bandits, the scourge of the borderlands between Bornu and Kaneem. Obviously the rogues were loath to slay the woman, or they would have long since done so. The two corpses at her feet and the wounds dripping crimson across the dark skins of the others indicated that the outlaws would have to pay dearly if they indeed wanted to take her alive.

In comparison to her attackers, the woman was splendid. She stood taller than at least three of them, and she fought like a lioness. The longsword and dagger she held in her hands were red to their hilts with the blood of hill-bandits. Though somewhat hampered by the flowing silk pazia she wore, the woman was able to hold her own because of her assailants' reluctance to kill her.

As yet unnoticed by any of the combatants, Imaro rested his gaze on the battling woman. The swords of the bandits had torn great rents in her pazia, and expanses of bare ebony skin flashed through them. Her face was beautiful both in feature and its expression of courage and determination. Her bush of kinky black hair circled her head like a dark halo.

Perhaps, thought Imaro, this woman could help him to forget the forest girl, she who had been called. . . . NO! That name must be forever forgotten . . .

Shaking the morbid thought from his mind, Imaro swiftly loosened the thong of his axe and hefted the huge weapon like a walking-stick. Then he spurred his stallion forward. From his lips burst the terrible war cry of the Ilyassai.

Like a roar of a lion, Imaro's bellow had its effect: everyone except him was momentarily frozen in their tracks. Before the bandits could move, two of them were already dead. Imaro's axe hewed gory gouges that nearly tore their bodies in two. A third bandit turned and lifted his sword in desperation, but a mighty sweep of Imaro's arm sent him shrieking under the pounding hooves of Imaro's horse.

Yelling in exultant battle-lust, the young warrior wheeled his mount for another charge . . . and was dumbfounded when the beast suddenly collapsed beneath him. Imaro was thrown by the horse's unexpected fall, and with a jarring thud he landed rear-first on the ground. Then his battle-instincts warned him of the danger looming behind him. Looking up, he saw yet another hill-bandit rushing toward him. The man was almost as huge as himself, and his sword was raised high over his head, and an evil, triumphant grin split his brutish face.

The curved sword swung down like the cleaver of a

butcher. But Imaro, still sitting, parried it with a deft thrust of his axe. With a loud clang, the bandit's blade shattered. Imaro jabbed his axe upward, and the spearlike point between its twin blades plunged deep into the bandit's burly breast. As the point pierced his heart, the bandit fell, blood gushing from his open mouth.

Imaro was about to rise to face the last of the bandits when a heavy weight struck him from behind. Again he was knocked sprawling to the ground. Snarling, Imaro shoved the thing from him . . . and was startled to find that it was the corpse of the last bandit.

What was even more startling was the dagger buried hilt-deep in the rogue's back.

Springing to his feet, Imaro noted that the object of the brief, bloody fray was standing calmly only a few yards away. In her hand her sword was still gripped tightly. On her face was a cryptic, unreadable expression. No word of gratitude did she speak to her rescuer.

The Ilyassai shrugged and turned to his fallen steed, which was at this time far more important to him than the mysterious behavior of the woman. He quickly discovered a sword transfixed halfway through the beast's breast. Apparently it had been thrust there blindly by the bandit Imaro had ridden under. In terms of eluding any Bornu soldiers still pursuing him, the barbarian might just as well have lost his legs.

Imaro was muttering curses that would have blasted the eardrums of a Kisiwan corsair when he heard a soft footfall behind him. He whirled about . . . and found himself confronted by the woman he had rescued, and who had apparently saved his life in turn.

But it was not gratitude that was written in the expression on her dark face. The point of her longsword hovered only a few inches from Imaro's chest.

"Drop it," she said coldly, indicating the dripping axe in Imaro's hand.

For a moment Imaro stared at the woman in open disbelief. Then he snarled, "By Ajunge, woman! I rescue you from these ragged dogs, lose my horse, and now you point a sword at my heart?"

"I was doing quite well for myself before you blundered in," the woman sniffed. "And chances are you only want what those jackals were after. Now, drop the axe!"

Imaro's eyes blazed like banked black coals, but he still tossed his weapon to the ground. Reflexively the woman's eyes followed the downward path of the battle-axe. Given that brief opportunity, Imaro struck.

With a blur of speed unbelievable in one of his size, the Ilyassai's foot flashed up and kicked the sword out of the woman's hand. As her weapon spun through the air, Imaro instantly recovered his balance. Before she could move, Imaro's hands shot out with serpentine speed and clamped like steel vises on her wrists. Although the woman stood less than half a head shorter than the giant barbarian, and was stronger than many men her size, Imaro was more than a match for her. The Ilyassai was even stronger than he looked, and the Amazonian-proportioned woman found herself helpless as a child in his iron-muscled grasp.

She did not like the fires that were igniting in the barbarian's obsidian eyes. And the lustful grin that was beginning to form on his lips frightened her. Still she bravely struggled on, maneuvering for space to drive a crippling knee-blow to Imaro's groin.

Suddenly the black warrior cocked his head, as if he were listening to something. Something heard, but unseen. Though the woman could hear nothing, Imaro's wilderness-honed senses were picking up a faint sound. It was like the drumming of distant thunder.

"Soldiers!" he growled, shoving the woman roughly aside. It was as if she no longer mattered.

Wildly casting his glance up and down the sloping, scrub-clad sides of the valley, Imaro searched for an escape route. The slopes were still high enough to make climbing difficult, but not impossible. But where would he climb? There was nothing but scrubby, low-growing trees beyond which he could see nothing.

Then he spotted a dark opening about halfway up the left-hand slope. It was a cave, which might offer protection and concealment if he acted quickly enough.

"I hear nothing," the woman commented as she rubbed her sore wrists.

"You will," said Imaro as he proceeded to strip the corpse of the biggest of the hill-bandits. When he finished, he removed his own scanty garments and hurriedly garbed the corpse in them. In the background, the woman looked at Imaro's naked, heavily-muscled body and speculation gleamed in her eyes. But whatever thoughts were passing through her mind at that moment were interrupted by the sound of faraway hooves. By now even her city-dulled ears could hear them, so they could not be far away.

Meanwhile Imaro had hastily donned the ragged, knee-length breeches of the dead outlaw. Then he drew his sword and chopped the face of the bandit into an unrecognizable red ruin. After planting his axe and sword near the bloody bodies, he stepped back to survey his handiwork. Strewn with butchered corpses and reeking pools of blood, the floor of the valley looked like the scene of a longer, harder-fought battle than the brief blood-letting that had actually occurred.

Then the barbarian walked toward the slope of the cave and began to climb.

"What in the name of Mulungu are you doing?" demanded the woman, as the pounding of the soldiers' horses grew louder.

"Not that its any of your concern," retorted the barbarian, "But I am going to climb this hill and take refuge in that cave. Hopefully the dogs of Bornu will fall for my little trick and think I am dead. If not. . . ."

He fingered the point of the dagger he had pulled from the back of one of the bandits. Then he turned and began to climb.

"Wait!" the woman cried. "Take me with you. The soldiers of Bornu are no friends of mine. Better you than them."

Imaro stopped and looked at the tall black woman. Though her demeanor was yet haughty, there was no mistaking the meaning of the look in her eyes. Through a long rip in her pazia, one of her large, round breasts was visible. Its nipple was painted a bright gold that shone against the darkness of her skin. She might, Imaro thought, make an interesting companion . . . if she didn't try to cut his throat first. But there was no time for further consideration. The soldiers were getting closer.

"All right, let's go," Imaro said. He extended his hand to the woman, and together they clambered swiftly up the rocky slope to the waiting cave.

Just as they scrambled into the cave's dark entrance, a clatter of hooves and jingle of armor announced the arrival of the soldiers of Bornu. Their loud voices drifted up to the listeners in the cave.

"By Baluga, this valley looks like a slaughterhouse!" commented one soldier.

"And there's our quarry," said another. "See the loinskin garments? Nobody in all Bornu would wear such a barbarous costume."

"It looks like the bandits caved the barbarian's head in for him all right."

"But he certainly took a lot of them with him. How in Motoni could these cursed hill-bandits have done what our comrades failed to do back in Jebbel Uri?"

"Never mind that now. He's obviously dead. We'll carry his head (or what's left of it) and his garments back to Jebbel Uri and claim credit for the slayings ourselves. Then we'll be the heroes! Let the vultures and jackals deal with the last of that cursed barbarian."

The hills echoed with the sound of their raucous laughter. And the pair in the cave exchanged sardonic glances, for they knew that events in the capital of Bornu would unfold exactly as the soldiers boasted.

Had either the soldiers or Imaro and his new companion seen the ominous sigil carved deeply into the rock above the mouth of the cave, their mirth would have quickly become cold horror. In the shape of an arrow was the mysterious sign. Its point was a human skull and instead of feathers it bore scorpion tails at its end. It was the sign of the dreaded Bwala li Mwesu, the Moon Pool...

A short while later, after the soldiers had departed, the woman suggested that they leave the cave and move on. But Imaro vetoed that idea.

"Before long, it will be dark. It would be foolish to risk another encounter with hill-bandits. And there is always the danger of beasts like the hill-panther and the rock ape."

"I am not accustomed to having my will questioned," the woman said with icy hauteur.

"Nor do I like having my ideas called 'foolish'. Do you not, barbarian, know who I am?"

"No," Imaro said shortly.

"I am Nakulla, an Ufalma of Ain Fara, capital of the kingdom of Darfur," she announced regally. But she was nonplussed in the extreme by Imaro's reaction to her revelation of her lofty rank. He gave a distinctly nonservile grunt and began to look over their hideaway.

Nakulla did not know that Imaro was not one to be impressed by status even such as hers, which was the royal family of Ain Fara. Among his Ilyassai people there was only one social class: warriors. Within this category was anyone who could wield a weapon, and status was determined by skill at arms rather than circumstances of birth. The only exception to this custom, Imaro reflected bitterly, was himself.

Since his exile from the Ilyassai, the young barbarian had encountered people who were considered (or considered themselves) "highborn". But for the life of him he could not discern any reason to perceive them as being much different from the so-called "lowborn".

To Nakulla he said, "Why are you not in Ain Fara now?"

Abruptly Nakulla's mood changed. Now her anger was directed not at Imaro but someone else . . .

"I was on my way to Bwarun, an outer province of Darfur," she began. "I was to be wed to Okatunji, its Ufalmo. My father and I accepted his suit over that of Idin Amni, the king of Bornu. Before I could reach Bwarun, my party was beset by agents of Idin Amni who had come into Darfur by a secret pass through the mountains. Had the skulking hyenas come by the regular route between the last mountain of the Gwarir-Milimas and the Khagga Swamp, they would have been cut down by our border guard!

"Instead, thanks to their treacherous cunning, they slew all my retainers and abducted me, carrying me through the same secret passage. I escaped by seducing and slaying the Bornu leader. I was attempting to find my way back to the pass when I was beset by the hill bandits. From their shouts I learned that Idin Amni had offered a reward to anyone in these parts who could deliver me alive and unmarked."

"I would rather die than be touched by that pig Idin Amni," she continued, shuddering at the thought. "That is why I did not wish to be found by soldiers of Bornu. But who are you, warrior? How is it that you were pursued by the soldiers?"

"My name is Imaro; my tribe was the Ilyassai," Imaro replied.

"Ilyassai . . ." Nakulla repeated wonderingly. "I thought that the Ilyassai were nothing more than a myth. When I was a child, my nurses would use the name to frighten me. Ilyassai . . . a tribe of fang-mouthed giants who feed lions to their children at breakfast. You do not look much like an Ilyassai to me."

At this naiveté the warrior burst into loud and gusty laughter. Scandalized, Nakulla felt the blood rush to her face and sudden rage kindle inside. But Imaro failed to notice the effects of his humor.

"No, I don't look much like my tribesmen," he said. "Most of them are not as tall as I. And we kill lions to protect our herds, not for food."

"Why did you leave your tribe?" Nakulla asked, interested despite her annoyance.

"I am a wanderer," he muttered, turning his head to hide the pain that shot through his eyes. It was always like that, when he remembered the cause of his exile . . .

"As for why the soldiers were chasing me: I had come to Bornu to sell my sword to Idin Amni in his war against Kaneem. I had heard that Amni was paying much gold to muajis, mercenaries. But when I came to Jebbel Uri, the capital, I found that the war is over and Bornu had lost. They believed that I was a Kaneem spy, and I had to fight my way out of the city."

Nakulla swayed slightly, her anger forgotten and her knees weak. She had never taken into account the possibility that Kaneem would defeat Bornu for despite his other faults, Idin Amni was a great warrior.

"And what of Idin Amni?" she asked, forcing calmness into her voice.

"From what the soldiers said, I think his head now adorns a stake outside the palace of Idris Alooma, king of Kaneem." Then he turned to walk out of the cave.

"Wait!" Nakulla cried. "Where are you going?"

"I go to collect some firewood from the scrub that grows around here. At night the bandits won't see the smoke, and the flames will keep beasts away."

With that declaration he left the cave, leaving Nakulla to her thoughts. Despite the many new implications and alternatives that raced through her mind, the Ufalma's dark eyes still lingered on the sea of muscles that rippled on Imaro's broad back. And a familiar desire began to stir in her loins.

As was traditional among highborn ladies of Darfur, Nakulla had enjoyed a high degree of sexual license. Thus she had made love to a wide variety of men, from princes to stable hands. But never before had she felt such sheer physical attraction as she did for this giant barbarian. Not even Okatunji, whom she supposed she loved. The thought of Imaro's bull-like body locked with hers made her shiver in anticipation. And the news that she was forever free of Idin Amni filled her with a different kind of ecstasy.

Hearing Imaro's returning footsteps, Nakulla quickly undid the four silver clasps that held her pazia together. The garment slid from her shoulders and formed a pool of crimson and gold at her feet. When Imaro re-entered the cave, his arms were filled with firewood. It dropped with a clatter to the rocky floor as his eyes devoured her naked splendor. The gold-painted nipples of her large, firm breasts were as startling in effect as the crescents and rows of golden dots that adorned her stomach and upper thighs. These were the marks of an Ufalma, and they made her a seductive vision in gold and black.

In no time Imaro was across the cave, enfolding Nakulla in a hot barbarian embrace. Slowly he drew her down to the cave floor, finding his fiery passion returned with an intensity he had never before experienced.

Outside, the skull-arrow chiseled in the rock above the cave-mouth seemed to grin in evil anticipation of what was to come . . .

It was much later in the night, and the fire Imaro had built burned low. A dull crimson glow was cast upon the dark bodies of Imaro and Nakulla as they slept deeply. They lay exhausted, and replete.

Suddenly the warmth of the cavern was broken by an unnaturally chill current of air. Wafting sinisterly from the deeper recesses of the cave, the current had a fetid, death-like smell. Gently it touched the face of Nakulla.

At that cold, detestable touch, the Ufalma sat bolt upright, her body as stiff as a statue. Imaro lay motionless, as if drugged. Nakulla's expression of lassitude and content was replaced by a grimace of sheer terror.

Until this moment, Nakulla had feared nothing. But as the tendril of cold air caressed the contours of her face and slithered obscenely down her body, she wanted desperately to scream.

But she could not utter a sound, and the current continued to weave its icy web around her mind. With terrifying portent, a word whispered like an errant breeze: "Come." Nakulla could not resist that whispered command. Stiffly, reluctantly she rose from the spread-out pazia and followed the lead of the cold air as it led her deeper into the darkness of the cave.

Now Imaro groaned in his sleep and fitfully thrashed his brawny limbs. But he could not awaken as Nakulla was swallowed by the inky shadows.

When the warrior finally did awaken, it was with a sudden start. His sleep had been troubled by images of grotesque, nightmare images against which his sword and strength were helpless. Shaken, he reached for Nakulla. To his astonishment, she was not there.

Like an endangered beast, Imaro sprang to his feet and searched wildly around the dimly lit cavern. He could see no sign of the Ufalma. Normally Imaro would have assumed that Nakulla had stolen what she could and slipped off into the night. But his nightmares had aroused a chill sense of foreboding within him. And, in the thin film of dust that covered the floor of the cave, Imaro could see the imprint of Nakulla's bare feet. The tracks led into, not out of the cave. And they indicated that she was walking in measured, even steps as if she were in a trance of some kind.

Imaro's eyes were grim as he poked an unused stick of wood into the fire to make a torch. The short hairs on the back of his neck prickled. He knew that he faced no foe that was beast or human. This thing smelled of sorcery.

Hastily donning his breeches and sword, Imaro began to follow Nakulla's trail. He stalked like a jungle cat, fighting down the primordial fear of the Unknown as if it, too, were a deadly foe.

The Pool of the Moon

After he had penetrated fairly deeply into the cavern, Imaro began to realize that the curious rock formations dimly visible along its walls were not the work of nature. When he examined them more closely, he repressed a violent shudder of revulsion. For it was impossible to believe that the monstrous figures carved into the stone was the work of human hands. The aesthetics and perspectives represented in the carvings were alien to his eye and mind. Imaro turned his head in disgust.

But before he did, Imaro noticed that a single image had dominated the weird sculptures. It was the same as the sigil carved outside the cave, unnoticed by Imaro as he had sought refuge in its depths. The skull-tipped arrow feathered with scorpion tails . . . the Sign of Bwala li Mwesu, the Moon Pool. All of the sigils were pointing in the direction of Nakulla's trail of footprints.

Imaro did not know how long he had been following Nakulla's trail when he first noticed the faint glimmer of light ahead. His torch was guttering dangerously low, however, and he was grateful that he would not have to grope his way in darkness when his light finally failed. Wondering how Nakulla could have negotiated the passage without a light of her own, Imaro closed his mind to several unpleasant speculations.

Vague memories stirred in his mind at the sight of the skull-arrows. But as Imaro's footfalls echoed softly in the tomb-like silence of the cavern, he was unable to recall its exact significance. Approaching closer to the spectral light, Imaro saw that it was an eerie, bluish-white phosphorescence unlike anything he had seen before. The portal from which it streamed was a circle of twelve feet in diameter. Blinking his eyes against the glow, Imaro peered warily inside, senses attuned to any danger lurking within. Satisfied that at least the entrance was safe, the Ilyassai stalked through the blue-white circle, sword upraised to strike any enemy.

But no foe attacked. Imaro's wide eyes stared in bewilderment upon a scene which was at once weird, unearthly, and terrible.

He was standing in a chamber hollowed out of solid rock. Pale moonlight shone through an opening at its top. On the sides sloping down from the opening, the twisted shadows of gnarled trees were blackly etched across four gigantic stone stairways. The stairways led to a wide, round pool, and it was from the pool's depths that the bluish-white radiance streamed. Between the stairways were flat surfaces inscribed with a pattern of horrendous implication...

These new carvings ran in three rows around the circumference of the chamber. On the top row was a progression of the phases of the moon, from the lean crescent of the new to the gorged corpulence of the full. It was in the second row that the horror lay. The prevailing motif in this row was a naturalistic rendition of a naked human female. The figure at the beginning of the series, at the new moon, was whole and complete. Each successive figure, however, depicted a hideous sequence of maimings and mutilations until at the end, beneath the carving of the full moon, there was nothing left but a skeleton. It was as though the woman had been devoured by the waxing moon.

And in the bottom row was the leering skull-arrow sigil of the Bwala li Mwesu. The evil symbols seemed to taunt the barbarian as they pointed to each abomination.

Only Imaro and the Sky Walkers would ever know whether the words Imaro muttered were prayers or curses. For on the floor of the chamber he could still discern Naklulla's measured footprints leading to the edge of the glowing Moon Pool. And he also saw grotesque, webbed imprints of the Thing which had awaited her there. At last Imaro knew the full, awful significance of the skull-arrow sigil and of Bwala li Mwesu!

Forcing down a spasm of superstitious dread, Imaro recalled a tale he had heard from Pomphis, the Bambuti pygmy with whom he had shared fantastic adventures along the East Coast of Nyumbani. Bwala li Mwesu . . . an eldritch, blasphemous ritual to the Mashataan once practiced by an inhuman race called the Kyaggath, one of many such which had dominated Nyumbai before the coming of the Sky Walkers. These fiendish creatures still survived, in myth if not reality . . . As Imaro recalled the more grisly details of Pomphis' tale, half-forgotten terrors tugged like insidious fingers at his backbone.

"By Ajunge, will the world never be cleansed of the Mashataan and their filth?" Imaro shouted suddenly.

Then he stared into the calm waters of the Moon Pool. He quickly found that its illumination did not originate in the water itself, but from a repellantly-shaped fungus which grew on its bottom. There were, however, some places in which the fungus did not grow. These dark areas took the form of yet another string of skull-arrows, pointing the way to an underground channel. Beyond that channel, the barbarian knew he would find Nakulla.

Imaro did not relish the prospect of swimming in the fungus-infested water. There was something about the plants that looked poisonous . . . But as long as there was still a possibility that Nakulla was alive, he knew that he must follow the path of the skull-arrows to its end, however horrendous that end might be. He owed her his life.

Slamming his sword back into its scabbard, Imaro filled his lungs with air and plunged into the deep water, shivering at its chill caress. Swimming with long, powerful strokes, he struck for the dark hole of the underground channel.

The longer the warrior swam through the tunnel the more endless it seemed. His lungs began to grow empty, and the blue-white opening at the channel's end seemed to mock his increasingly difficult efforts to hold his breath.

Dimly he wondered how Nakulla had made this swim.

Then he realized that she had probably not swum at all but was carried through the channel by the same Thing that had summoned her to the Moon Pool.

At last, when the Ilyassai's lungs seemed near to bursting, the roof of the tunnel disappeared and the surface became visible once again. To Imaro, it seemed as far away as the sky . . .

Suddenly two dark snakelike objects darted into the water and wrapped tightly around Imaro's upper body. Then he was pulled upward at frightening speed. Fiercely Imaro struggled to break the hellish hold. But the tentacles were as strong as steel cables. Then his body broke the surface, and he was being dragged forward. Shaking his wooly head and gasping for breath, Imaro blinked the water out of his eyes . . . and stared upon the face of Horror!

For the Thing which was hauling him onto the rough stone floor was alien to anything he had ever known. It stood upright on bent froglike legs with huge webbed feet, and its body was a round lumpy mass of gray-green slime. From the misshapen body protruded not arms but six octopus-like tentacles, two of which were already wrapped around Imaro's body. The others were whipping toward him with serpentine speed.

It was the Thing's face, however, that was its most horrible aspect. Half froglike, half hideously anthropomorphic, that face was dominated by a wide slash of a mouth filled with row upon row of needle fangs. Its eyes were lambent green, and burned with both intelligence and an eternal hatred and contempt for all things human. The creature was a Kyaggath, the last of its demon-spawned kind.

Behind the hulking monstrosity Imaro could see a high wall set with tiers of rusting iron cages. Nakulla must be in one of them . . . but was she still alive?

Fighting off the crippling fear that the loathesome creature inspired, Imaro struggled to his feet and strove to free his arms from the slimy tentacles. But the rubbery, boneless things were like a nest of pythons and they were squeezing the Ilyassai unmercifully. The Kyaggath, which even on bent legs stood taller than Imaro, was slowly dragging the warrior's head into its gaping, fang-filled jaws. . . .

Imaro's dark eyes blazed with the fury of his hatred of things Mashataan. Planting his heels firmly, he tensed all of his powerful thews to rocklike rigidity. Like a tower of black iron, he resisted the inexorable tug of the tentacles of the Kyaggath. But even if he managed to free his swordarm, at these close quarters his weapon might not be effective . . . still he fought on, locked in a silent struggle of death.

Surprise glimmered in the demonic green eyes of the Kyaggath as it began to realize that it could not drag the black warrior any closer to its deadly jaws. This time it was not dealing with a mesmerized, swooning victim, but a fighting-mad warrior like those which had decimated its kind centuries ago.

But strength was not the only weapon of the Kyaggath. From tiny pores on the undersides of its tentacles, a virulent venom began to trickle. The effect was immediate; wherever the tentacles touched, white-hot pain shot through Imaro's body. Roaring like a maddened buffalo, Imaro reflexively threw himself backwards just as the monster made a redoubled effort to pull him into its jaws. The result of this action was astonishing and unexpected!

The strain of such a giant surge of strength was too severe for the boneless, pulpy anchorage of the Kyaggath's tentacles. With a sickening rip of rubbery flesh, four of the snakelike members were torn from the creature's body as Imaro pitched backwards to the floor. Taking quick advantage of his opportunity, Imaro yanked out his sword and hacked off the remaining two tentacles.

As the warrior freed himself from the severed growth, he heard the Kyaggath utter its first sound. An ear-splitting, croaking shriek of inhuman agony filled the chamber of Bwala li Mwesu. Scrambling to his feet,

Imaro advanced upon the now-helpless monster. Croaking pathetically in a language dead for millennia, the creature retreated awkwardly on its misshapen legs. Thick white fluid oozed from the gaping round wounds down the front of its bulbous body. The flaming green eyes now mirrored only terror and pain rather than the previous cosmic contempt.

With a grim, merciless smile on his lips the barbarian stalked the crippled monster. As he raised his sword, the demon-spawn must have recalled the time long ago when other black men had arisen and sent other Kyaggaths back to the nighted hells of the Mashataan . . .

Like a shimmering arc of death, the barbarian's blade streaked toward the Kyaggath. Imaro's stroke sheared completely through the pulpy half-flesh, and the monster's torso fell in one direction and its legs in another. The two parts of the Kyaggath's corpse lay twitching in widening pools of stinking white gore.

Breathing heavily from his exertions, the warrior had not time to savor his triumph, nor to think about the lingering pain of the Kyaggath's venom. Frantically his eyes searched the long rows of iron cages. He called, "Nakulla! NAKULLA!"

"Here . . ." a small voice answered from the bottom tier.

Following the direction of the voice, Imaro saw a dark shape huddled against the bars of one of the cages. As he ran to her, the warrior saw that the other cages contained ancient human skeletons, each bone of which was scored with the imprints of unpleasant-looking teeth. As to how long the last Kyaggath had squatted in its cave awaiting human victims, Imaro did not care to guess. Through the bars of the cage Nakulla was looking at Imaro with an expression of incredulous relief on her face.

"Did that hell-creature harm you?" Imaro asked with a concern rare for him.

"No . . . but how will you get me out of here?" the

Ufalma replied hopelessly. "Only that . . . that Thing knew the way to unlock the door."

"There are no others?" Imaro asked suddenly, voicing his only fear. One Kyaggath was bad enough. He did not care to face a horde of them.

Nakulla assured him that there had been only one of the monsters in the cave. Then Imaro grasped the bars of Nakulla's cage firmly in his huge hands. He pulled, the thews of his back, arms, and legs standing out in bold relief. Imaro did not know the limits of his strength, which far surpassed that of men even larger than himself. But this latest exertion was approaching them as he strained to the utmost of his power. For a long moment the ancient bars resisted the warrior's super-human effort. Then, with a loud screech of protest, the entire door of Nakulla's cage was torn from its hinges.

Wide-eyed and passive with awe, the Ufalma allowed herself to be lifted in Imaro's arms and carried out of the cage. A quick glance showed the barbarian that this chamber also had stairways leading to an opening at its top. Thanking his bloody gods that he did not have to make that cursed swim again, Imaro walked heavily up the steep stairway. His endurance was almost at an end, but when he reached the top and breathed in the free night air, he shouted in exultation. Nakulla kept her face buried in his broad breast.

EPILOG

One week later, Imaro and Nakulla were at the mouth of the secret passage that led through the Gwaride-Milima Mountains. They both wore hill-bandit garments, and were riding double on a stolen war-horse. On their faces they each wore smiles.

"You never told me where you were bound, Imaro," Nakulla said over her shoulder.

"I'm headed for Cush," the warrior replied. "I intend

to look up an old friend named Pomphis, just to see the look on his face when he discovers I'm still alive."

"Dharfur lies on the way to Cush. Were you to deliver me safely to my father's house in Ain Fara, he would reward you with enough gold to make your sojourn in Cush a pleasant one."

"And what reward is promised by you?" Imaro asked ironically.

"Oh, you have already collected it," Nakulla purred, pressing her ample rump into the warrior's lap. "And before we reach Ain Fara, you shall collect it again . . . and again . . . and again!"

Laughing lustily, Imaro spurred their horse into the narrow mountain pass.

Appendix

THE YEAR'S BEST FANTASY BOOKS

I. ORIGINAL FICTION

1. *Flashing Swords! #3: Wizards and Warriors,* edited by Lin Carter. Original anthology; 272 pp.; $1.25, Dell. Five new novelets, a Eudoric by L. Sprague de Camp, a Fafhrd and the Gray Mouser by Fritz Leiber, a Witch World by Andre Norton, an Amalric by Carter, and the first story in a new series by Avram Davidson. Sword & Sorcery—more or less.
2. *Gate of Ivrel,* by C. J. Cherryh. Novel; 191 pp.; $1.25, DAW. Stunning debut by a gifted new writer; vies with the McKillip for best of the year.
3. *Camber of Culdi,* by Katherine Kurtz. Novel; xx + 314 pp.; $1.95, Ballantine. Fourth volume in this author's popular Deryni series: overlong, talky, but hard to resist. A "prequel" to the others.
4. *The Riddle-Master of Hed,* by Patricia A. McKillip. Novel; 228 pp.; $7.95, Atheneum. Lean, flawless, gripping: superb first novel in a new series by the author of *Forgotten Beasts of Eld*. The best novel of the year, except possibly for *Gate*

of *Ivrel.* (Why are so many important new fantasy writers pretty girls?)
5. *Count Brass,* by Michael Moorcock. Novel; 158 pp.; $1.25, Dell. First book in a new series related to the Dorian Hawkmoon cycle. Moorcock simply gets better and better.
6. *The Sailor on the Seas of Fate,* by Michael Moorcock. Collection of linked novelets; 160 pp.; $1.25, DAW. A new Elric book, brooding, gloomy, morose, doom-fraught, and gorgeous.
7. *The Tournament of Thorns,* by Thomas Burnett Swann. Novel; 167 pp.; $1.50, Ace. The first of a few posthumous novels by this late author: slight, shallow, but richly imaginative as are all of his works. We lost a good man here . . .

II. FANTASY ANTHOLOGIES

8. *Kingdoms of Sorcery,* edited (with an introduction, notes and recommended reading list) by Lin Carter. Collection; xvii + 218 pp.; $6.95, Doubleday. Sixteen stories, or excerpts from novels, ranging from Voltaire to *Watership Down,* including Lewis, Tolkien, CAS and Poe, arranged to illustrate some of the major schools and traditions of fantastic literature.
9. *Realms of Wizardry,* edited (with an introduction, notes and recommended reading list) by Lin Carter. Collection; xvii + 269 pp.; $7.95, Doubleday. Companion volume to the above, tracing other themes in fantasy through sixteen selections from Cabell, Haggard and Dunsany to Vance, Moorcock and Zelazny.
10. *The Second Book of Robert E. Howard,* edited and with notes by Glenn Lord. Collection; 368 pp.; $1.95, Zebra. Twenty-two stories and poems, familiar and un-, expertly demonstrating

Howard's extraordinary range, variety and vigor. Couldn't be better.

III. IMPORTANT REPRINTS

11. *The Complete Enchanter,* by L. Sprague de Camp and Fletcher Pratt. Omnibus; 420 pp.; $1.95, Ballantine. The Magical Misadventures of Harold Shea, the first two books compiled into one volume. But be warned!—it is *not* "Complete," lacking the two hard-to-find stories which make up the rare third book in the series, *Wall of Serpents.* Great stuff; glorious fun.
12. *Tales of Three Hemispheres,* by Lord Dunsany. Collection; xviii + 140 pp., with decorations and illustrated by Tim Kirk; $9.00, Owlswick Press, Box 8234, Philadelphia, PA 19101. The complete text of Dunsany's last great collection of tales, first published in 1919. Beautifully printed, bound, and illustrated: and it just happens to contain some of the finest fantasies ever written—by the finest fantasy writer of them all. Unreservedly recommended!
13. *Heart of the World,* by H. Rider Haggard. Novel; 347 pp.; $3.95, Newcastle Publishing Co., 1521 North Vine Street, Hollywood, CA 90028. Another of Newscastle's handsome reissues in soft-cover of Haggard's marvelous old Lost Race romances, which are beginning to be rare and hard-to-find. With black-and-white illustrations of the period. Good work, you chaps!
14. *The Well of the Unicorn,* by Fletcher Pratt. Novel; xi + 388 pp.; $1.95, Ballantine. One of the best (and best *written*) heroic fantasies in the entire literature, rescued from oblivion into which Lancer's bankruptcy plunged it. Let's

hope this time it stays in print forever: thank you, you Del Reys!

IV. RECOMMENDED NON-FICTION AND RELATED

15. *Literary Swordsmen and Sorcerers: The Makers of Heroic Fantasy*, by L. Sprague de Camp. Collection of essays, with an introduction and essay on de Camp by Lin Carter xxix + 313 pp.; $10.00, Arkham House. In eleven essays, de Camp epitomizes a history of heroic fantasy through studies of key authors in the genre: Morris, Dunsany, Eddison, Pratt, Tolkien, Lewis, Lovecraft, Leiber, Smith, Howard, etc., his rather arbitrary cut-off date being 1940. Scholarly, well-researched, very insightful—but how he can consider T. H. White and Lovecraft and Clark Ashton Smith as authors of *heroic* fantasy beats me! Still, a very valuable, major addition to the slender (but growing) apparatus of fantasy scholarship, criticism, and history.

16. *The Last Celt,: A Bio-Bibliography of Robert E. Howard*, edited and compiled by Glenn Lord. Compilation; 416 pp., innumerable illustrations, photographs, reproductions of *Weird Tales* covers, etc.; $20.00, Donald M. Grant, West Kingston, R. I. And worth every last penny of it, too. A gigantic, perfectly magnificent monument to Howard's memory: exhaustive bibliographies of every last appearance of every single poem and story, together with descriptions of unpublished fragments, biographical sketches, memoirs of Howard, and literally everything else you could hope such a book might contain. *Bravo*!

17. *The Father Christmas Letters,* by J. R. R. Tolkien, edited by Baillie Tolkien. Collection; unpaged, with numerous drawings by the author; $8.95, Houghton-Mifflin. Warm, humorous, imaginative sequence of letters, presumably from Santa Claus, which Tolkien wrote to his children over the years. Slight, light, but charming.

The above seem to me the best and most important books relating to or of fantasy published in this country during 1976. The honor-role, let me caution you, reflects only my own personal and possibly biased taste, and not necessarily that of my publisher.

As with the two previous *Year's Bests,* I have limited myself to listing the seventeen books which seemed to me the cream of the crop. I don't exactly remember how I got myself locked in to that arbitrary figure in the first place, but I guess I'm stuck with it now. Unfortunately, it forced me to squeeze out some excellent runners-up, like Andy Offutt's *The Undying Wizard* and Gordy Dickson's *The Dragon and the George.* Sorry, fellows: if it makes you feel any happier, I had to leave my own novel, *The Immortal of World's End,* off the list, too. This was a very good year for original fantasy fiction . . . and next year promises to be even better.

Happy Magic for 1977!
—LIN CARTER

- [ ] **THE BIRTHGRAVE** by Tanith Lee. "A big, rich, bloody swords-and-sorcery epic with a truly memorable heroine—as tough as Conan the Barbarian but more convincing."—**Publishers Weekly.** (#UW1177—$1.50)

- [ ] **DON'T BITE THE SUN** by Tanith Lee. A far-flung novel of the distant future by the author of **The Birthgrave.** Definitely something different! (#UY1221—$1.25)

- [ ] **DRINKING SAPPHIRE WINE** by Tanith Lee. How the hero/heroine of Four BEE city finally managed to outrage the system! (#UY1277—$1.25)

- [ ] **BROTHERS OF EARTH** by C. J. Cherryh. One of the most highly praised sf novels of the year. A Science Fiction Book Club selection. (#UW1257—$1.50)

- [ ] **HUNTER OF WORLDS** by C. J. Cherryh. A brilliant and complex novel of three races under the domination of an ancient predatory star folk. A Science Fiction Book Club Selection. (#UE1314—$1.75)

- [ ] **VOLKHAVAAR** by Tanith Lee. Shaina the slave girl versus a world's most powerful magician—an adult fantasy novel of high coloration. (#UW1312—$1.50)

DAW BOOKS are represented by the publishers of Signet and Mentor Books, THE NEW AMERICAN LIBRARY, INC.

THE NEW AMERICAN LIBRARY, INC.,
P.O. Box 999, Bergenfield, New Jersey 07621

Please send me the DAW BOOKS I have checked above. I am enclosing $_____$ (check or money order—no currency or C.O.D.'s). Please include the list price plus 35¢ per order to cover mailing costs.

Name_____

Address_____

City_____State_____Zip Code_____

Please allow at least 4 weeks for delivery

☐ **THE SAILOR ON THE SEAS OF FATE** by Michael Moorcock. The second Elric novel—now first published in America. (#UY1270—$1.25)

☐ **LEGENDS FROM THE END OF TIME** by Michael Moorcock. Strange and diverting adventures of the last decadents on Earth. (#UY1281—$1.25)

☐ **THE JEWEL IN THE SKULL** by Michael Moorcock. The First Book in the History of the Runestaff. (#UY1276—$1.25)

☐ **THE WEIRD OF THE WHITE WOLF** by Michael Moorcock. The third novel of the saga of Elric of Melnibone. (#UY1286—$1.25)

☐ **THE MAD GOD'S AMULET** by Michael Moorcock. The Second Book in the History of the Runestaff. (#UY1289—$1.25)

☐ **THE VANISHING TOWER** by Michael Moorcock. The Fourth novel of Elric. (#UY1304—$1.25)

☐ **THE SWORD OF THE DAWN** by Michael Moorcock. The Third Book in the History of the Runestaff. (#UY1310—$1.25)

☐ **THE RUNESTAFF** by Michael Moorcock. The Final Book in the History of the Runestaff. (#UY1324—$1.25)

DAW BOOKS are represented by the publishers of Signet and Mentor Books, THE NEW AMERICAN LIBRARY, INC.

THE NEW AMERICAN LIBRARY, INC.,
P.O. Box 999, Bergenfield, New Jersey 07621

Please send me the DAW BOOKS I have checked above. I am enclosing
$_____(check or money order—no currency or C.O.D.'s).
Please include the list price plus 35¢ per order to cover mailing costs.

Name_____

Address_____

City_____State_____Zip Code_____
Please allow at least 4 weeks for delivery

DAW PRESENTS MARION ZIMMER BRADLEY

"A writer of absolute competency . . ."—Theodore Sturgeon

☐ **THE FORBIDDEN TOWER**
"Blood feuds, medieval pageantry, treachery, tyranny and true love combine to make another colorful swatch in the compelling continuing tapestry of Darkover."—**Publishers Weekly.** (#UJ1323—$1.95)

☐ **THE HERITAGE OF HASTUR**
"A rich and highly colorful tale of politics and magic, courage and pressure . . . Topflight adventure in every way."—**Analog.** "May well be Bradley's masterpiece."—**Newsday.** "It is a triumph."—**Science Fiction Review.**
(#UJ1307—$1.95)

☐ **DARKOVER LANDFALL**
"Both literate and exciting, with much of that searching fable quality that made **Lord of the Flies** so provocative."—**New York Times.** The novel of Darkover's origin.
(#UY1256—$1.25)

☐ **THE SHATTERED CHAIN**
"Primarily concerned with the role of women in the Darkover society . . . Bradley's gift is provocative, a top-notch blend of sword-and-sorcery and the finest speculative fiction."—**Wilson Library Bulletin.**
(#UJ1327—$1.95)

☐ **THE SPELL SWORD**
Goes deeper into the problem of the matrix and the conflict with one of Darkover's non-human races gifted with similar powers. A first-class adventure.
(#UY1284—$1.25)

DAW BOOKS are represented by the publishers of Signet and Mentor Books, THE NEW AMERICAN LIBRARY, INC.

THE NEW AMERICAN LIBRARY, INC.,
P.O. Box 999, Bergenfield, New Jersey 07621

Please send me the DAW BOOKS I have checked above. I am enclosing
$_____(check or money order—no currency or C.O.D.'s).
Please include the list price plus 35¢ per order to cover mailing costs.

Name_____

Address_____

City_____State_____Zip Code_____
Please allow at least 4 weeks for delivery